# PAGAN SIEGE

Sam Taw

This is a work of fiction. Names, characters, organisations, places, events, and incidents are either products of the author's imagination or are used fictitiously.



Cover art supplied by Carantoc Publishing Ltd
First edition, 2021
ISBN 978-1-9163059-6-0
Carantoc Publishing Ltd.
www.carantocpublishing.com

Please note that this novel was created by a British author. Except for Cornish words, slang and dialogue, spelling and grammar are corrected to **British English**. There are also scenes which may offend more sensitive readers. It is not deemed suitable for children.

# CHAPTER ONE

I hated that crossing point. Every time I went near to the bridge over the River Sid marking the edge of our lands, I came away scared out of my wits or grieved beyond words. This time looked set to be no different. The new leader of the Durotriges sat high on his horse, wearing a frown that would give no quarter. I couldn't tell if he was about to double-cross us or keep his promise.

For a little more than a moon, he'd kept my friend Renowden and his fellow Sea Warrior captive. They secured the Chief's claim over a vast quantity of tin my nephew had pledged to pay. No matter how I twisted my neck to see past the long line of men on the opposite river bank, I couldn't spot my friend.

A dozen fears erupted in a tangled mess inside my mind. What if Ren and Massen had been tortured for details about our mines or starved to death? What if they were killed without honour and the whole deal was just a ruse to leave my nephew vulnerable to attack on the bridge? These and many other possibilities crowded my senses until I could hardly breathe.

Tallack had insisted that all our men turned out in force, in case things turned sour. His Sea Warriors were well ordered and prepared to fight, but the Head Hunter

Clan lounged near to their horses smoking hemp and teasing one another. It took three sharp barks at those idle layabouts from our Chief to garner their attention. This is what happens when they are left without a leader for too long. They grow bold and rebellious.

Even with my old eyes, I could see the Duros smirking. They were keen to lay their hands on our rare metal ingots. It was a handsome sum indeed and now that my nephew had seen justice done, when the Duros overthrew Brea and handed her over to us, he seemed reluctant to pay up.

It gladdened my heart that Tallack had not exchanged me in return for Brea that day, but I couldn't help thinking that my nephew might choose to lose his two best warriors instead of passing over the tin due. That would surely undo the peaceful negotiations and set us back on the same troublesome path as before.

I held my breath as Tallack and two of his largest men led their horses onto the bridge. The Duro leader did the same, until they were facing one another, just as before. Tallack looked tense, but I was glad he was on his mettle. There was no way of knowing whether we could trust this new leader. He was just as likely to attack as consolidate the truce.

The two Chieftains locked eyes. I crept closer, weaving between my nephew's men until I could hear them.

"I was beginning to think you'd never make contact." Fane held his composure, before a broad grin spread across his face. He needed the tin. Despite the fact that we could ill afford his extortionate terms, I would have given double the ingots to get Ren back. Not that the original deal included him or his shipmate, Massen. The tin was in payment for the traitor, Brea, we just didn't have the metal ready at the time of transfer.

"We had a few issues to deal with, otherwise we'd have been here sooner."

So far so good. They were not snapping nor sniping. It all sounded perfectly amicable. Maybe the peace treaty would hold.

Fane looked at his men and then back at Tallack. "Did Brea die well?"

I couldn't figure out why the man who took over her position would care how she ended her days, until I recognised an evil streak; that glint in the eye showing how they revel in brutality and vengeance. Brea was not liked during her short reign. She too bore all the markings of a vindictive leader.

"Let's just say that there are a number of wolves who won't need to hunt for a while." Tallack's face cracked into a smile and the pair of them snorted in shared amusement. It made me wonder whether Fane had fallen for her allure in the same way Tallack had.

When their mirth had passed, my nephew frowned. "We have the tin. I need to see that my men were treated well."

Fane twisted on his horse's back and nodded to the line of warriors, each holding a shield and spear. They parted, allowing two women in cloaks to walk forward. From their spry steps, I guessed them to be young, no more than fifteen summers, perhaps a little more.

Tallack squinted into the midday sun, shielding his eyes with his hand. "What's this? Where are my men?" His raised voice unsettled the horses. They jostled and whickered, taking a firm hand on the reins to stop them from bolting.

Fane raised his hand. "It's fine, your men are back there and unharmed. I simply wish to extend the deal."

Tallack pursed his lips, but held his temper well. He must be well accustomed to slippery negotiations after all his summers trading our tin with foreigners and other tribes.

Fane gestured for the women to move closer to the bridge, allowing us all a clearer view. "We are allies, are we not?"

"We are."

"Then we should bind our families by blood." He flicked his fingers, beckoning the two young women to the far end of the bridge. One was fair and pretty, one was dark, with a pinched face and a glower that could sour milk. Both had a sullen demeanour.

Tallack looked back over his shoulder at me as though searching for guidance. Hadn't the poor dolt understood what was being asked of him? I shrugged my response. Only he could decide on taking a wife, even if the notion was thrust upon him unexpectedly.

"Show me my men first. When I can see that they are as you say, we can talk about further deals another time."

Fane sucked his teeth. He barked out orders to a younger version of himself; a broad lad with the swagger of a clan leader. I took him to be one of their Chieftain's sons, although neither of the leaders were at the stage in the alliance where cordial introductions were possible. With the presentation of the two young women, I sensed that might follow in haste.

The warrior stuck two fingers into his mouth and whistled to his men. Within moments, Ren and Massen were brought in front of the line of Duros. Their wrists were tied, their ankles bound with just enough slack to allow a painful shuffle towards the bridge. Both were gaunt and weak, but Ren looked to have suffered the most. He was a lean and sinewy man before his captivity. Massen could afford to lose a little bulk. His fondness for fatty meats served him well.

I scanned my friend from top to toe. There were no evidence of bruises nor cuts. Apart from their extreme loss of fitness, they were indeed unharmed.

Tallack nodded at our warriors who both attempted a smile at their Chief. "Good." He kicked the flanks of his horse, urging it forward until he was within reaching distance of Fane. "The tin, as promised." My nephew held out the bag of ingots to the Duro Chief. One of our warriors hopped down from his horse to cut Ren and Massen's bindings as they hobbled over the central line of the bridge.

My relief was profound. I hurried to my friend and offered him my arm for support before remembering that everyone was watching. He had his dignity and reputation to uphold and I had revealed my feelings.

My face flushed hot as I resisted the urge to fuss over him. "Are you in any pain? I have resin or willow, whichever you prefer."

Renowden stopped at my side, looked down at me and smiled. "It's good to see you too, Mel."

My chest swelled and tightened. What was wrong with me? I was giddy with emotion.

Before we could all turnabout and leave, Fane put his ambition forward more forcefully. "Chief Tallack. In the spirit of friendship, I must insist that you take my daughter as your wife. It will cement our alliance for generations to come."

He was right, although having been in a similar situation myself in my youth, I pitied the man's offspring. Those bindings made through fondness and affection were more successful and long lasting than those forced upon them, as recent history would attest. We all froze on the bridge awaiting Tallack's answer.

He pulled on the reins of his horse until he was facing upstream across the bridge. "I understand your urgency, Chief and I will give it serious thought. You will have my answer by midsummer." From his tone of voice, it was clear that Tallack meant to conclude matters once and for all.

Fane let out a noisy breath. He was not appeased. "Then I have another request to make of you."

This was rapidly turning into an untenable situation. The man had kept his word but the alliance was far from an easy one.

Tallack held Fane's gaze. "Name it, by all means, Chief. If I can accommodate your wishes, it shall be done."

"We are in need of a healer."

Tallack glanced back at me and my stomach lurched. "We have only one who is skilled in the arts of medicine and I cannot spare…"

"I understand, Chief. You made that apparent during our last meeting. My request is that you take my niece. Step forward girl." He barked at the dour girl with the puckered face. "If your healer can take her as an apprentice, I'd be most grateful."

Tallack's tense shoulders lowered, slackening the rigid frown lines in his face. "Of course. My aunt would be delighted to be of service, wouldn't you Aunt Mel?"

I closed my eyes and sighed. Would my trials ever end? "If it pleases you, Chief, certainly." There was nothing else I could say. The surly girl huffed and puffed her discontent as she made her way across the bridge. I narrowed my eyes at the wretched creature as she passed me. There was not a hint of compliance in her manner whatsoever. No doubt this was foisted upon the girl against her wishes. At least she was not to be wed to a stranger, unlike her poor cousin on the opposite bank. The fair-haired young woman seemed mightily relieved by Tallack's reluctance to bind with her. I could tell from Fane's expression that this would not mark an end to his requests and demands.

In that moment, I chose to focus on my friend Ren and his poor state of health. She would require firmer handling than a skittish horse and I was ill prepared for the task. Ren and Massen had just enough strength to mount the ponies unaided. I stayed close by their sides, passing water bladders and bread, cheese and whatever else I'd had the presence of mind to pack.

Both were ravenous, but their stomachs had shrunk from lack of food. I wrapped what they couldn't force down and kept it handy for the ride back to camp. Ren perked up a little when he'd had time to digest. I told him about the journey out to the Teign River and the wolf pit where Brea met her end, plus the deeply moving burial of our two former Chiefs.

"What? Scampering about the tors on his own?" Ren said, when I mentioned Tallack's half-brother, Paega.

"Yes, the Chief saw him too. He followed us all the way to the cromlech where Aebba and Blydh were laid to rest. I didn't see him after that."

"Do you think he was plotting?"

I sucked in my lips and shrugged. "It's hard to tell. He was never the sharpest blade in the toolbox."

"But the most conniving."

I nodded. He was right enough there. Paega was more slippery than wet clay. Just when you thought you had him pinned down in one place, the kyjyan always managed to escape to cause chaos elsewhere.

Ren thought for a moment, scratching at his straggly beard. "You think he's looking for his priestly kin on the moors?"

"That would make the most sense."

He took more water and handed the bladder across to Massen. I wanted to tell him about the incident at the cromlech, but we were surrounded by too many curious ears, least of all those belonging to the new Duro girl. She kept her horse's nose stuck to the tail of mine all the way home. It made me wonder if she was sent as a spy in our camp rather than to learn healing skills for her tribe.

When I was sure that Ren was mending well, I cantered to the front of the line to speak with Tallack. I had to say my piece before the Duro girl caught up with me.

"Chief, I need a word." I knew I couldn't rest until I had spoken my mind about the leader of the Alchemist Clan. He was a shrewd man. Too shrewd to be fooled by the pack of lies my kin had fed him over the past quarter moon.

Tallack slowed to the speed of my old pony. "You're not going to refuse to teach her, are you?"

"What? Oh, no. Fane left us with no other choice."

"Then what's all the fuss?"

"I think you should take Kenver aside and tell him the truth about his daughter's passing. Regardless of your faith in young Treeve, I'm not convinced he believed a word of his ridiculous tale about keeping her quill necklace safe for him. It was a lame excuse and badly delivered. Kenver was not taken in for one moment."

"You worry too much. What can he possibly do?"

I frowned at my nephew, staring at his features to see if he was joking. He wasn't. "He's the leader of the Alchemists. There's a lot he can do. He controls all the tin for our entire tribe."

Tallack took a long breath. "Fine. I'll speak to him when we get back, but I think you're worrying unduly. I can reinforce the story that she was killed defending our compound during the attack. He's a reasonable man. He understood the risks his child took in leaving the mining settlement."

"Those risks didn't include Kerensa siding with our enemies and betraying us." I lowered my voice to a whisper.

"Well, I'm not about to tell him what really happened. That's just asking for trouble. There's no way he'll discover the truth. Her body is long gone."

I grumbled under my breath, but he wasn't listening to me. Anything that might cast poor light on his favourite crewman was dismissed. That preferential treatment didn't go unnoticed by the men. If Tallack was to retain the respect of all our warriors, he would need a fairer approach to governing tribal members than his current one.

I let my pony slow down until I was back at Ren's side. The poor man was exhausted, hanging onto his horse with what little strength he had left.

"What was all that about?" Ren asked. One eyelid drooped, but he was intent on catching up with the news. I think he sensed I was holding something critical back from him.

I peered over my shoulder at the Duro girl. "Tell you later."

The journey home was uneventful, punctuated with regular stops for the horses to take water at the streams and for us to refill our supplies. A dry spring had turned into a scorching summer. The earth baked into sharp peaks on the rough track. I steered my pony out of the ruts, but the hard ground was tough on his bones.

As we neared the palisade walls of the compound and the ingenious lifting bridge over the River Exe, all I could think about was how I should brew some teas and tinctures to help Ren and Massen's recovery. They were mere shadows of their former selves. I didn't give a thought as to where I would put the young Duro girl, until we rode into camp.

Kewri was chopping logs outside our hut. He dropped the axe to the ground and waved. It was only then I wondered how he might react to another woman sleeping under our roof. He was a constant puzzle to me. Neither slave nor clansman, this giant of a man was charged with my protection, a duty he'd taken to the extreme.

He and I had grown accustomed to one another in an odd sort of way. We'd fallen into a comfortable routine together. He helped with lifting and carrying, keeping the fires going as well as building shelters and such, and I took care of his meals and linens. This Duro girl could not be left to sleep in the shelter next to the goats. She was of Chieftain blood and would no doubt complain bitterly if her treatment was less than satisfactory. It was no use. She'd have to sleep in our hut with us.

I was about to question the girl, find out her name at least, when Treeve pushed through the door skins of the Long Hut and ran at full pelt towards Tallack and me in the horse enclosure. He was so fleet of foot, I thought he might have a hot ember in his leggings. I knew the boy was Tallack's favourite, but to be so blatant with his familiarities was a mistake. All the warriors could see the young man's keenness to be with my nephew.

"Chief! Thank Cernonnus, you're back." He panted, skidding to a halt. I'd mistaken his urgency for affection. I was wrong. The lad's face was crumpled with deep concern.

"For kyjya's sake man. What's happened?"

"It's Kenver. He went for a walk in the marshes."

"So?"

"He came back spitting with fury. I couldn't figure out why until I went along the track a short way…"

"Spit it out, Treeve." Tallack and I both knew what had happened, but he needed to hear it anyway.

"The water level has dropped. Kerensa's body was sticking out from the silt."

"Where's Kenver now? I'll go and try to smooth things over with him, although I have no clue how I'm going to talk my way out of this one."

Treeve looked like he might burst into tears. "It's too late for talking. He left the compound and took his ship from the estuary this morning."

# CHAPTER TWO

The three of us stood in the pony pen, dumbfounded. Of all the things that could possibly go wrong, that was the most unlikely. What was the leader of the Alchemists doing in the marshlands of all places?

It wasn't the first question that popped into my nephew's head. "How did he know it was his daughter's body? It could have been a slave sacrifice or an accidental drowning."

Treeve shook his head. "He asked your mother where he could trade for some woven trinket to take home to his wife. Cryda sent him to the weaver women, but they were out cutting stems in the marshlands. By the time I found out he'd gone after them, it was too late. Kerensa was poking out from the mud and silt, half eaten and rotting. He recognised her tunic as one his wife had made for her."

Tallack rubbed his forehead with closed eyes. He let his horse run off still carrying his bedding and weapons.

As he strode out of the enclosure, I scurried after him. "What are you going to do?"

He turned and snapped at me. "The only thing I can do. Send a messenger to patch things up with Kenver."

That sounded like a cop out to me. He should have raised the men and sailed after him immediately. Tallack's Phoenician ship was the swiftest vessel on the western seas. We could've easily caught up with him, even though he had a head start. I opened my mouth to protest, but when I saw his angry stare, I closed it again.

The Duro girl was loitering near to our horses, listening to our conversation. Blowing out my cheeks, I set about removing my bag and furs from my pony. "Do you have a name, girl?"

She nodded.

"Well?"

"Alvina, but only my mother calls me that. Most folks call me..."

"Right, well make yourself useful and carry these over to that man with the axe." I left her standing there, mouth agape and scowling. I had more important things to do than worry about an annoying slip of a girl. Latching the gate behind me, I stood on the boardwalk trying to decide which direction to take. If I followed Tallack into the Long Hut, it would probably end with us falling out over his decision. Failing that, his mother would distract us with more whining about how she'd struggled to cope with everything while we were away from camp.

I headed south in the end, straight to Ren's hut. As exhausted as he would be, I was in need of his sound advice. He knew Tallack better than anyone on the island. Outside his shelter, I suddenly felt nervous. Clearing my throat, I took a breath and steadied myself.

He must have heard me. "Meliora, is that you out there?" I could hear him grunting as he moved the skins hanging over the doorway aside.

"Yes, it's just me."

As his arm flung the drapes back, I could see his ribs poking through his skin and his belly caving in above his hips. He was in worse shape than I thought. The poor man was skin and bone. I didn't wait for him to invite me inside. "What did they do to you?" I couldn't keep the shock from my voice. My feelings balled up in my throat; I was so close to tears I had to look away.

"Nothing. I'm alright." He moved like every one of his joints was on fire. In the privacy of his home, I took his elbow and helped him to his bunk. He let me.

"Did they beat you? Torture you?"

"No, nothing like that. They gave us scraps and water. The cage had a roof so we were better off than our prisoners here."

"But you are in such bad shape. Massen is nowhere near this wasted." I touched him and a spark flitted between us.

He chuckled. "I got sick that's all, and you were not there to give me tonics and remedies." As he lowered himself down on the edge of the bed, he caught hold of my hand and raised it to his lips.

I found myself stroking the back of his head and smiling. "Well, I'm here now. I will make you some mallow tea and a little broth." He had more than enough problems to occupy him without me adding to them. It was too hot for furs. I fetched some cold water from the stream and helped him to wash the filth of the Duro camp from his body.

Leaving him to finish cleaning his private areas, I headed home to collect some food and medicines. Kewri was standing in the doorway of my hut, holding all my kit in his arms and blocking the girl's way.

"You have to let me in, I'm her apprentice." She screeched, tearing at his arms and pushing against his massive bulk with all her might. Kewri would not budge. I could see him grinning from halfway down the boardwalk.

When I was close enough for him to hear me, I flicked my hand at him. "She's telling the truth, Kewri. Let her in."

"An apprentice, but I'm your…" He stopped and pulled a face. Clearly, he had no idea what he was to me either.

"Let's not get into it now. Her name's Alvina and…"

"Vina. I'm called Vina." She interrupted.

"Yes, yes. Don't flap, child. The Duros insisted that I train her so, for the time being, she'll be staying here with us."

Kewri snatched my belongings from the girl and dumped them on my bunk. He followed me to the bench containing all my tinctures. "But we haven't enough room."

"Then we'll make room. It's Tallack's command." I gathered together my pot of flour, the last of my dried meats and roots, together with my medicines and hastened back to my friend.

Before I was back on the boardwalk, I heard Vina shrieking at Kewri. "I want this bunk, it's furthest away from the door." I had to titter. She was already bossing the poor giant about, demanding the comfortable bed he'd built for himself on the far side of the hut. She was going to be a whole handful of trouble, that one.

On my return to the south end of the island compound, I watched a number of elders with their families lining up outside the priestess's hut waiting for their blessing. Resources were already tight after Tallack had encouraged them to donate what metal they could spare for tributes to another tribe. These people obviously had stashed some away for leaner days. They carried beaver pelts and pots of grain, Frynkish wine and many other exotic traded goods in offering to the gods.

The priestess stood at her door, accepting the gifts and laying her hands on those fraught with troubles or ailing from whatever was blighting their lives. It was fascinating to watch.

Endelyn looked the penitent up and down, first deciding which of the deities carved into the wooden trunks would best suit their needs. When she'd stripped them of their goods, she ushered them in front of the icon and pressed them down by the shoulder until they were kneeling with heads bowed.

A short time later, she threw her arms in the air and begged whichever god she'd chosen to hear her plea. If I had not felt the wrath of the gods myself, I should think it all complete nonsense, but it's never wise to toy with such blasphemous notions. The last time I renounced the gods, we were struck with such misfortune that I was forced to eat my words.

Endelyn finished her entreaty and followed it with an eye-rolling babble of god speak. The elder at her feet peered up at her, passing something small and shiny into her palm. I knew this part of her rituals too. They were paying her with a tin grain or two for a sacrifice. It made me wonder what the old man had done to warrant such an offering. Endelyn obliged with a smile, pocketing the tin and gesturing to her friend, Senara.

It wasn't exactly what I had in mind when I sent the shield maiden to the priestess. She was supposed to protect her, make her feel safe after all that had occurred in camp during the spring moons. Instead, the two women had become inseparable, with Senara reduced from fierce warrior to servant and play thing of the priestess. Senara dragged a duck from a wooden box sitting behind their hut. I didn't need to see what happened next. It was something I'd observed dozens of times before.

Ren was back in his bunk and smelling a lot sweeter when I returned. I let him doze while I stoked his fire and chopped the meat and roots into a cooking pot. It was hard going without my knives. All I had after the unfortunate trip into Belgae territory was a dagger on loan from my nephew. Its edge dulled so quickly against roots and dried venison strips. Tallack had promised to have new blades forged for my healing kit, but without tin and copper we could not make bronze. I knew it'd be some time before he could make good on his promise. Until then, I had to make do.

The heat in Ren's hut was intolerable. With the drapes pinned back and the broth bubbling away, I walked through the east gates and into the marshes. Tallack had sent some of his men to remove Kerensa's body from the water. Treeve stood there, shouting at the Sea Warriors, who did not look pleased to be ordered about by the illicit lover of our Chief. I didn't linger. As soon as I'd cut what vegetation I needed, I hurried back to Ren's place.

While the broth cooked, Ren snoozed. I plaited the reeds I'd gathered into a flat paddle with a handle. It was perfect to waft in front of my face, providing a cooling breeze while the air about us was so still. When the broth was almost done, I pounded some dough and spread it out on one of the flat hot rocks to cook. That was when I saw two little faces peeping in through the doorway. Both were grimy; their eyes watery, their cheeks hollow.

At first, I thought that they were looking for Renowden, but one of them took a long sniff at the air with closed eyes. I could hardly ignore them.

"Has your mother sent for me? Is someone injured or sick?" I said, smoothing out a second flat bread to cook. When neither answered me, I looked up at them. "Then what is it? Did you come for Ren?"

They shook their heads. Heaving myself up from the fireside stool, I wiped the sweat from my brow on a sleeve and struggled to the door. They were startled, jumping backwards beyond the thatched eaves.

"Please, Fur Benyn." The taller of the two boys ventured. "Can you spare some of that stew for us?"

The other grew emboldened. "I haven't eaten for two days."

I could well believe it; they were in a similar shape to Ren, only they hadn't caught an ague. "I haven't seen either of you about camp before. Who's your mother? Where are you staying?" I looked all about the huts at the south eastern side of the compound for their parents, but saw only those I knew already.

The boys looked down at their feet. "Our mother's dead." The tall one said.

"And your father?"

"He came back half drowned from a fishing accident in the estuary a quarter moon ago."

"You live downstream in the stilted huts?"

They nodded, clutching their groaning bellies. How could I turn them away? I found a couple of wooden bowls and gave them a third of the broth, watering down the remainder to stretch the meat and roots. When the bread was cooked, they near snatched my hand off. The slurping and belching woke Ren, who wondered how I'd attracted such waifs into his home.

At nightfall, all the broth was gone and I sent the lads back to their father with a couple of strips of dried venison. It was all I could spare. The boys spoke of the difficulties the fisherman was having in bringing home a decent catch. It seems the warm water had chased the shoals out into the tricky currents of the bay. Half the families living alongside them were just as starving. The women and children foraged for what shellfish, crabs and seaweed they could find but the shoreline was already stripped bare.

When Ren was settled, I left him to speak to my nephew about the food shortages. Stopping at the raised grain store, I muttered my greetings to the guard and peered into the open hatch. The warrior held a torch aloft for me to see inside. A small mound of barley sat in the middle, no larger than the circle of stones around my own hut fire. It would barely be enough to feed a family for a quarter moon, let alone everyone in camp. I had to urge my nephew into action.

Two large torches illuminated the cracked earth and brown patches of grass either side of the Long Hut door. I could tell from the noise within, that my nephew was indulging the warriors with another feast. After the shameful state of those two young boys, I was more than a little cross with his extravagance. He was happy to ply the Head Hunters and Sea Warriors with fine roasted boar and goat, in return for them riding out to the River Sid to look menacing while our fishermen and their children starved.

I stood in the doorway and scanned the top table at the far end of the room. The two tall chairs belonging to Tallack and his poor dead brother, Blydh, were both empty. Treeve sat in pride of place in the seat reserved for the first wife of the Chieftain. How that young man had the nerve, I'll never know. If Tallack's father was looking down on the state of this tribe from the Summerlands, he'd come back and haunt us all.

Before long, Tallack made himself heard. He was sitting among the Sea Warriors, his eyes misted with tears. "That was when we stood back to back and fought them off, with flaming branches and bronze swords, we sent the whole pack scampering away yelping with their tails between their legs." He sniffed and banged his cup down hard on the table. "There was none better than Blydh the Brave." The men stamped their feet and hammered their fists on the table in praise of the fallen warrior. He was feasting his brother's passing. Something we'd not had the chance to do since the burial at the cromlech near to the moors. This would be a harder discussion than I thought.

Tallack caught sight of me loitering behind him. "Aunt Mel, come and drink to the best of warriors, the finest Chieftain since Aebba the Wild, maybe even Cador, eh?"

I shook my head. "Don't liken him to my brother." He shuffled along the bench and made room for me to sit down next to him. "Cador was pure evil. Blydh was nothing like him, thank the gods." It was stretching the truth somewhat, but there was no harm in it, now he was gone. Tallack hadn't the luxury of grieving. He had to hold himself together while he ruled the tribe alone.

One of his warriors pushed the ale jug closer and found me a cup. These were Tallack's men. Every one of them was loyal to him. Blydh's Head Hunter Clan sat on the opposite benches, sneering and muttering their private jokes together. While my nephew was in his cups, there would be no chance to talk some sense into him. He'd already mishandled Kenver, several times over. Now he looked set to lose the respect of his brother's men too.

"Tallack, the grain store is almost empty. There's barely enough for bread, let alone to replenish your ale stocks."

His movements were slow and ungainly. He was having trouble focusing on my face. "So, we can trade for some. We have new allies now you know."

"Yes, I was there, remember? We don't have any tin with which to trade." I waited for my statement to sink into his addled brain.

"Good point. Then I will send to the mines for more tin first and then trade for grain."

"Except you have just let Kenver go back to the Bentewyn mine in the certain knowledge that you know who…" I flicked my head towards Treeve sitting above us all in the Ruvane chair and lowered my voice to a rasp. "Killed his daughter."

Tallack swayed backwards on the bench and looked up at his lover. "He didn't kill Kerensa, Aunt Mel. I did. He just got rid of the body." The room went silent. The Head Hunters made low grumbling sounds and tuts. "She was working with Brea and those kyjyan Skotek Novantae. Going behind our backs… what else was I supposed to do?"

I was wasting my time. The more he spoke, the less the men respected him. Without Ren to lend a hand, I cast my stare at Massen for his help. He's a good man. He mobilised Treeve and the Sea Warriors and encouraged them all to sing a song composed just for Blydh the Brave. While the men were all carousing, I tugged on my nephew's arm and pulled him to his feet. "Treeve," I gestured towards the lad. "Get the Chief back to his hut and mind he doesn't do anything else stupid tonight."

He jumped down from the top table platform and pulled Tallack's arm over his shoulder. Together, they staggered towards the door with me following on behind. When we reached the cool night air, Endelyn was waiting under the stars.

Her long fair hair hung in loose curls over her shoulder, glowing in the torchlight. "You're not leaving now, are you? I have some wonderful news to share."

Tallack lifted his head and gave her a dreamy smile. "What is it, Priestess? Tell me your good news. We are all in desperate need of some."

"I'm carrying Blydh's child."

# CHAPTER THREE

I expected Endelyn's announcement, but hoped that she'd prove me wrong. Her reaction following Blydh's assault was not what I'd expected. Twice she refused my offer of a tonic to hasten the bleed, claiming that it was the will of the gods. I'd never known such acceptance in one so violated as she. "How can you be sure?" I squinted at her flat belly in the torchlight. "Isn't it too soon to tell?"

Endelyn stepped forwards and took my hand in hers. "Dear, Fur Benyn. You have always been kind to me. I just know that the seed of Blydh grows within me." She did that infuriating slow blink up at Tallack while twirling a lock of her hair around a finger.

Poor dazed fool grinned. "You heard her, Aunt Mel. She knows. She is a priestess after all. This is marvellous news. We must celebrate."

I dropped Endelyn's hand and steadied my nephew as he swayed between his lover and Massen. To the latter he said, "Take a couple of men and ride out to the northern mine for tin at first light. Clemo is still a sensible man. He'll give us no problems."

It was a logical plan, but for one tiny snag. "Except he will be furious that we left his boats in Duro territory and managed to get his nephew killed by the Belgae. I can't see him cooperating, especially if he's had word from Kenver."

"Pfft. Why must you always see the bad side of every situation? It'll be fine. We'll get the tin, trade with the Duros for grain and feast the coming of the new wolf." He didn't wait for me to gainsay him. I left him to embrace the priestess and revel in the uncomfortable news. More than anything, I wanted to return to Ren and talk this latest development over with someone sober and practical, but I knew that he'd be asleep. He needed to rest and regain his strength. Instead, I scampered back to my hut in the certain knowledge that Kewri and Vina would still be at each other's throats. I was not wrong.

As late as it was, Vina was clinging to the posts at the end of Kewri's bunk refusing to move. Her possessions were stashed beneath and his bedding lay in a heap on the rushes. Kewri paced about not knowing how to handle the situation. Any other man would have scooped her up and physically removed her, but not the gentle giant. His snorting and sighing was pitiful.

I strode through my house and took in the whole scene in moments. "Vina, move yourself. You get the patient's bunk over there. Behave yourself and we might make you a more comfortable bed in a moon or two." I pointed to the low wooden structure that was little more than a wide bench with a rim to stop the bedding straw from spilling onto the floor. She grumbled and muttered but did start to move away. I kept my eye on Kewri. His shoulders slumped and his spine slackened with relief. The pair of them glowered across the room in between stretching out their furs. This was going to be a long summer.

Massen and the Sea Warriors rode out of the northern gate when dawn broke. I heard the hooves hammering on the compacted earth as they cantered through camp. With a couple of horse changes at various homesteads, they would not be long in their mission. They woke both me and Vina, but not Kewri. He stayed in his bunk long after dawn, probably pretending to be asleep to avoid the girl.

I can't say I blamed him. The Duro was an entitled child. From the moment she awoke, she demanded eggs and cooked oats, and all manner of other items.

"Your Chieftain blood won't wash here. Get off your kyjyan arse and see to the goats. When you're done with that, tidy up your mess and prepare my horse. We're going out foraging." I figured that I should keep her out of Kewri's way for as much of the day as possible. If I could wear her out, she would have less energy to argue. Shoving a bowl in her hand, I pointed to the goat pen and set about my chores. I could hear her grumbling and moaning from inside the hut. When I went outside to see what was taking so long, I found her wiping milk from her face and hair. With my hands resting on my hips, I scowled at her for an explanation.

"I've never done this before. How was I to know that these stupid creatures would wriggle about and step on the bowl?"

It took all my powers of concentration to keep a straight face. How foolish could you get, expecting goats to stand still and wait for you to steal their milk from their young? "Clean yourself up and be quick about it. We've a lot to do today and no time for your antics." I ducked into my house and allowed myself a moment to laugh. By the time she was back inside with a half empty bowl, I'd managed to recover my sternness.

Vina strapped my empty hemp sacks and bags on my horse and walked it to the southern gates. I took a short detour to check up on Ren before meeting her. He too was not surprised by my news of Endelyn's pregnancy. If she was indeed bearing my dead nephew's child, her status within our tribe would be assured for all time. The young wolf would be of Chieftain's blood, and unless Tallack took a wife and issued an heir, the priestess would become the future mother to our tribal Metern after Tallack's time.

We both recalled that dreadful night when Blydh lost his senses and accused her of working with our enemies. The cruel punishment he inflicted upon the innocent woman was heard throughout camp all that night. Ren looked up at me. I could tell that he had a question but didn't want to give it a voice.

Had she brought the assault on herself following days upon end of whispering into his ear? What had she promised him while he was half addled from the evil spirit that took him over? It was certain that she was reeling him in and positioning herself to become his wife. It was doubtful she could have predicted that he would attack her. One thing was evident; we would never know what prompted him to take such brutal action.

Safe in the knowledge that Ren was on the mend, Vina and I walked out along the river heading south. Sullen at first, the Duro girl relaxed a little when we found some duck eggs along one of the tributaries. The birds themselves flapped out of our grasp, but we were able to paddle through the shallow waters to collect all that we could find. We were lucky that not many people knew about this spot. My age does have some advantages. There were still a few choice foraging areas I kept secret from the youngsters.

Wandering towards the estuary, I scanned the marshlands and drier banks further along and was saddened to see so many people poking sticks into the silt of the low tide, scratching about for something to eat. Everywhere we looked, the plants had withered and died. With nothing to feed them, animals move on. Our people had nothing left to hunt. “Come on.” I said, warming to my new helper. “Let’s try the forest at the northern side of the camp.”

I could have left her to scurry alongside my horse, but the day was scorching and I didn’t fancy nursing her back to health after a bout of heat sickness. Offering her my arm, I helped her up onto my pony behind me and together we ambled along the trail to the woodlands. At least here it was cooler. The dense canopy shaded us from the stinging sun.

We found a cool place in which to rest and unhitched the bags from the horse. As Vina led him down to the water, he broke free from her grasp. She panicked at first, but I reassured her that he was a faithful old boy. When he’d taken his fill of the cold water, he would return to us. The horse folded his legs and sat down in the stream, frolicking about like a new foal. After a full morning of gathering, we’d taken just eight eggs, a small amount of willow bark strips, and a handful of herbs. Slim pickings indeed.

We ate some dried venison and refilled our water bladders from further upstream, before moving through the dense undergrowth. I showed her the leaf shapes to avoid, and those that could be of use, but it seemed to me that she had no interest in learning the arts of healing at all. It couldn’t have been her idea to train under my guidance, but that of her uncle. That made me like her a little more, especially since I too had little interest in teaching her. It was my mother's wish that I should become the tribal healer after her time was over. My earliest memories were of wanting to be a shield maiden and fight battles and lead raids like my dear father. My cruel brother put paid to that notion as soon as he became Chieftain of our tribe.

As it happens, being the only medicine woman in the tribe has proven more useful than I could have ever imagined. The rarity of my skills has helped me out of a tricky situation more times than I care to admit. Training this youngster could be the only chance I have of passing my knowledge onto the next generation, and if that helps to cement ties with our new allies, so much the better.

We passed thick patches of brambles and scraped moss from fallen logs and rocks, listening out for the rustling sounds of animals nearby. The forest was surprisingly quiet for the season. What noises we heard turned out to be small birds; sparrows, crows and the like, none of which make good eating and are pretty hard to catch.

"Can you hunt, Vina? Are you good with a bow and arrow?"

She shook her head.

I sighed. "What can you do?" It was meant to help me figure out what I needed to teach her, but it came out a bit strong. She thought I was mocking her.

She folded her arms across her chest and pouted. "Well not much of any use to you, obviously."

We'd started off on the wrong foot, and if we were to make a success of this alliance, I had to turn that around.

"I didn't mean it like that. What did you do to occupy your time in the Duro camps?"

Her arms flopped to her side, her gaze distant and wistful. After a long moment she looked back at me. "I can't think of a single thing. We had slaves to cook, clean, take out the piss pots, do everything really." I looked at her with fresh eyes. No wonder she struggled with every task I gave her. It explained everything, the uncooperative manner, the sullen pout and her soft hands free of callouses. She was used to luxury. I had no intention of giving into her petulant whims and whines, but I made a decision to be more patient in her tutelage.

By mid-afternoon, we broke canopy to ride along the main track through the forest to the furthest end in search of useful plants and if we were lucky a few mushrooms. It was a long shot, given the dry conditions, but worth a few moments to check out the sites that I knew. As we turned the final bend in the path, I heard laughter. The banter was deep and manly, coming from a clearing off the trail. Safe in our own lands, it could only have been warriors from our camp.

I urged Vina to jump down from the pony and ushered her along. "Go quietly, girl. Don't blunder through the bushes. I want to see what they're up to." Tying the reins of my horse to a sturdy branch, we crept along until we could see them. There was more than twenty men from the Head Hunter Clan, lounging around a fire. Suspended above the flames roasted a whole hoglet. "Tallack must have sent them out to hunt." I whispered.

"Well, they don't seem to be in any hurry to take the spoils back to camp." She made no attempt to lower her voice. I feared that they would hear us and ruin my opportunity to watch them. She was right though. If they managed to kill a young boar so easily, why were they now waiting to devour it themselves instead of going after the rest of the herd? That hog would feed a family for a quarter moon or more. I was in half a mind to stomp into the midst of them and give them a sound reprimand, but I thought it might undermine Tallack even more, having an old aunt of the Chief give them orders.

I hesitated, watching their interactions. Four of the men were shooting arrows at a target scored onto a tree trunk. Others snoozed on their bundles in the shade. One man stood out among them. He was tall, well-built and commanded respect from the others. When he spoke, they listened. When he moved, they watched intently. When he suggested something, they were keen to please him. I knew his name of course. I'd watched him grow up under the command of the twin's father, Aebba. This man was Kitto, as strong and fierce a warrior as you'd ever meet.

There was no strutting nor preening, like you sometimes see with the younger men. His self-assured manner had a massive impact on the others. If they approached the cooking boar with their impatient fingers, he only needed to gently shake his head and they backed away without a murmur. I remembered him as a child. He was younger than the twins' father by a considerable amount, but Aebba respected him. Despite the age gap, they had trained together, fought alongside one another and protected themselves from all kinds of danger.

When Kitto was old enough to join the clans, he chose the Head Hunters. I recalled Aebba being disappointed, hoping that he would join him in swelling the Sea Warrior numbers at the time, but when Aebba became Chieftain, he did not choose Kitto to be the new leader of the Hunters. It always puzzled me until this very moment. Kitto was too much of a threat to Aebba's leadership to award him the honour of leading his men.

Aebba had the sense to keep him pliant with ale and trinkets, trusted missions and his confidences, but never to let him lead. Without Blydh in charge of the warrior clan, Kitto had assumed the role without invitation.

I'd witnessed all I needed. Kitto was unlikely to return to camp for some days while they were pretending to hunt for our people. I shoved Vina back towards the horse and we began the short journey home at a reasonable amble. It was too warm to rush anywhere.

I'm not sure which was more irritating, the constant soggy mud of the winters or the choking dust of the summer. Everything we'd collected, plus our clothes and hair were coated in a fine powder from the track. The horse had taken on a paler colour over the course of the sultry day. He just about yanked my arm off when I relieved him of my bags, removed the reins and set him loose in the enclosure. The old boy rushed straight to the stream and drank his fill, kicking about until it was churned with silt.

Vina carried the eggs as though they were made of gold. With them cradled in the crook of her arm, I told her that she was welcome to a couple for her help. It was the first time I'd seen her smile since the crossing at the Sid. Perhaps she wasn't so bad after all. I caught her up along the boardwalk and together we went through each of the plants in my bundle. I was just explaining the uses of mallow to her when she stopped outside the shelter Kewri had built for my patients. His feet were poking out of the door.

I peered around the shutters at him lying on his oversized bunk. "What are you doing?" I asked, wondering why he'd dragged his enormous bed out of my house and into the tiny shelter.

"I can't sleep under the same roof as her." He jabbed his thumb in Vina's direction. It was too late in the day for this kind of battle.

"Can't or won't?" I smirked.

He responded by narrowing his eyes at me. There was no harm in him staying outside, it was preferable to being indoors with the stifling heat making sleep so hard to achieve. I left him there, snorting and puffing with indignation. It suited me that he'd solved the bickering, but I did feel a little guilty that he'd been ousted from his home by Vina. If I could find a way for the two of them to get along, they could both assist me.

As we approached my hut, chatting about the process of extracting the pith from the willow bark for pain relief, she looked up into the sky and took a long sniff at the air. Her features fell into a contorted frown.

"What is it?" I asked, curious as to what her keen young senses had detected.

"Can you smell burning, I mean, more than the camp fires?"

I sniffed the air and moved to where it was the strongest. Further away from the hut, I could detect the unmistakable aroma of burning plants. It was not the sweet, mellow smell of seasoned logs, but that acrid stench when leaves, moss or heather catch fire. I looked to the north and saw a great plume of dark brown smoke rising up to the clouds and drifting out towards the sea.

# CHAPTER FOUR

Vina came and stood beside me, head tipped back, mouth drooping open. "Is that some sort of signal you Dumnos use?"

"It's too big for a signal. That's wildfire." With no idea how close the blaze was to camp, I thought it prudent to raise the alarm. Leaving Vina to deal with the supper, I walked to Tallack's hut, making plenty of coughing and stamping noises to forewarn him of my arrival. "Ho there! It's me."

His response was quicker than I thought it would be. Virtually every time I appear at his hut, he tends to be otherwise engaged with Treeve. "Come in, Aunt Mel." He croaked. I ducked under the drapes and found him laying across his bunk with just a small cloth to cover his bits. "You haven't got any willow tucked in your pocket, have you. My head is splitting." He rested his forearm across his eyes as though the late sunlight pained him.

One glance at him told me that his suffering was the result of his gluttony with ale the night before. "Water would put you straight, boy. Go and lay in the river like my pony. You smell like him too."

Treeve tittered from across the hut. He was slicing up cold meat left over from the feast and splitting it between two bowls. I flicked Tallack's ankle, encouraging him to move his leg for me to sit on the edge. As I lowered my creaking bones onto the bunk, I thought about which of my news was the most pressing, the idle Hunters relaxing in the forest or the billowing smoke from the north.

"There's a wildfire not far away, I think it would be wise to see how close it is to our camp. The wind is blowing the smoke in this direction." I waited a moment for him to react. When he said nothing, I jogged his leg.

"Yes, Aunt Mel, I'll send someone. Now leave me in peace."

I wanted to tell him that our tribe's folk looked to him to keep our people safe, to provide a reliable source of grain and solid trade links. He seemed to be failing on all counts. The elders would give him a few days to grieve his brother, but that amnesty would not last forever. "I'll send Vina over with some willow tea in a while. If you were sensible, Nephew, you would consider Chief Fane's request to wed his daughter before midsummer. We worked too hard to achieve that alliance for it all to fall apart now."

He lifted his head up from his bedding and glowered at me. "I know you mean well, Aunt, but don't meddle in affairs you don't understand." His expression was fierce, his tone of voice sharp and hurtful. It shocked me. I hurried away from his hut, holding back the tears. He seldom spoke to me in such a terse manner. Why was this such a raw topic to discuss?

Every tribal Chieftain was expected to take a bride to secure relations with our allies. Tallack's binding should be no different. His father's wedding with Cryda, brought a long-lasting peace between us and the Cantii at the far end of the channel. Why should he be spared from doing his duty? My own past came back momentarily to check my judgement. Had I not done the very same thing when presented with a forced marriage during Cador's reign?

I tried to avoid Vina on my return to our house. I didn't want her to see the emotions welling up inside me. As it happened, she was fending off an emotional situation herself. While she stood outside the Long Hut in the middle of the island watching the fire smoke, some of the compound children gathered around her, jeering and spitting at her feet.

In response, she'd chased them away but I could tell that she was upset. Everyone knew that spitting at the feet of enemies was a Duro custom. To have it targeted back at her must have been the highest insult. Our tribe would take a long time to forgive the Duros for their killing sprees and attacks on our compound over the many generations. She folded her arms across her chest, hugging herself for comfort while she dashed into my hut.

I should have gone after her, given her the benefit of my wisdom, tended to her homesick heart, but I too was wounded. My chest was crushed by Tallack's words. Instead of going home, I went back to see Ren. He was up and about, tidying his hut and sharpening his blades. It was good to see him with colour in his cheeks. He saw me through the open door and began pouring me a cup of ale before I'd set foot in the place.

We sat and drank his beer for half the evening before hunger called me home. Ren offered to find me something to eat, but I knew that he was not strong enough to go hunting just for me. I'd avoided it for long enough. I had to sort out the grudge between my two young friends. My head spun a little when the cooler evening air hit me outside. My first attempt to mount the boardwalk resulted in a misstep that sent me tumbling along the ground. Nursing a bashed head, I righted myself quickly and peered about to see if I was spotted losing my dignity. I think I got away with it, although you can never be sure who is watching about camp.

Embarrassed and bruised, I hurried towards Kewri's shelter to find him lying on his bunk with his head poking out of the door. Opposite him, the skins covering my door were pinned back, allowing Vina to hurl abuse across the way.

"Well, you're an ugly brute who's freakishly tall." She screamed.

"You're mean and bitter," came his retort, bellowed at the top of his voice.

"At least I don't stink like a pig with the squits."

"No, you just reek of being a Duro spy. No wonder the camp kids spit at you."

That was one snipe too far. She howled in anguish. I feared that this feud would not be quelled with a stern talk and a pat on the back from me. This rivalry was far too deep rooted for that. In the absence of a solution, I took a breath, blew out my cheeks and headed inside. The poor little mite was all snot and tears. Her first instinct upon seeing me was to back herself into a corner defensively and hold her fists high in protection.

"No one will hurt you, child," I said. "Come here." I held open my arms and beckoned her towards me. After a moment or two of pondering, she let the tears flow and ran into my embrace. Rocking her to and fro for a time, the hysteria lessened.

She pulled away and wiped her eyes. "I want to go home." She sniffed.

"I know, but that decision is out of our hands. If I can teach you quickly, and you agree to learn all you can, I can send you home to be the Duro healer in no time at all." I lied. It would take many full cycles of learning to absorb all I had to teach, supposing she was prepared to learn.

"You know Kewri is a lovely person when you get to know him, child. You'd do well to make your peace."

"Will you stop calling me that, Fur Benyn? I'm not a child. I'm almost sixteen summers now."

I couldn't stop myself snorting. "Dear girl, I have tunics older than that. You are a child to me, but I will do my best."

My small gesture of compassion seemed to spur her on. She walked to the fire and raked the coals, before placing a cooking pot into the embers. Cutting a nob of butter off into the pan, she cracked two of my duck eggs and stirred the sticky mess until it was fluffy and golden. When she tipped the mixture out into a single bowl, I gave her an odd look.

"I couldn't wait, I had mine earlier."

Satisfied that she'd taken care of her own hunger, I spooned a heap into my mouth. With a pinch of salt, they tasted like gifts from the gods. It was after I'd cleared the plate that I thought about Kewri, dangling half out of the shelter. It was too much to ask her to cook some more. I cracked the rest of the eggs into the warm pan and fluffed up a fresh batch.

"You know, the quickest way to make peace is to give them something they want, a small token of friendship." I emptied the pan into a clean bowl and tipped my head towards the door. "I shall need both you and Kewri to help me in the coming moons, and that can't happen until you stop bickering." I held out the scrambled eggs for her to take.

For a moment, I thought she might return to her old wilful and stubborn self, but she took the bowl with grace and walked to the door. Curiosity got the better of me. I sneaked closer to see in the failing light. Vina walked so slowly, I thought she was going to bolt, maybe hide away and eat the food herself. Kewri had turned himself around on his bunk. As she neared the huge feet, once again poking out of the door, she quickened her step.

"Fur Benyn thought you might be hungry." Her small frame was not much bigger than mine. Next to Kewri, she was tiny.

His feet retracted from my view and then returned with him standing outside the doorway. He reached out a massive hand and gently took the bowl from her. "Thank you. That was kind of you to bring it over." His smile was awkward as though he begrudged giving it to her. They stood for a short while, each waiting for the other to fill the silence. It was painful to watch.

Eventually, Vina took the initiative. "I don't want to fight anymore. Fur Benyn needs us both. If you want to bring your bed back into the house, I won't make a fuss."

Not the best apology, but certainly not the worst. I wondered if Kewri would take offence at the notion that Vina considered my house as hers to do with as she pleased. I decided who stayed and who left. Kewri had more than earned his place at my table and here she was pretending that he was only welcome if she deemed it so. At least she tried. With bowl in hand, he turned his back on her and sat on his bed.

I moved away from the door, pretending that I was ignorant of their exchange. She huffed and puffed at his rudeness before launching herself onto the patient's bunk in a sulk. There was so much for her to learn. If she couldn't make amends with easy going Kewri, then it would be impossible for her to win over the rest of the tribe.

Yet another humid night prevented restful sleep. Every move I made seemed to make me feel worse. Coupled with the anxiety of not knowing how close the fire was plus the soft whimpers of my homesick apprentice, I was wrung out by dawn. I used the piss pot and wandered outside as the sun crept over the horizon. Its orange glow blended with the smoke high in the air until the smell was all but a trace in the breeze.

From across the island, I could hear Tallack's little sister crying out. Knowing that his mother, Cryda would be wide awake and exhausted, I decided to pay her a visit. Cryda was pacing about the rushes, carrying a squawking Delen about in her arms when I arrived. One look of desperation cast in my direction was all it took for me to step up and take the babe from her. She's a dear little thing, but not a good sleeper. Cryda took the opportunity to throw herself down on her bunk and close her eyes. I needed her to stay awake.

I lifted Delen up until she was laying close to my shoulder and almost upright. Within moments, she calmed, her bawling ceased.

"Why can I never get her to do that? She hates me."

I chuckled. "She can feel your angst. The more tired and desperate you get, the more she wails. You just need a rest." I sat down and kept my upper body swaying to soothe her.

In a matter of moments, Cryda sat up and peered towards the thatch above. "Oh, blissful silence, my old friend." As she cast her sight back to me, she noticed my red and swollen eyes. "What's wrong, Meliora. Who has upset you?"

I swallowed hard. Just thinking about my exchange with the Chief brought a lump in my throat. "Tallack and I have fallen out."

She stared at me with waspish eyes. "I shouldn't worry about it, you know you're his favourite, just like his father before him. It'll pass."

I shook my head. "Not this time, I fear."

"What did you fall out over?"

I couldn't see any harm in telling her. She would see the situation the same way that I did. "I only mentioned that it was worth considering the Duro offer of binding with the Chief's daughter. He snapped my head off."

She sucked in her lips and nodded. I knew that she'd understand. She too was of Chieftain blood and knew the responsibilities that accompanied the title. In her case, she was lucky that Aebba adored her and pursued an alliance with the Cantii in order to wed her. Other tribal daughters often don't have that luxury.

"I'll have a word with him. He can't fall out with his own mother or the goddess will never favour him again."

It comforted me to know that she shared the same mind as I over this issue. Despite Tallack's current preference for his crewman, he would need to declare a first wife and Ruvane of our tribe at some point. It made sense that the Ruvane should be chosen carefully to benefit our trade links and alliances.

I stayed for a while, chatting over the events at the cromlech and how badly Treeve had handled the whole matter with Kenver of the Alchemists. There too, she agreed with me, but she made no offer to include it in her discussion with her son. Cryda was only brave to a point and no further. When her slave returned from washing their clothes at the river, I passed the sleeping child into her arms and said my farewells.

Taking the long route home, I walked beside the eastern palisade walls and stopped to watch the pigs snuffling in the wooded area behind the Hunter's tents. From there, I skirted the Long Hut roasting pits. As I turned the corner, I could see the grain store guard struggling to separate two weaver women from a large man carrying a sack.

The women were kicking his shins and scratching his arms, trying to snatch the bag from him. The guard tried to remove the women, but they clung tighter than a limpet. By the time I got to them, one of the ladies had jumped on the man's back and was throttling him from behind. His eyes bulged as he gasped for breath. The other bit the guard's arm while he grappled her around the middle.

"Hey, hey! What's all this?" I yelled. The woman riding the strangled man recognised me and released her grip. She slid down from his back and hung her head in shame. The guard let go of the second woman who stood before me, hands on hips in defiance.

"That stinking greedy kyjyan has taken the last of the grain." She screamed, although we were all close enough to hear her without the vitriol.

I looked at the man. "Chief Tallack's orders. Got to malt the last of the barley for ale. He's almost out."

I turned my gaze to the furious women.

"We've not had our ration this quarter moon and our children are starving." Now I could see why they were fighting. The poor man was covered in angry red welts from their scratches. He was only carrying out his Chief's orders. It wasn't his fault. Much to his surprise, I took the sack from him and handed it to the women. "Split this as best as you can. Make it last as there will be no more for a while." They hurried away before the decision could be altered. The large man looked deeply perturbed.

Turning to him, I said; "Tell Chief Tallack that you went to the grain store but found it empty. If he questions you further, tell him that I was there as a witness." I gave the guard my sternest look until both nodded in agreement. "The empty bellies of children should always come before the ale of a Chief." I can't recall a time when petty squabbles such as this got out of hand. People were getting desperate, and it looked set to get much worse.

Glancing about the island, I could detect a subtle change in the atmosphere. Where once it was languid and purposeful, it was now fraught with worry; the furtive looks of envy whenever the elders' wives displayed their metal jewellery, the children sent to pick every grain from the parched earth that was spilled from the store, the ravenous camp dogs snarling over the fragments of bone cast aside on the midden pile.

I spun about and aimed myself north towards home. Before I was half way along the boardwalk, I heard the horn of the watchmen blow. The gates swung open and the bridge lowered over the river. There stood a half hundred men, women and children, their belongings dragging behind them.

# CHAPTER FIVE

There they stood, gaunt, sweating and exhausted from their journey. These were our homesteaders, driven in desperation to seek our help. There were no livestock, nor pets. Not even a horse among them. I could tell from their ragged clothes and lack of shoes that they had traded or eaten everything but their children.

The horn brought many out of their houses to see who was at our gates. Even Tallack was moved from his bunk to slip on his leggings and walk to the north side of the island to greet the visitors.

His long strides allowed him to reach them before I could. "Hail, friends, what brings you here?"

One of their menfolk responded. "Did you not see the smoke, Chief? The moors are on fire. Our homes, cattle, everything has gone. All we have is what you see." He was holding it together for the sake of his family, but I could tell his level of distress from the tremble in his voice.

Tallack looked at them but said nothing. The shock of having so many displaced people at our gates threw him. The man waited patiently for an answer, an instruction, anything to reassure him that they would be welcomed with open arms. When none was forthcoming, the man grew desperate. “Chief, we have paid our tributes every season since my grandfather’s generation. You cannot fail us now.” He was right. It was the unspoken tribal law. In return for a portion of their harvests, our warriors did all they could to keep them safe. They heeded the call for new recruits, sending their most able children to us for training and induction into the clans. If Tallack failed to provide for them in their time of need, things would turn nasty.

“Of course, yes. I was just thinking about the best place for you to go.” He twisted on his heels, scratching his head until he spotted me. His mouth hung open; his eyes widened. He had no idea how to deal with such a problem. After his sharp tongue earlier in the day, I was tempted to let him flounder, but the homesteaders didn’t deserve that. They needed food and healing herbs to set them straight. One or two looked to be nursing burns on their hands and forearms, incurred no doubt when they tried to save their homes.

“Perhaps they could stay in the Long Hut for the time being, Chief, just until new huts can be built?”

“Yes, splendid idea. That’s where you should go.” He gave them his most charming smile and directed them to the centre of the island. Treeve took them inside and began dividing the space and stacking benches. Tallack approached me. I waited to see whether his mood had improved. I wasn’t about to forgive his outburst on the turn of one of his smiles.

“The Head Hunters should be back by now. I can’t imagine that they would find it difficult to hunt down a few boar or a couple of deer to keep us all going. I wonder what’s delayed them.”

I probably should have told him what I’d seen in the forest the day before, but I was still annoyed with him. If he can't manage men such as Kitto, Tallack is in for a rough ride as Chieftain.

My silence surprised him. He frowned at my lack of interference. "Aunt Mel, how will I feed all these extra mouths?"

I shrugged. The lad had to learn. I wouldn't be around forever to bail him out. It was churlish of me I know, but I walked away and left him to sort out his own mess. I sauntered back to my hut and began stringing up the few bunches of herbs from the foraging trip to dry. Vina had returned to her sullen uncooperative self. Perhaps it was too hot for hard labour, but this was easy light work and a chance to learn the plant names. It took some nagging, but eventually she shifted herself from the bunk to help.

With Vina occupied, I ferreted Kewri out from the shelter. He looked as wrung out as I felt. His hair was wet with sweat and stuck in cords to his forehead. I was reluctant to ask, but we needed food. "Kewri, can you go to the forest and see what you can find for supper? We are out of dried meat; the salt is down to a pinch or two and the grain store is completely empty."

Credit where it's due, the lad didn't moan one bit. He collected the bow and arrows from my hut, secured his knife in his belt and walked to the pony enclosure to ready his carthorse. He was the one person in the whole world on whom I could rely. I thank the goddess every day for bringing him to our camp. Before settling to my work, I went to see that my goats had enough water and leaves to eat. When I let myself inside their enclosure, I sensed something amiss. They crowded around me as they usually did, but were less insistent in their jostling. Normally, one large brown nanny would butt me in the arse if I took too long with their food. I spun about, but she was nowhere to be seen. My best milking goat was gone.

I checked the hurdle fencing for scrapes dug out from the dry soil or breaks in the weave, but found no weaknesses in the pen. Securing the gate behind me, I searched around my hut and the shelter, but saw no sign of her. If she escaped, the others would have vanished too. It looked more and more like someone had stolen her, but who would do such a thing? Everyone in camp knew they were my animals. No wonder the rest of the little herd were jittery.

Vina had no answer to give me about the missing creature when I asked and there was no way Kewri would have let her bolt. He'd learned his lesson about captives the hard way. I'd barely stepped foot back in my hut when one of Tallack's slaves came for me. The Chief sent word that my assistance was required in the Long Hut and I was to bring my medicine kit with me. I grabbed my things and scuttled over the brown grass to find that Cryda, Endelyn and Senara had also received summons from our leader.

Cryda ran out of the noise and commotion as soon as she saw me. "It's chaos. There simply isn't enough room for them to stay inside. The slaves have a thin stew cooking, but it won't be enough to feed them all."

I watched the homesteaders marking out sections for themselves with benches, moving the boundaries of their neighbours and causing upset in the process. They were moments away from a full-on fight. "It's not cold at night. They can set up camp in the southern reaches of the island. When the stew is done, they can file in and collect a bowlful one family at a time. While they wait in line, I will patch them up and tend their burns. Get some of the Sea Warriors to maintain order among them." Senara heard my orders and ran off to organise things. When she was no more than half a boat length away, I called her back. "And tell them to watch their metal and livestock. We have a thief in camp." She nodded and ran like the wind.

"What about us, Fur Benyn. How can we help?" The priestess said in her wistful yet dramatic way of hers.

"I'd appreciate some help with the sick and injured, Endelyn, if you will? Cryda, make sure the slaves dole out equal portions of stew or we'll have a brawl to match the Duro attack." For once, the former Ruvane took my suggestion without complaint, taking charge of what little food was on offer.

Treeve set up a couple of benches and tables near to the front entrance of the Long Hut for me to assess their health. Most of the children were undernourished and covered in lice. One or two of the men complained of toothache while the women suffered silently, their backs aching and their will broken. Endelyn cared for those who were heavy with child. At first, I thought it was because she felt empathy with them. When I got the chance to listen to her wittering on, she was boasting about the blood line of her unborn child to all who would listen.

My efforts were best placed with burns and cuts. It was fortunate that I had a stock of plantain paste in my stores. The lice infestation would have to wait for another day. When the homesteaders could see that everyone was treated fairly, order was restored. It was only then that Tallack showed his face. This was a side of him for which I was not proud. He'd washed his hands of the problem, allowing us women to arrange the solution.

I had just finished stitching a gash in a man's leg when Tallack sidled up behind me and whispered in my ear. "The cooking pot is almost empty. There is nothing else to give them."

He would not be content with an obstinate shrug from me this time. I had to say something about the Head Hunters and their dereliction of duty. "You know Vina and I saw the Head Hunters in the far reaches of the forest just yesterday."

"Oh, did you speak to them? How much food had they stockpiled?"

"So far as I could see, just the one hoglet that was roasting for their supper while they snoozed the day away." I looked up from my work and held my nephew's stare. Handing my patient some willow bark to chew on, I waited until they had hobbled away and could no longer hear me before continuing my observations. "If you'll forgive me for saying, Chief Tallack, I fear you may have problems with the Head Hunter Clan. Kitto has assumed control over them. He actively encourages discord within the tribe. They were in no hurry to find food for us all and looked set on staying away."

His concerned frown turned positively sour. I wasn't sure whether it was from me overstepping my boundaries again, or the news that Kitto was usurping him.

He took a noisy breath and sighed. "I'll send Ren to track them down. They'll listen to him."

"Ren's too weak. That might finish him off. Send someone else."

"There is no one else, unless I go myself. Kitto is not easy to sway at the best of times. You're right, Aunt.

I've let things go unpunished for too long. Maybe I should make an example of him."

That idea frightened me more than the thought of Kitto overthrowing my nephew as Chieftain. "Is that the best way to deal with him, Chief? Your father gave him missions and responsibilities to keep him at arm's length. Would that not be better than turning the rest of the men against you for flogging someone they respect as a leader?" I'd said too much, not giving my choice of words enough thought, but it was too late to take them back.

Tallack sneered. "I'm the only leader of this tribe since my brother's death, Aunt. Don't you forget that." He stomped away from the Long Hut in a southerly direction. Despite my warnings, he was intent on sending poor Renowden after the unruly clan.

By late afternoon, the smell of burning was so strong, it made us all cough. I tied a cloth over my face and carried on stitching and pasting until I was out of cattle gut and plantain. My back ached and my stomach felt as though it was trying to eat itself. I wandered out into the grassy space at the south of the island to stretch my legs and click my spine. Ren's wooden panel was wedged in the doorway of his hut. That was sign enough that he'd followed Tallack's orders despite his weakness.

When the sun dipped below the horizon in the west, the gate horn blew a second time that day. More tired and dusty homesteaders had arrived from their abandoned settlements around the moors. Senara loomed up behind me as the newest group of our tribe fanned out and started foraging for whatever they could find. "Secure your belongings, Senara, or you might find them wandering off. These are desperate people fallen on hard times."

Within moments I heard the unmistakable sound of pigs squealing in the western wood. The loudest of them fell silent abruptly. One of the visitors had killed a pig. I hoped to Cernonnus that it wasn't one of the suckling sows, leaving starving piglets to rear to add to our problems. Our islands' delicate balance was shattered the moment the homesteaders arrived.

This must be how they felt whenever their homes were raided by neighbouring tribes. A few of the Sea Warriors captured the men making off with the hog and took them straight to Tallack. Treeve directed the Long Hut slaves to collect and butcher the sow for the pot. At least that solved the immediate food shortage, even if her little piglets went without a mother.

My wits were frayed, my bones ached and my muscles were sore. I returned to my hut and wedged the panel in the doorway. With so many strangers abroad, I no longer felt safe in my house. Kewri returned shortly after dark. When he discovered all that had happened, he vowed to protect my goats from anyone lurking in the night. I believed him too. If it meant staying up until morning, Kewri would guard us all. The reliable giant stood outside with a deer slung around his neck as though it was a collar to keep him warm.

Vina's eyes brightened when she saw his haul. "Oh, thank Cernonnus!" She clapped her hands together at the thought of so much meat. "You are clever." I could see that it slipped out of her mouth before she realised what she was saying.

Kewri gave her an uncomfortable grin. His cheeks flushed with a rosy glow. "I'll bleed and butcher it around the back." He went to step away and stopped. "If you like, in the morning, I'll start preparing the hide for you." She didn't realise that he meant her, until he glanced back and smiled.

"Oh, yes. I'd like that."

A part of me wanted to say, told you so, but I was too tired to argue with her. She'll learn, or she won't. The night was almost as warm as the day. The mild breeze dropped, leaving us all without relief. It was good to have Kewri back. At least we could reopen the door and wander to the cool stream to sluice ourselves down.

Cooking was impossible inside the hut. Vina built a fire while Kewri prepared the meat. I was too hungry to wait for a sizeable roast, and it didn't seem like the decent thing to do with so many starving people about camp. We sliced thin strips of the venison and fried it in a pan with some duck fat I was saving. We had no bread to mop up the juices, but it was still the tastiest thing I'd eaten in an age. With prudent management, we would have enough to last us for some time, providing it was properly preserved with salt and dried. At least that was something Kewri could do without needing my instruction.

The morning brought more homesteaders from the north. Not such a large crowd as the day before, but still enough to have us bursting at the seams. Their reports were of vast fires skipping along the dry heath lands, sending the wild ponies racing off into the distance. Our loss would no doubt be the Duros gain. Tallack grilled their elders until he was sure that the fires were heading away from our island compound.

We were not at risk; for the present. I knew how quickly the wind could change up on the moors. In the blink of an eye, it could turn south and put us all in danger. There was enough panic in camp without me fanning the flames. Without ale, Tallack was sober, clear headed and fully aware of his responsibilities. He ordered his Sea Warriors to fell trees, gather materials and start to build shelters on the south-western training grounds outside the compound.

We all knew that being outside our palisade walls would set them apart from our community, but there simply wasn't enough room to house them all within. Thanks to our new alliance they were safe from Duro raids, but without the advantage of integrating with the families and warriors inside the walls. It wasn't an ideal situation, but Tallack assured them that it was a temporary arrangement. Some muttered their discontent, claiming that their tributes were worth better treatment, but they fell silent when some of the warriors closed in on them, heavily armed.

Tallack stood with his mother on his left and me on his right. Between the homesteaders and us was a wall of muscular fighting men. Their presence alone was enough to quieten the dissenters.

"Even if Massen comes back with the tin we need…" I said in little more than a mutter. "You know Fane won't trade with you unless you give in to his request to bind with his daughter."

"She's right, son. Duty is duty. You'll have to wed the girl." Cryda said, backing up my statement.

"And make a Duro Ruvane over our tribe. I'd rather slam my pintel between two rocks than let that happen." His vehemence was understandable given all that had occurred between our tribes over the generations.

"Well," his mother said, flipping her long hair over her shoulder. "You won't get an heir by tupping your crewman."

I couldn't stop myself. My snort of amusement almost erupted from me. None but his mother could get away with such a blunt insult. Neither could he deny her statement. What shocked us more was his solution to the problem.

# CHAPTER SIX

"I shall bind with Endelyn. She already carries the heir to the tribe." Tallack announced to us both, although thankfully, none of his men heard him.

"Don't be ridiculous. She has no Chieftain blood. She's just some priestly spawn left to go feral on the moors. What good would that do for our tribe?" Cryda scoffed.

"She's a Dumno, born and bred in our camp. She will make a fine Ruvane and our tribe will stay in good hands when the wolf cub takes over on my death." It took a few moments for his plan to sink in, for I was sure he was teasing his mother. With every objection Cryda brought up, Tallack countered it with a sensible reason for his choice.

"What about the Duros? Fane will see it as a slight on the alliance." I said, interrupting the mother-son dispute.

"That's easy, Aunt Mel. I'll take his daughter as my second wife. He made no mention of her becoming Ruvane, nor did he say that I must take only one wife."

I couldn't argue with his logic. There was a certain beauty in that arrangement for all parties involved. Endelyn would have the status she so craved and reassurance that her son would one day lead our people.

Fane's daughter would become a wife in name only, while Tallack and Treeve could continue their relationship right under the noses of the whole tribe. I couldn't see Treeve taking the news well though. He looked set on being the first ever man-wife of a Chieftain, making the Dumnonii a source of derision and mirth among the Chieftains at the midsummer gatherings. That would never do. There was little more I could say or do to alter his mind, not that I had the energy or will to see it through anyway.

For the rest of the day, Vina and Kewri went in search of more willow, plantain and goose grease, while I prepared the back strap from a couple of hares for stitching and fresh leaves to cover burns. Every child I examined seemed to be riddled with lice, making me scratch my own head every few moments. I was sure that the mucky creatures had given them to me too.

Every now and then I wandered to the south, squinting at Ren's hut to see if he'd returned with the Head Hunter's. Each time I was left disappointed and concerned.

Although Vina and Kewri had set off at different times to complete their tasks, they returned to camp together. I couldn't make out if this was just a happy coincidence or whether they had designed it that way. Were they finally starting to warm to one another?

Everyone around the compound was industrious. Sea Warriors put their superior carpentry skills to use building new shelters, slaves toiled over huge cooking pots of watery stew for the extra mouths to feed, while elders and their families kept a weather eye on pilfering and potential looters.

It was as orderly as you could expect, considering the cramped conditions and intolerable heat. The calm turned back into a storm when Massen rode in through the northern gate, leading two horses by the reins with his two crewmen slung over their backs. One of the men was still alive, just. The other man had three arrows embedded in his back. Screams from the womenfolk brought people from their huts, including the Chief. One glance was all it took to convey their failure in collecting tin from Clemo at the northern mines.

Massen's horse skidded to a halt in the dust. It foamed about the mouth and neck. People ran from all directions to lend a hand, lifting the men from their steeds and carrying them into the Long Hut. I went straight to the man with only two arrows sticking from his leg and side. He'd lost too much blood. There was little I could do to help him, but I tried. His mother shrieked her distress and tried to tug the bolt from his side.

"No! You mustn't. Take that out and he'll lose the humours he has left." She deferred to my experience, sobbing quietly into her husband's neck behind me. Vina brought clean binding cloth, while I made a small cut in his leg to remove the less dangerous of the two arrows. There was such a crowd around me, it was hard to concentrate. If I could get the arrow out of his side, he would either bleed out in mere moments and die, or live long enough for me to slip a few stitches into any of the leaking guts inside and hope he lived out the rest of the day.

With his life in my hands, I decided to try and give him long enough to say his farewells. Kewri moved the crowd back, giving me space to work. I lined up my best bone needle and finest back strap next to Kewri's knife. It was sharper and easier for me to handle than Tallack's dagger. After a quick blessing from Endelyn, I took hold of the shaft in one hand and braced his ribs with my other. "This will hurt. Try not to move." As soon as the words left my mouth, I yanked with all my strength.

The warrior wailed loud enough to summon spirits from the Underworld. I had to work fast or he was set to join them there. Blood gushed in great spurts, hot and bubbling. It told me that he'd punctured the bag of humours sitting under the lungs. Try as I might, I couldn't get my fingers inside the hole to find the fissure. A quick nick with Kewri's knife gave me more room, but the cavity was filling up fast and obscuring my view.

Red bubbles fizzed about his mouth and he struggled to breathe. A shattered rib must have sliced through his lung too. All about me the crowd went silent as the warrior's life ebbed away before our eyes. I had just one chance to save him. I plunged my fingertips inside his chest and felt about in the soft innards. Poking my finger under his ribs, I located the hole in the blood bag. I pinched the two sides of the gap together between thumb and forefinger and the flow lessened. Holding tight I screamed at Kewri. "Get me a jug of salted water and all my clean cloth from my kit."

For such a big man, Kewri was remarkably nimble. He stood at my side, jug in one hand and rags in the other, awaiting my directions. I couldn't afford to let go for one moment. Pouring just a splash at a time, Kewri flushed and dabbed until the innards were as clean as we could get them. My knuckles were white with the pressure of holding his entrails together through the narrow gash in his side. I squeezed so tightly; the poor man passed out from the pain. Those around me gasped, thinking it was all over and that the man had fallen into the arms of Cernonnus. I knew better. His chest still rose and fell, albeit too quickly for my liking.

Vina threaded the fibres of back strap through my bone needle and handed it to me. It was a fiddly job, but a few over stitches were all it took to secure the hole in the blood bag. Whether he would survive having lost so much fluid was another matter. I closed his skin as fast as I was able, not caring about my messy stitching. When I had finished, I looked down at my tunic. It was drenched in the warrior's humours. So too were my hands. I even had dried globs of the stuff on my chin.

The crowd waited for me to speak. I knew he would not last out the night, but that was not what they wanted to hear. His parents and siblings were trembling at the front of the group, their hands clasped together in anguish.

Facing them, I looked directly at the warrior's mother. "I have done all I can, the rest is in the hands of the goddess. May she bless him and restore his vigour so that his mother may hold him again." The poor woman understood all and crumbled into her husband's arms. Endelyn stepped forwards with her coloured clays and paints and daubed a smudge of ochre on each of the foreheads of his family.

She was gifted at exploiting people's attention. Normally, I would have scoffed and wandered away from her antics, but this day I was glad of the distraction. Death was hard for me to reconcile. Grief was too close to the surface for me to cope with anymore. I slipped away to the stream to wash myself, ridding my skin of the dying man's blood. There was not much I could do about my tunic. After a quick change back in my hut, I left the cloth to soak out the stains and returned to my patient.

Tallack was standing near to the door watching the elders and their family's response to Endelyn's rituals and chants. She summoned just about every god in living memory and asked each and every one of them for their favour, throwing her head back and babbling the way she always did when she was pretending to converse in gods' speak. The crowd lapped up her fervour with metals and jewels thrown at her feet in offering, as though they could buy the life of the warrior through the priestess.

I turned to my nephew. "Are you sure it's a good idea to make her the Ruvane?" It was a risky question, given his terse warning back in his hut to mind my own business. It seemed such a drastic step to give a priestess such power over the tribe.

"Of course, it is. She's lovely. Look at how the tribal elders adore her. She soothes them after troubles and we've had more than our fair share of those recently. Look how she dealt with the whole Blydh incident. I'd say she possessed remarkable maturity. She'll make a fine Ruvane."

I'd seen these blind infatuations of Tallack's before. His judgement of character was worse than mine. His love for a Phoenician Prince did not end well, and this decision gave me an ache in my belly; a sense of foreboding that I couldn't quite define. We watched them for a while, the elders and their wives kneeling in adoration with Endelyn prancing about in her thin tunic holding them in thrall.

Senara stood near to the priestess, guarding her with pride, the puppy on a leash at her side. I knew that the shield maiden was bright, but I didn't realise her skill in manipulation. In a short space of time, she had earned my trust, broken Kewri's heart after claiming deep affection for the giant, and now stood to become the most trusted adviser to the next Ruvane. I couldn't help thinking that given enough time, those two women could end up ruling over half the land in the whole world.

When Vina and Kewri had bundled my things together, I checked on the patient one last time and made my excuses to leave. It was uncommonly warm and oppressive in the Long Hut, and I was of a mind to be alone. Vina went for a walk in the early evening sun while Kewri guarded the goats in their pen. I ate a couple of strips of the venison to tide me over but my appetite was lost. Everything tasted of ash.

By nightfall, most of the elders had returned to their homes, leaving those closest to the warrior to watch over him. I dragged a stool to the doorway of my house and watched the smoke thicken in the sky until it blotted out the twinkling light from the gods. It was marginally cooler for one, but I could also keep an eye out in case Ren returned with the Hunters.

A short time after the darkness was fully on us, Tallack's men lit the torches along the boardwalk and in other strategic places about camp. He was not taking any chances with the new people and their thieving ways to use the night against us. Predictably, Endelyn's hut was lit up like a midsummer festival. Her recent performance had attracted new believers into her clutches. Even the night time did not halt her blessings and offerings to the wooden gods outside her door.

It may have just been concern about Ren, or that Tallack appeared to be reluctant to deal with Kenver, but my unease and restlessness would not abate. I stayed up until long after dark, grinding and mixing pastes and potions with a sense that they would be needed in the coming moons. When most people had turned in for the night, and the priestess had exhausted the line of offerings and tributes, I saw Tallack strolling over to her hut. He carried with him a circle of twisted willow withies. After just a few moments, Senara and the pup exited. She did not look at all pleased to be put out of her latest home.

I didn't need to guess what my nephew and the priestess were discussing. He'd already made up his mind and he was never one to wait patiently for the right moment to act. He would make his offer to bind with the priestess, presenting her with the eternal circle of life, woven in green stick wood and decorated with flowers. Neither did I need to know her answer, for the elated shrieking coming from within her hut said it all. She had accepted him and within a few moons, would govern by his side over us all. It was a dark night indeed. With hope fading in my heart, I went to my bunk and tried to sleep.

The news of Tallack's proposal spread quicker than the heath fires. Women all across camp were buzzing with excitement. Endelyn set herself up outside her hut, receiving visitors and well-wishers, traders and kind hearted Sea Warriors paying their dues to the next Ruvane.

In the absence of my morning milky grains, I walked to the Long Hut to see the warrior and his family. As I anticipated, he did not live long. His father took my hands in his and fixed me with his watery stare to thank me for the short while they had with the patient during the night. There was no need to exchange words, for nothing I said could comfort him, nor his wife and daughter.

I knew they'd already given everything of value to the priestess in offering, but still he tried to pay me with his only blade. It was a tempting offer, given my need for such a fine knife, but they could ill afford the loss after all they had endured. Instead, I told him that the gods had guided me to help his family, and he needed to take care of them in the days ahead. That seemed to appease him, as many about camp believed I had the ear of Cernonnus through the rare white hart I'd befriended, just before my nephews had him sacrificed.

With hunger and grief so commonplace within our tribe, I thought Endelyn might have the decency to wait before making her preparations for the ceremony, but I was wrong. She spun about in a dream of opulence that made me nauseous. I was on my way back home when she saw me and glided across the cracked earth to my side.

"Isn't it fabulous news, Meliora? I'm to be Ruvane. Did you hear? I thought I'd see you at first light this morning. Why didn't you visit?"

So many questions, such an absence of decorum and sensitivity, I hardly knew which of them to address first. More irksome than those, was her use of my given name. Through respect for my position in the tribe, Endelyn had always called me as others do, Fur Benyn, or wise woman in our tongue. The very moment Tallack elevated her status so that she would become the next Ruvane, she declared herself my superior. I knew it would be so, but I thought she'd take longer to adjust to the change.

When I failed to answer her many questions, she thinned her eyes. Was that scorn I detected or something worse?

"Come and speak to the woman who will dye the cloth for the gown I'm having made. I want that luscious deep colour between purple and red that Tallack has on his ship. The dyers say it can't be done, but they must be wrong. You'll know what to use, surely?"

I did know and the dyers were right. The only reason such a colour existed on Tallack's ship was because it had sailed all the way from the shores of Tyre on the other side of the world. "It isn't possible to achieve that colour with any plant or rock from our lands." I said, trying to pull away from her tight grip on my arm.

"Then we'll trade for some. What do we need?"

I closed my eyes. Whether it was exhaustion or exasperation I could not say, but she irritated me beyond reckoning. All around us, children infested with lice were starving and homeless, mothers grieved for their sons and all she could think about was the colour of cloth for her binding ceremony. I lifted my face to the skies and sent a silent message to the Summerlands to bring me deliverance. Perhaps I was once again in the gods favour, for the guards in the northern watchtower sounded the horn and opened the gates.

In they came, whooping and hollering in their usual way, but not with our enemy's heads strung from their horses. They came with meat; deer, boar, beaver, and many other animals besides. The noise brought out a long line of tribe's folk to greet them. Kitto led the Head Hunter Clan into the heart of the compound, waving and grinning at the cheering crowds. I knew what they were all thinking. It was written all over their faces. Kitto was their saviour, a strong warrior who not only kept them safe, but provided for them in their time of need.

Tallack's hold over the tribe was weakening.

# CHAPTER SEVEN

Renowden was at the rear of the procession of returning Head Hunters. He was in terrible shape, barely hanging onto the reins of his pony. While the Hunters took their victory laps around the central paths of the island, revelling in the praise, Ren stopped his horse outside my hut and almost fell from its back. I hurried to help him inside away from prying eyes.

"Are you hurt?" I panted, fearing the worst.

He shook his head and coughed for a long time. "Just need to catch my breath. I'll be fine in a bit."

We both knew that to be a lie. It was a foolish errand. Tallack never should have sent him. He took some water with a little honey that I'd been saving for a special occasion. These days, special occasions were a rarity. I also knew that the sweetness would perk him up until I could get some good food into his belly. He needed bread, something easy to digest, but there was no flour nor grains to be had anywhere in camp. With Vina out searching for roots and Kewri slicing up some venison, I sat and listened to his story of how he found the Hunters.

After I'd spotted them at the far end of our northern wood, Ren tracked them to the edges of the moors. The heath fire had already passed that area, blackening everything in its path and forcing all the creatures east. It took another half day for him to catch up with them on the borders with the Durotriges land, where they'd set up camp and looked as though they were prepared to stay there for some time.

"I spoke at great length to each of the men, trying to convince them to return. They are loyal to Kitto now that Blydh has gone." He said, before gulping down the honey water.

I nodded agreement. It was worse than I'd feared.

"Kitto has them all believing that Tallack wanted his brother dead so that he could take full control over the tribe without him. They blame him for the strange behaviour, the attack on Endelyn, the failed trip to the sacred springs, everything."

The news was difficult to swallow. I knew how close the twins were, but few of the men had the same privileges that I'd enjoyed. In public, my nephews often disagreed, more so towards the end, when Blydh was overcome by the dark spirit from the Underworld. His head injury preyed heavily on my mind every night. I laid awake wondering if there was anything else I could have done to save his life that day but all my ruminations came to nought.

Without my procedures to remove the shattered bone from his brain, he would have certainly died. If only I could return to that moment and warn myself against using the golden sun disc to protect his head from further damage. That was a mistake I had to live with for the rest of my days and one my family would always have to hold against me.

"So, how did you get them to come back?"

"I didn't really. In the end, it was Kitto's decision. He suddenly roused everyone from their slumber and ordered them to hunt like their lives depended upon it; said that the tribe's folk were relying on them. As soon as they had enough butchered and wrapped, we rode like the Morrighan was on our tail all the way home."

I stared down at the rushes. Kitto was a shrewd man. He had the Hunters obeying his every word. They'd stayed away just long enough for our people to get desperate, then returned in the nick of time to be hailed as heroes. "And they all follow him without question?"

Ren nodded slowly. This was disturbing news indeed. Tallack's number of loyal Sea Warriors was dwindling fast. With the Alchemists slaughtering the two men alongside Massen at the northern mines, and the losses we'd incurred during the Duro attack and the fated trip into Belgae territory, the Head Hunter Clan was almost double the size of the Sea Warrior Clan. If Tallack couldn't bring them back under the control of his Chieftaincy, there was a strong possibility that our family would cease to rule over Dumnonii lands. If that should happen, Kitto would have all our heads skewered on posts at the gates before the sun set.

Ren didn't need to explain what this meant. We both knew the risks involved. When I told him about Tallack's proposal to Endelyn, he blew out his cheeks and shook his head. "They will not respect a Ruvane from the Priest Sect, not after the incident with the poisoned water last winter."

"But she was never part of the Sect. She practiced at the Nine Maiden Stones on the moors."

"Doesn't matter. As far as the Hunters are concerned, all priests are the same."

I sat on the bunk beside him and rested my weary head in my hands. We stayed like that for some time, lost in deep thought with no need to speak. For what could we say? We both knew that our family faced tough challenges ahead, and neither of us wanted to admit that Tallack was too inexperienced to meet them. He was not a cruel leader like his grandfather, nor a disciplined one like his brother. Instead, he'd embraced clemency before earning his reputation as a fierce warrior in battle like his father, Aebba. Without the respect of all the clans, he would have a short reign and a short life to match. What then would become of Cryda, little Delen and me? A shiver passed down my spine.

Ren saw me close my eyes and shudder. He lifted his arm around my shoulder and tipped his head against mine. "We'll think of something, Mel. Don't give in just yet."

I wish I could say that I shared his optimism. With all the mismanagement over the last quarter moon, I didn't think things could get any worse. He stayed until the meat and roots were cooked and for once, all four of us sat around a table to eat together. This was my own little family of misfits. How many moons had I left to enjoy them?

For most of the day, I had queues of incomers lined up at my door for healing remedies. The one benefit of having such warm weather was that many of the plants surviving the drought had seeded early, including angelica. I couldn't trust Vina to pick the right plants, since they look so similar to some that are potent poisons. Instead, Kewri walked out to the edges of the marshlands to pick the seed heads ready to crush.

Many of those at my door were the mothers of lice ridden children. With a quick dunk in the stream and some soapwort rubbed into their hair, Ren set about shaving their heads before passing them along to me. I sprinkled the crushed angelica seeds on their skin and moved them along to Vina, who grumbled while she smeared any cuts and scrapes with plantain paste. By the time we'd finished, there was a whole collection of shiny pink scalped youngsters sitting on the grass squabbling over food scraps.

One or two of the mothers asked us to treat them too, until eventually, we'd shaved entire families. Whether or not the lice had spread, the whole procedure made us all itch. It was hot and tiring work. When all the seed was gone, and we'd sent the visitors on their way, Ren and I went down to the stream and dangled our feet in the cool water. It tingled and revived me, but I still felt grubby. Ren must have felt the same because he slipped off the bank and sat half-submerged in the tributary fully clothed.

I had to laugh. He cared not what other people thought. While I was distracted, he yanked me by my ankle until I too was laying on the stream bed. Spluttering, giggling and soaking wet. The moment of silliness cheered my old heart no end. Ren flicked and splashed water at me until others from the camp saw us. I thought they might jeer at us old folk having a bit of fun, but they saw it as permission to do the same. Before we knew it, Kewri, Vina, the elders, mothers, children and the camp dogs had all jumped in with us.

We frolicked about as though we were all half-addled by the heat until the stream was a giant muddy mess. That did not please those who needed fresh water for washing clothes or making their stews, but it did us all the power of good.

When the fiercest heat of the day had passed, Ren helped me out of the stream and together we walked up to my hut to let our clothes dry on our bodies. Kewri had built a fire outside the shelter rather than indoors. It kept the leftover food from our last meal bubbling gently. I find it odd that when you have no grain, you hanker for bread and porridge, and when meat is scarce, that's all you want to eat. We had food in our bellies and that was more than some. There was a lot for which to be thankful, despite the bleak uncertainty ahead.

As the sun lowered behind the palisade walls to the west, Kewri went in search of his friends from the recruits' tent, and Vina left us alone to talk. I found that Ren and I had kept pace in terms of thinking about our worries and fears. The issue of Kitto and the Head Hunter's couldn't be put off any longer. When the warriors left their building work outside the compound and returned to their families, Ren decided that it was time to speak with Tallack.

The plan was simple. Ren had some ale stashed away. His intention was to invite Tallack back to his hut for a drink, where he would list the most pressing issues for our Chief to consider. Just before he left to find him, Ren asked if I would join in the discussion. My initial reaction was that my presence might make matters worse. The relationship between my nephew and I was less than amicable and any interference on my part might well be met with prejudice.

"Don't say that, Mel. He loves you more than anyone in the tribe. He probably snapped at you because he knows you'll forgive him. It must be a terrible strain to be a Chieftain at such a young age. He doesn't realise it but he needs you."

It was all I needed to hear. We walked to the centre of the compound and parted ways at the Long Hut. Ren turned towards the warrior shelters at the eastern fringes of the island while I continued south to Ren's house. Dipping beneath the thatch, I took in the neat surroundings, the tidy bedding and his few possessions lined up on a shelf next to his bunk, and smiled. Always the sailor, even on land. Everything was shipshape and in its place.

My clothes were still damp from the early evening romp in the stream. I didn't want to soak his bedding furs so I sat on a small bench next to the unlit fire. It wasn't long before I heard them approach. Tallack was expressing his concern about his old friend's fitness, as well he should. He was leaner than ever and hadn't yet regained his old strength. When my nephew ducked beneath the door skins, he saw me.

His face dropped from a smile into a deep frown. "What's this, Ren? An ambush?" His snarl turned towards his trusted ship mate.

"It's not like that at all. Your aunt and I are worried and we thought we would have a word with you in private to see if there was anything either of us could do to lend a hand. You have so much to deal with right now, we figured you could use our help." His diplomacy never ceased to amaze me, but then Ren had endured more summers on our ships with tricky leaders than he could count. I dare say steering the clan leaders was as important a skill to learn as navigating the oceans.

"I can manage." Tallack said, his snippy tone unrelenting.

Ren gestured to the bunk for him to sit down and poured the ale from his secret stash into three cups. He chose to sit next to Tallack, despite his leggings being as damp as my own. “Great blessings for your binding with Endelyn, Chief. She’s a fine woman.” He raised his cup to meet Tallack’s and then to mine.

“Blessings indeed.” I said as heartily as I could muster.

That seemed to break his glum mood. “Thank you. I do believe it will be well favoured. The priestess does seem to have the ear of the gods, and the tribe’s folk love her. It’s a good match.” We drank in celebration, sipping at the precious beer. He was starting to relax, lowering his defensive posture. “So, what’s on your mind?” He directed the question at Ren and I was happy for him to do so, for every time I made mention of tribal affairs, I was bluntly told not to interfere.

“While I was out with the Head Hunters, I made some troubling observations you should know about.” Ren went on to explain how Kitto had a strong and loyal force behind him and how if it came to a fight, they would overthrow the might of the Sea Warriors with ease. Ren had mastery of the conversation, dropping in hints and suppositions until Tallack was forced to come to the same conclusions as we already had.

“This sounds very much like Kitto is mobilising the men to take over the tribe.”

“It does, Chief, and if you take into account the Alchemists’ revolt, we are in a particularly weak position. If Kitto and Kenver join forces…”

From the look on my nephew’s face, I’d say he hadn’t considered half of the things Ren pointed out. I dare say he truly believed that leading a tribe would be nothing but ale and feasts. His father had done little to prepare any of his boys for rule. Faced with such a weighty task ahead, Tallack did the sensible thing and asked what his most trusted adviser would do under the circumstances.

Ren stifled a smile. He was getting through to him at last. "You need to secure your place among the men. Announce who you choose to replace you as clan leader for the Sea Warriors first."

"Fine, that's easy, I choose you, Ren."

Renowden chuckled and then poured more ale into Tallack's cup. "I'm honoured, Chief, really I am, but I'm too old to lead the men. I need a warm bunk at night these days and the comfort of undisturbed sleep. Whoever you choose, I will gladly assist for a while. Just until they find their sea legs and learn to navigate our waters."

For a moment or two I panicked, thinking that Tallack would immediately choose the young upstart, Treeve to take charge of the sailors. That would alienate the rest of his men.

My nephew pouted, staring down at his feet. "Who would you pick?"

"Honestly, Chief, you'd go a long way to find a better man than Massen. He's a favourite among the warriors and Head Hunter's, he's fair and even tempered and stronger than an auroch bull. He's also loyal to you and your family, so you really can't go wrong with him."

"Good. I agree. What about the Head Hunters?"

Ren sucked in his lips and shook his head. "That is one tangled mess to sort. Kitto is the obvious leader, but he'd rise up and take over the tribe in less than a half moon. He's a dangerous man to have about camp and has too much influence over the warriors when they're away."

"That's not a solution, Ren. That's just reaffirming what we already know."

"If we are to retake control of the mines from the Alchemists, you're going to need the support of every one of our men." Ren looked up at me. He seemed to be stumped as to how to resolve the crisis. I had no answer for him.

Tallack scratched his forearm, bringing red welts to the surface. "Are you suggesting that I have him killed? Claim he is plotting against us?"

"No, I'm not saying that at all. That would set the men against you forever. They admire him. The trouble is, if you'll pardon me for saying…?"

He waited until Tallack nodded, giving him permission to speak candidly.

"The men respect Kitto more than they do you. He's had many summers to prove himself in battle compared to your few." Ren twitched and fidgeted raising the subject, but Tallack needed to hear the truth.

I watched as my nephew processed the information laid at his feet. It was a hard lesson for him, especially so soon after his twin's death. He and Blydh kept one another on an even keel. They confided in almost everything. Now poor Tallack was cast adrift with only a few trusted fellows to guide him.

He drained his cup and placed it on the table. Neither Ren nor I felt the need to speak, the decision was his alone to make. I thought he might conclude that Kitto should be sent on a mission far from our lands until his popularity waned. Perhaps a scouting trip to the top of the world to assess the situation with the Novantae after we had slain their Chieftain and all their heirs, but Tallack had another plan. One that was doomed to failure.

# CHAPTER EIGHT

"I shall tell the Head Hunters to hold leadership trials to root out the best of the best. Whoever they put forward must defeat me in single combat for the honour of becoming the next clan leader of the Head Hunters." Tallack announced, taking to his feet and puffing out his chest with pride.

I couldn't believe what I was hearing. Whatever trial he could come up with would be won by Kitto, who would go on to slay Tallack at the first opportunity. Tallack was handing the tribe and my head over to Kitto without the need for battle. I couldn't let him follow such a flawed plan without speaking up.

"Nephew, with respect…" I began, but he curled his lip as I started to speak. "Please, hear me out, I beg you."

His posture returned to a defensive one. He sat back down on the bunk, folded his arms and glowered. "Get it off your chest, Aunt, but don't expect me to follow your suggestions." This was why Ren was better at this than me. He was a man with an esteemed position in the tribe. Even though he and I viewed most situations in the same way, I was nothing more than an interfering old crone. It crushed me to think that I'd lost his affection.

"From what Ren says, the men would rather let Kitto win in the trials to assure that he got to fight against you for the title."

"So?"

Was he really ignorant of the warrior's superior fighting skill, his massive body mass and experience? How could he believe that it would be an honourable duel between them?

Ren butted in to rescue me. "I think what your aunt is trying to say is that given the chance, Kitto would take advantage of the situation and fight dirty. It wouldn't be fair to put you in that kind of position."

"You don't think I'm up to it, that's what you're saying." Tallack looked affronted. "You forget that I have the mystical blade. I am favoured by all the gods. With that against his feeble bronze sword, I will carve him into pieces and then appoint someone trustworthy in his place." The hubris of youth, will they ever learn?

"You plan on killing Kitto? Then what would be the point of holding warrior trials?" Ren said, utterly missing the part where Tallack believed himself invincible.

"I can then choose the second best to lead my Head Hunters. They will bow to me having beaten Kitto, and I will earn their respect."

Every aspect of his plan was idiocy, but no amount of cajoling or persuasion would alter his mind. He was determined to go through with the whole thing. There was enough food in camp for maybe a quarter moon, if no one squirrelled away more than they needed. Most people supplemented their rations with what other items they could scavenge in the marshlands or along the coast.

That gave Tallack a little time to get himself organised before sailing along the south-eastern coast to Bentewyn to regain control of the mines. That assumed he would be victorious over Kitto and could bring the Hunters to heel. It was an ambitious assumption.

Tallack left Ren's hut shortly after his announcement. He said he wished to spend time with his mother and little sister. I know my nephew well. Under times of extreme stress, he returns to the comforting arms of his mother. He knew full well that he was unlikely to beat Kitto in single combat, with or without a sword made from an unknown metal.

Ren dribbled out the last of the ale into my cup. "He can't win." He muttered.

I shook my head.

"Then you know what will happen?"

Sniffing, I nodded. He had no need to say it out loud. It would mark the end of many generations of our family rule over Dumnonii lands. Cryda, the babe and myself would be beheaded, if Kitto was feeling merciful. If not, ritual humiliation, torture and a slow death to discourage anyone from standing against his claim.

"I won't let that happen to you, Mel. We need to make contingency plans."

I understood his meaning. He wanted Cryda and I to escape from the compound with little Delen. He thought we should disappear into the wilderness to live out our days eking out a living from the land like every other family. There was just one problem with that course of action. We were of Chieftain blood, so too was Endelyn's unborn child and Tallack's half-brother, Paega the Wily. Every one of us had the right to challenge Kitto's claim to the Dumnonii. Our tribal alliances were deep rooted, forged over time from the binding ties of wedlock and kinship. Kitto would run us down, right to the ends of the world, to kill us all.

Cryda could legitimately seek refuge and protection from her birth family. Her brother was the Chieftain of the Cantii. In theory, she could also run to the mountain people to be with her daughter Derwa and her husband and heir to the Ordoviches, Glaw. I couldn't see that being an option though, after they were banished from camp for helping Paega to escape his cage.

Despite all those options, I had an inkling that Cryda would refuse to leave. She was loyal to the tribe in the fiercest way. Could I really leave her and the babe to die alone? I'd had my long life and was grateful for every summer and spring but I was also tired. Perhaps this would be the season to end all seasons and I would seek my place next to my ancestors at last.

I lifted my hand and cupped Ren's cheek. "You're a good man, but it won't do any good to flee."

"Nonsense. We can pack and prepare everything in advance and, if the fight goes sour, we'll walk out of the compound and ride across the border. I'll come with you. I know loads of places where the Head Hunters have never been. They won't find you. I'm pretty sure Kewri would come too, if that's what's bothering you."

It wasn't. I was also sure he'd be willing to accompany us. It was an attractive proposition but I knew that Cryda would not survive without her luxury and comforts. For her to make a new life for herself, she had to be with her kin. "If you want to help me, you dear man, please make sure that Cryda and Delen get to the Cantii. That is my fervent wish."

His eyes narrowed. He understood what I meant to do. I would provide the distraction needed for him to get the young ones away. He nodded his head just once. We had an agreement. I turned to leave.

"Stay. We don't have many nights left to us." He looked so vulnerable, so pale. My resolve left me before I could get to the door. He skirted around me and lifted the wooden panel across the opening. What harm could it possibly do? We both deserved a little warmth and succour before the end.

The next day, I heard Kewri rushing about outside the hut. His footsteps were easy to distinguish from others. They pounded the dry earth like no other. When his great fists rattled the door panel, Ren jumped from a deep sleep and grabbed his sword.

"Ho there, Ren. Have you seen Fur Benyn? She didn't come home last night." Kewri gushed in a panic.

"I'm in here, Kewri. There's nothing to worry about." I yelled, throwing my tunic over my head and crouching in search of my pattens. When Ren moved the panel Kewri averted his gaze, although I was perfectly respectable by then. "Um, er, if it's all the same to you, Fur Benyn, please don't disappear like that. I've been searching the woods since dawn thinking you'd been half-eaten by a wolf pack."

I had to stifle a cackle. The poor giant was more affected by the slow and painful death of our enemy Brea than I thought. I wondered how many other young ones were haunted by the sight of a woman being torn to pieces by those ravenous beasts. I recalled that he was quite looking forward to the spectacle at the time.

Ren grappled my hand as I slipped past him. "Will I see you later?" I gave him a mischievous wink and traipsed across the island back to my house. Despite my determination to remain in camp should the worst come to pass, I needed to know that Cryda and Delen would have all they needed to make it to the Cantii. While Ren went off to train with Tallack in the woods, I packed a few tonics and pastes that I thought might come in handy for her journey. I stacked all the little bundles by the door with the intention of giving them to Ren just before they left.

By midday, the smell of smoke was strong in my nostrils. The wind had changed again and was shifting the heath fires in a southerly direction. Treeve walked about camp banging a blade against a shield and shouting the latest orders from our Chief. The warriors, elders and family of the Chieftain were called to a meeting outside Endelyn's hut. It made sense to use her place as the temporary central point while the Long Hut was crammed with homesteaders and their screaming children.

I cleared away the mess from an ointment I'd been preparing and rinsed my hands in the stream. When I got to the priestess's hut, most of the warriors were already crowding around. Some of the elders parted ways to let me sneak to the front, mainly because they could still see over my head.

Tallack and Endelyn stood in front of the carved icons, with Senara leaning against the doorway behind them. It was an odd scene, seeing one of my kin joining forces with someone of the Priest Sect. When his father tried the same, it proved to be nothing but a constant thorn in his side. I hoped that it would be different for my nephew.

"Come closer, this is a joyous day and one we will all remember." Tallack began. Everyone shuffled forwards around him. "It is with enormous pleasure that I introduce you to my bride. Endelyn has agreed to bind with me at midsummer." His grin was so broad, dimples appeared in his cheeks. He was genuinely pleased with his choice. While the Sea Warriors cheered and stamped their feet in support of his selection, the Head Hunters glared and frowned at one another. I kept my eye on Treeve's reaction. He was standing on the opposite side of the group to me. His face was utterly neutral, making it hard for me to gauge his thoughts. Tallack held Endelyn's hand and pulled her towards the crowd. She fluttered her eye lashes and acted all coy, but the display failed to stir the warriors. The elders, mesmerised by her performance, kept the stomping and cheering going for much longer than was required.

"Thank you, thank you all." She effused. "You have all welcomed me into your embrace and made me feel a part of the tribe as no other could. I promise to serve you well as your Ruvane."

That was when the Sea Warriors stopped their cheers. They were puzzled. It was obvious that they thought she would become his second wife. Each of them was present at the crossing on the River Sid, when Chief Fane proposed that his daughter should bind with Tallack at the earliest opportunity. Having the priestess become their Ruvane was beyond imagining, despite the Sea Warriors being used to Tallack's unconventional leadership style.

"I'm glad you all approve." Tallack said. The rest of the noise from the elders died immediately, making it clear that they did not, in fact, approve. I caught Cryda smirking among the crowd. It was just as she had said. Endelyn was fine as their priestess, a second wife even, but not as their Ruvane. She simply didn't have the right blood to make it a worthy match. She brought nothing to the tribe by way of increased alliances or trade partners, unlike the Duro girl.

The tense atmosphere continued as my nephew followed that shocking news with his choice of clan successor. "With my growing commitments in camp, I have appointed Massen as the new clan leader of the Sea Warriors." The tribe were at least pleased with that, raising their voices and patting him on the back so heartily he almost lost his balance. It left Kitto scowling at the Chief. He anticipated the same reaction for his own elevation, expecting Tallack to name him as Blydh's successor to the Head Hunters.

"I know my sailors well…" Tallack continued, ignoring several snorts of derision. "But only my brother knew the Hunters well enough to choose from among them. I have respect and admiration for you all, but to make it fair, I have devised a trial to select the worthiest."

The Hunters had not predicted this turn of events. They shifted uneasily, moving apart from each other and the rest of the crowd as though a little competition would make them all sworn enemies.

"You will fight in friendly bouts until the victors are reduced to one. Poles and sticks only, no metal. When there is one clear winner, they must beat me in a single bout. If they can best me, they will become the next leader of the clan." Tallack glanced at Endelyn and grinned. Was she already directing him?

Over the course of one night, he'd gone from fighting and killing Kitto with his mystical sword, to a wrestling match. It was less risky, but there was still nothing to stop Kitto from throttling the life out of our Chief, sharpening a pole into a spear or hiding a dagger until the last moment and plunging it into Tallack's throat. He was far larger and stronger than Tallack would ever be. He might survive the trial, but he was more likely than ever to lose face in front of the entire tribe.

Our family's reign would end on a whimper instead of a roaring, bellowing battle between two warriors. Not one person asked what would happen should the winner of the trials be defeated by Tallack; they all knew that Kitto would be the outright victor. How was it that everyone could see the obvious except my nephew?

I'd heard enough. There was no sense in his actions at all. As I turned to walk away, I noticed that Treeve did too. He disappeared behind the Long Hut and out of view before I could catch up with him. It always worries me when he goes quiet. That's when I distrust him the most. He may look small and weak, but beneath the feeble exterior lies a wilful and bitter man.

I waited outside the shelter to try and catch Cryda on her way home. There was still a high probability of her son being killed by one of the strongest men in our tribe. I had to try and convince her to leave camp while she could. When the crowds dispersed, I craned my neck to see which route she would take across the compound. Before I could catch her, Endelyn bounded up to me, oozing charm and insincerity.

"Meliora…" I don't know why it grated so much. She was entitled to use my given name. "Do you have any valerian root spare? I'm finding it hard to drift off to sleep."

I spotted Cryda ducking behind the Long Hut, just as Treeve had done. "Take what you need, Endelyn. My apprentice will show you where I keep it." I hurried away before she could stop me. The more time Cryda had to prepare, the better. Scurrying as fast as my old legs could carry me, I cut across her path on the opposite side of the Long Hut.

"Cryda. We must speak. It's really important."

She moved in a half-circle around me and carried on walking. "Must we? I'm shattered and my slave needs to go and wash more linens through for Delen. Her stomach is upset."

I offered to examine the babe if she was willing to speak with me at the same time. When we got back to her hut, the slave was jogging the child in her arms trying to soothe her. Nothing seemed to work. When she saw Cryda, the girl offloaded Delen into her mother's arms and dashed out with a basket of stinking cloths and mucky moss. It says a lot when a slave would rather wash infant kawgh from bindings than listen to the incessant wailing of a baby.

I checked her over. There was no extra heat to her skin, her cheeks were rosy and she had no rashes nor swellings. She was simply irritable from the dry heat of the summer and too many leaves in her food. After I'd declared her fit, Cryda loosened the pin on her tunic and presented a nipple to the child. It latched on like a barnacle, making her mother wince.

"Teeth coming through?"

Cryda nodded. I did all I could to approach the conversation with tact and diplomacy, but I am not Renowden. My words came out as a slur on her son's abilities.

"Don't be ridiculous. Tallack is a superb warrior. He'll beat any man in the tribe. Just you wait and see."

When I suggested that she and the child leave to visit her relations on Cantii ground, she laughed in my face. "I'm not going anywhere. This is my home and my place is with my children. Honestly, Meliora. You were never this cowardly before. What has got into you?"

I didn't answer her, there was no point. At least my conscience would be clear if the worst happened. Out of the corner of my eye, I spotted Treeve moving outside. Loitering in Cryda's doorway, I squinted in the sunlight, watching him duck into Tallack's stores behind the guard's back. Sometimes I wonder why my nephew even bothers to put a watch over that place. His men are hardly on their mettle. Within moments, the young crewman flitted back out the way he came with a small jug in his arms.

Cryda was still mocking me when I left to follow him. I have never trusted that lad, especially after hearing him threaten Kerensa when she admitted that her end game was to become Ruvane and wife of Blydh before his injury. Treeve was fleet of foot, making it difficult for me to keep pace with him. Several times he glanced back to see if he was being observed. The first couple of times, I dipped behind a warrior tent or the empty grain store. When he hurried across the brown grass, there was nowhere for me to hide.

Straining my eyes to their fullest capabilities, I saw him approach Endelyn's place. Here, he slipped behind the carved icons of the gods. For a moment or two, I was unable to see what he was doing, until he reappeared without the jug and wandered away. What is that boy up to? I should warn Endelyn. Treeve may not have killed Kerensa, but I had no doubt that murder was on his mind.

# CHAPTER NINE

I ambled back to my hut filled with worry. Endelyn was nowhere to be seen. Even a cursory glance at the jug gave me no clues as to what he could have laced it with. For most of the day, I watched and waited for her to return, completing as many of my chores outside next to the shelter.

Vina was in one of her cooperative moods. "The priestess took your jar of valerian and some other bits she said she needed. Shall I go out and look for more to replace what she took?"

"Yes, that's a great idea, Vina. Thanks." The sooner she was out of my hair the better. She took Tallack's dagger and a hemp bag and headed for the meadows through the western gate. It left Kewri and I to fall into our old routines. He fixed, mended and chopped while I stripped leaves, pulverized and mixed various ointments and tinctures. All the while we worked, thoughts of my nephew's demise encircled my mind.

By late afternoon, Kewri came back from the wooded area at the western fringes near the pony enclosure fastening his belt around his leggings. "Fur Benyn, have you seen any of the new folk loitering about here?"

I walked towards his shelter drying my hands. "No, why?"

"Another one of your goats has gone."

"For the love of Cernonnus. This is getting tiresome. There'll be none left at this rate." I fumed. "It's no use. You'll have to move your bunk back into the hut and take the goats into the shelter. It's the only way we can keep them safe." He grumbled and moaned, but even he had to see that he couldn't watch them all the time. Those homesteader children were faster than lightning and experts in hiding from view. My poor goats would be sliced up and in a pot before sundown.

A little later, I saw Endelyn and Senara folding a long length of fabric outside their hut. Dropping everything, I hobbled down the boards to warn them of what I'd witnessed. They saw me coming and smiled.

"Isn't this just the finest weave you've ever seen, Meliora?" Endelyn smoothed her hand along the material. "You can almost see right through it."

"It's lovely. I came to speak to you about…"

"Yes, I'm glad you're here. You were telling me about the dyes, in particular the colour of that tiny banner on Tallack's ship. I want that for my binding ceremony gown." She handed the bundle of fabric to Senara who went inside their hut.

"What? No, as I said before. It's not possible to achieve that colour without a particular sea snail."

"Well, where can I get those? I want the ceremony to be special."

I sighed. She was not going to let the matter drop. "A Phoenician Prince once told me that the snails live on the other side of the world. There is no such colour like it anywhere. You can have pale purple, but only when the elder or bramble fruits ripen in the autumn, or you can have red if you're prepared to dig up enough bedstraw root to crush, but then Tallack won't be too pleased if you do. His warriors rely on that. Your best bet is a nice bright ochre, as vivid as the sunset."

She pouted. "And what would I need for that?"

"Alder bark, lots and lots of the stuff. It's the inner part you need, so be prepared to get your hands well stained. There are plenty of those trees upstream along the river bank." She had thrown me off my purpose. I almost walked away without telling her about the jug. Stepping closer to her, I lowered my voice. "I spotted Treeve here earlier today acting suspiciously. He left a jug behind the carved gods over there. Make sure whatever it is, you throw it away. I don't trust that lad."

Endelyn flitted to the carved trunks and glanced behind them. "What jug?"

I was stunned for a moment and followed her gaze. It was gone. "But it was there, I'm sure of it."

The priestess lifted the back of her hand to my forehead. "Have you been out in the sun all day? Maybe you should have a cool drink of water and a bit of a lie down."

"I'm not sick. I saw him do it. He took a jug from Tallack's stores and left it here."

"Perhaps he meant it as an offering to the gods, but changed his mind. It happens from time to time." The look she gave me wavered between mockery and pity. Why was everyone treating me like a simpering old crone?

I scowled at her. "Pardon my interference, but you'd do well to heed my warning. Stay away from Treeve. He means to do you harm." Her smirk was more than I could take. I stomped towards home furious with her condescension. How quickly she had taken on the mantle of Ruvane was astounding. Before I could set foot in my door, the watchtower horn sounded again. My spine crumpled with the thought of more homesteaders to delouse and feed, but when the gates opened and the bridge lowered there was a single horseman waiting to enter. I recognised him at once. It was Perren, the scout from the Durotriges Tribe.

There was no mystery as to the message he carried, but I went to greet him anyway. His approach was justifiably cautious until he saw me. Any solitary Duro riding into a former enemy's camp would be the same. I stood outside the Long Hut and waited until he was level with the door. His dismount was sprightly considering the distance he must have ridden.

"Well, if it's not our favourite spy." I said, but not so loudly that others would hear.

He grinned and held his arm out for me to grasp in greeting. "You look well, Fur Benyn. The summer treats you with kindness, I see."

"Ah give over. Save your flattery for Senara." I laughed, but then noted his puzzled look. "Are you not taken with our fair shield maiden?"

"Fond of her, certainly. Senara has no aims to make it more than that." His perplexed frown slackened into one of sadness. I'd touched upon a raw topic. Common decency dictated that I changed the subject.

"You have brought word from Chief Fane, no doubt?" I gestured for him to walk with me in the general direction of Tallack's hut.

"I have indeed."

"Then when you've delivered your message, you must come and eat with Kewri and me. I am determined to repay your kindness."

That put a smile back on his face. When we arrived at Tallack's door, there were familiar sounds emanating from inside. Tallack was otherwise occupied with his crewman.

"How about I take you to see Senara first, eh? Let you catch up for a while and as soon as I find the Chief, I'll bring him to you." Perren understood my distraction fully and played along like the fine fellow I knew him to be. I hoped to Cernonnus that he didn't know with whom our Chief was busy, the Duros are not fond of deviations from what's considered normal. Some might call them a prudish bunch.

I altered our destination and quickened my step, calling out to the priestess and her close friend as we walked. They welcomed the scout into their home, introducing the young pup and offering him a whole range of exotic foods to sample.

Endelyn poured him some Frynkish wine and served a few olives from across the ocean in a bowl. Perren had never encountered them before. He bit into one and shuddered as his teeth hit the stone. Its dry flesh and tangy taste shocked him. His face contorted and his tongue protruded until we were all in fits of laughter at his expense. While he was providing the entertainment, I slipped back outside and stood just beyond Tallack's doorway.

"Chief Tallack, your presence is requested. A Duro scout has arrived with a message from Chief Fane." I practically bellowed it so that there was no way he could say he hadn't heard.

The muffled talking and bumping about inside continued for a short while. His rutting really was becoming most tedious. "He's waiting for you at the priestess's hut." I shouted, irritated by his complacency over his relationship with Treeve.

"Tell him I'll be right there, Aunt Mel."

I could have continued walking south to Ren's place, but I was curious as to how Endelyn would react to the news from Fane. Instead of leaving them to their own business, I returned to Endelyn's hut and enjoyed the entertainment while I could.

Tallack did not leave the scout waiting for long. Perren had drunk less than half a cup of the wine when he arrived, smoothing his hair down and folding his arms behind his back. A Chief did not greet lowly scouts in the same way that I had done. This was Tallack's idea of exerting his authority over those of us in the room. It worked too, since Perren shot up from his stool and bowed his head to my nephew.

"Chief, I have an urgent message from Chief Fane of the Durotriges."

"Out with it then. I don't have time to waste."

"Right, yes. He asks that you give your decision immediately or he'll take this delay as an indication that the truce no longer holds." The poor lad couldn't look Tallack in the eye, yet he was a good few summers older than my nephew and much taller.

Tallack tipped forwards on his toes and frowned at the scout, feigning deep thought.

Endelyn was all charm as usual. "What decision is this, my love?" I'd completely forgotten that she was not present at the borderlands when the two Chiefs last spoke together. Had Senara kept the news from Endelyn all this time or was she using it as a way to butt into the conversation?

"Nothing for you to worry about. Walk with me… what's your name, lad?"

"Perren, Chief, if it pleases you."

Tallack backed out of the priestess's hut gesturing for Perren to follow. "Aunt, if you will come and arrange for the care of his horse and such."

To be honest, I was shaken to the core that he wanted to include me in his negotiations after shunning me so viciously before. His moods were as changeable as his brother's of late. I trotted after them, leaving Senara to break the news to her companion, if it was indeed news.

When I caught up with the long strides of the men, Tallack was telling Perren that he'd be delighted to accept Fane's daughter as his wife, and that his Chief should send her directly to our camp where his mother; "Would guarantee her safety until our binding on midsummer's eve."

I almost choked on my own breath when I heard him say that, for I was sure that Endelyn was planning their binding on the same day and there was no way she would share that ceremony with a Chieftain's daughter from another tribe. I said nothing, preferring to listen and watch while he dealt with the fallout from his actions.

"If you'll permit me to speak my mind, Chief?" Perren said, increasing in boldness.

They stopped walking and faced one another. Tallack nodded.

"I know Fane's daughter, Chief. She is… delicate and sensitive." He tilted his head as though he was searching for the right words without causing offence. Now I saw why Fane valued him as a messenger. "If I were of a mind to avoid outbursts and unpleasantness, I would build her a home of such finery, that she had little to complain about."

Tallack grinned. "Is that so? Well, tell your Chief that his daughter will know no hardship whatsoever. Nothing will be spared in her honour. She will have so many furs and slaves she won't know what to do with them all."

So, this was how men spoke about us women behind our backs. For some reason, my mind wandered to Tallack's horse slaves. They too were given similar instructions since my nephew valued his steeds above all else.

After they'd shared a knowing chuckle between them, Tallack invited Perren to stay a day or two to watch the Head Hunter trials.

"That's kind of you, Chief, and believe me when I say that nothing would give me greater pleasure, but I am under orders to return this very night." I was disappointed that he couldn't stay. On more than one occasion he'd shared his food and shelter with Kewri, Senara and me in the borderlands. I felt I owed the man.

Before he left, I scuttled back home and wrapped a few cooked strips of venison for him to take and wished him safe travels. Tallack left us at the gate and returned to Endelyn to explain the deal he'd made with our new allies. I couldn't imagine that would be a particularly jolly conversation in light of all her preparations for her binding day.

When I got back to my hut, I found Vina and Kewri scowling at one another across the room. His bunk was back in its usual place and the goats were bleating in their new home under Kewri's shelter. The atmosphere between them combined with the sultry heat made me snappy and tired. The bench with all my herbs and potions was a mess. Powders scattered, flowers crushed and jars upended as if Endelyn's puppy had tumbled across the table.

Tutting and mumbling, I picked a few of the items up and scraped the mess onto the rushes. "Did the priestess bring the valerian root pot back?" I asked Vina. She answered in the form of a shrug, while maintaining her glower at Kewri.

There was something amiss with my things. The spilled blackthorn flower heads were everywhere. It wasn't like Vina to be so sloppy. When I can get her to do some work, she was always neat and tidy. In light of the recent spate of goat thefts, I suddenly wondered if anything else had been taken.

"Have either of you been at my poppy resin?" I must have sounded terse, for it broke their staring match in an instant.

"No, not touched it," they chorused. I was sure that the pot was three quarters full. There was barely a fraction left. If it wasn't Vina or Kewri, then we would have to board the door every time we left to prevent further pilfering. If any of the men were injured during the trials, they would have to make do with willow bark for pain relief. I had no more tin to trade for resin.

Things were looking desperate for more than just the homesteaders. Tallack had promised lavish goods and slaves to his new Duro bride, with no way of paying for them. The longer my nephew left it to deal with the insurrection at the mines, the greater the likelihood of Kenver forging trade links with foreigners behind our backs. We'd lose control over the mines for good, unless he acted quickly to restore order. That was, of course, providing he lived through the trials.

At dawn, Treeve started banging that infernal shield again, calling all the Head Hunter contestants to the clearing beyond the river opposite the southern gates. Some of the men carried benches from the Long Hut so that the elders and those heavy with child could sit and watch the fights. Tallack ordered that the wooden paling structures be pushed back to give the warriors space to move freely. All that was left to organise was the pairings for each bout.

Eight men stood in a line in front of Tallack and his Sea Warriors. Endelyn rubbed her belly and arched her back, exaggerating her suffering from the early stages of her pregnancy. My nephew took the cue. "Shall I have our chairs brought out for us, my dear?"

"That would be wonderful. Thank you, Tallack." She simpered. His order to carry out his bear head chair was not surprising. What floored us all, was that he also demanded that his men collected his brother's tall chair for the priestess; the Chieftain's wolf's head seat.

I caught Treeve's expression as the men set the chair down next to Tallack. His scowl would not ease. I cannot fathom that young man at all. His manner is too forward, his arrogance irks all the men and elders in camp, and yet his devotion to my nephew is astounding.

Senara swooped down with a bundled sheepskin to cushion the seat. With her customary lazy grin, Endelyn lowered herself into position next to her intended. There was no way she would give way to a Duro bride. She had every intention of becoming the Ruvane, no matter the cost. That was evident to all as she sat there surveying the grounds before her.

We all waited for the men to finish preparing the site, but there was simply not enough room. The new homesteaders' shelters sprawled right across the former training grounds. Even with our defences moved back, the space could not accommodate the bouts for eight men at once. The Head Hunters were all for demolishing the huts, the Sea Warriors tried to bring about a compromise and the homesteaders squabbled over their new homes. Tempers were more than frayed and looked set to spill over into an all-out battle within the tribe.

I looked to Tallack to take control, display his status and power by acting swift and decisively. The whole point of the exercise was for Tallack to regain the men's respect. With the situation balancing on the edge, Tallack sat frozen in his tall chair.

# CHAPTER TEN

Kitto smirked as the Head Hunters pushed and shoved the Sea Warriors. The Homesteaders set loose their wives to kick and punch at anyone nearing their huts, the men standing behind them with spears in hand ready to defend their homes. With the camp dogs nipping at everyone's heels and barking incessantly, the noise was deafening. Still Tallack did nothing, sitting with a wide-eyed stare at his tribe as the bickering took a fearsome descent into chaos.

I watched as Kitto scanned across the sandy ground until his eyes met those of Tallack's. This was precisely what the wily older warrior wanted; more opportunities to undermine the young Chief. I leaned forward from my bench and hissed at my nephew.

"Tallack, do something… anything!" By the time I'd gained my nephew's attention, it was too late. One of the Head Hunters threw a punch at a Sea Warrior. Rather than knock him to the ground or rattle his wits it merely incensed the man. He pulled back his fist and slammed it into the jaw of the Hunter. Within moments, the anger of those jostling around them boiled over until our finest men were engaged in a vicious brawl. Knuckles and jaws collided, blood and spittle flew, until many were reduced to wrestling their opponent to the ground.

Senara fidgeted next to me, keen to wade into the fray. Even she was spoiling for a fight. All the pent-up aggression and posturing over a potential war with our neighbours had left our warriors restless. Kitto must have known that before he took the Head Hunters out to replenish our meat supplies. My poor nephew was out manoeuvred at every turn.

I tried to rouse him to action once again. “Tallack, please, you have to stop this before someone gets killed.” At first, I thought he’d not heard me. I stood up and followed my nephew’s line of sight as he watched a figure leaving the western gate and hurry across the trickling gravel beds of the stream. He looked to be in pain, his back hunched and his gait was ambling and cautious. When my old eyes focused on his face, I recognised him.

It was Ren. My breathing quickened in fear as he made his way towards the gaggle of fractious men. What I couldn’t see was what he clutched to his chest. I covered my mouth to stop myself from calling out. He was too weak to stand between the warriors; he’d be smashed to pieces by their superior strength. Even Tallack shook himself from his daze and stood up, preparing to protect his old friend.

My heart pounded in my ears, I was dizzy with fright but just when I was sure that Ren would put himself in harm’s way to stop the fighting, he stood on the periphery and lifted a horn to his lips. With a single blow, the shrill noise halted all action at once. The men looked up from their squabble and saw the battered old sailor staring at them all.

"Call yourself Dumnonii? You should be ashamed of yourselves. These homesteaders are our people. Are we not one proud tribe?" He went red in the face with the effort of yelling at them. Most of the men immediately let go of their wrestling partners and hung their heads, staring at their feet. Kitto folded his arms across his chest in defiance. Ren was not finished. As weak and sinewy as he was, he still commanded great respect. He turned to face Kitto.

"And you of all people should know better." The two men locked stares, neither backing down. "You who expects to be promoted to clan leadership, yet allows the men to succumb to their childish ways." There was a lengthy silence in which neither shifted their scowls. I thought Ren had more to say, but he remained quiet, allowing his age and standing in the community to bear down on the great warrior. Eventually, Kitto dropped his gaze to the ground. Only then did Ren spin about to address the men.

"Enough of this pettiness. Settle your differences and accept that these are troubling times. We pull together as one tribe. That's the way it is and will always be."

It was Tallack who led the foot stamping and rapping on wood in support of the crewman's speech. As much as I applaud Ren's mastery over troubled waters, it did little to assuage the men's doubts in my nephew's ability to lead. He couldn't expect Ren to bail him out of all his leadership issues and still gain the respect of our tribe's people.

Tallack relaxed in his bear head chair, chatting to Endelyn and Senara while Ren arranged the fighting bouts as fairly as he could. I watched him gather up a series of small stones from the sandy ground and show them to the men. From what I could see, he was assigning each rock to half of the warriors. I assumed that they were all distinctive in size or shape or the sorting process would return to chaos once again. One of the homesteader women fetched a bag in which the stones were placed.

Ren shook the rocks inside the cloth and held the bag out to each of the men who did not have a stone assigned to them. As the pebbles were drawn, the pairings for the bouts were fixed. Most drawings received a little chorus of cheers, until they could see that the youngest and as it happened, smallest of the competitors was left to pick Kitto. The cheers faltered. It was hardly a fair fight, but then, the lad was foolish to stand against so many others with more experience.

While the men prepared themselves, guzzling water and stripping off to their essentials in the heat of the afternoon, Ren marked out a circle in the sand with a big stick. Only one bout could occur at a time in the limited space. For those from the homestead settlements, this was a new and exciting spectacle, worthy of a ring-side seat. For those of us who are long in the tooth, it meant a tedious afternoon of stinking sweat, grunting men and the application of too many cattle gut stitches and plantain paste.

For the life of me, I couldn't figure out why Tallack was so adamant that he should fight the victor. Everyone knew that he would have to face Kitto in the ring at some point, and that would spell disaster. If the seasoned warrior allowed Tallack to live, we would be banished at best, or slaughtered as a warning to others at worst.

The drummers and pipers sat on the scorched grass on one side of the training ground, whipping the crowds up into fevered anticipation. Kitto graciously asked Ren to remain on the side line as referee, should there be a need to intervene. This was not meant to lessen the numbers of our best men by way of murder, only to demonstrate strength and agility.

When the first bout began, I slipped away to my hut in search of my medicine kit and a long cool drink. The ale supplies in camp were at an all-time low and I had no thirst for warm milk. I had to make do with water like everyone else. Before leaving my house, I took a long look at the few possessions I had left to me. With my knives taken by the Belgae on that ill-fated trip and my tin all gone, I had nothing left of value.

If the worst happened, there was only my bedding furs to offer to the gods for my passage into the Underworld. I am no warrior maiden, nor a great leader of men. There would be no seat next to my forefathers in the Summerlands on my passing.

Would Cernonnus take his vengeance out on me for my kin slaughtering the white hart? I swallowed back my tears. My life had been long and full. There was little point in fleeing. Kitto would've me run down in no time at all.

I dragged my weary limbs back to the fights to find that the first was already over. Both warriors appeared to be evenly matched in size and strength but one of them, a young man who I knew relatively well, had out matched the other in mere moments. Senara's account of the bout told me that she greatly admired this untested warrior who used his quick mind over brute force to win the bout. The Head Hunters were keen to take the man's arm and praise his fortitude. His opponent sat dejected but unharmed outside the circle, cradling his head in his hands.

“Remind me of that lad’s name, Senara.” I rasped, leaning over closer to where she sat.

“They call him Skentel.”

I screwed my face up at her, confused. “What’s his given name?” His parents wouldn’t have chosen that for his proper name. It had to have been a nickname of sorts, referring to his quick-wit and intelligence.

She shrugged. “That’s all I know of him. You’ll have to ask someone who knows him better.”

Well, that should have been me, only my memory had clouded. The men were so fond of bestowing nicknames on people. From the way he was received by both the Head Hunters and the Sea Warriors, I’d say he enjoyed a great deal of respect for one so young. He took his fill of water from the jugs at the far end of the training ground and rested alongside Kitto. I watched their interactions closely. Would Kitto see this young fellow as a potential threat, or recognise his value as a worthy ally?

Skentel nodded and smiled to the warrior as he lowered himself down on the cracked earth. Without altering his dour expression, Kitto returned the nod and glanced away. Before I could inquire further about the pair, the second bout was underway. The crowd roared once again, sending the dogs yapping and snapping into the ring, much to the amusement of all. After a brief hiatus, giving Ren time to shoo the mutts away, the bout began in earnest.

Armed only with hazel poles, the two men moved about the circle, baring their teeth and goading the other into striking first. A lunge was countered by a swift side-step, a swipe with the stick in return had them both ducking. It was quite some time before the crowd lost patience with their dance. Calls of, “Bash his head in!”

and "Get on with it!" came from the homesteaders, who were eager to see the men bleed.

When the fight truly began, the crash of the sticks sent splinters flying until both men held two halves in each hand. Neither of them would let go, lashing out with the jagged ends to catch the other in the face or neck. I could see the bout ending in a lost eye or worse, requiring my skills with a needle and hot blade at any moment.

Thankfully, Ren foresaw the same. He called out to them, forcing them to discard the broken shafts and continue the fight without weapons. For a short while the warriors glared at each other, waiting for a sign that their opponent would comply with the order.

"Do it now, men or forfeit the bout." Ren yelled, prompting both to drop the sticks immediately. It's times like this when I admire Ren the most. He has an astounding sense of fair play. If only he were of Chieftain blood. He would've made a brilliant leader. The fight continued without interruption; pounding fists, shattered teeth and an arm lock that almost squeezed the life out of the shorter of the two men. When the poor lad's face was almost purple with lack of air, he tapped his opponent's arm and conceded to the stronger man.

On it went for the rest of the afternoon until it was time for Kitto to fight with the youngest contender. The crowd stopped their yelling and cheering, hushed at the difference in stature. Kitto spat on the ground and pulled off his tunic, revealing rippling muscles and extensive tattoos across his torso. The summer heat had given him a bronze glow that glistened with a dewy sweat. He had quite a fan group of young maidens, bickering over who of them he preferred the best. Kitto flexed and preened, making a show of stretching his arms out and clicking his bullish neck.

His opponent stood at the far side of the ring, blind terror flickering in his eyes. We could all guess what was passing through the poor lad's thoughts. He had no way of backing out now, unless he was willing to be teased and belittled for the rest of his days. The lad took off his belt, but kept his tunic on. It was soaked through with nervous sweat in huge stains about his armpits and chest. Ren passed him a hazel pole and patted his back.

Kitto lifted his weapon over his head, reigniting the cheers and whoops. I watched intently, curious as to how this wily brute would handle the young warrior. Would he smash him down in mere moments, toy with him like a bird of prey teaching her young, or let the lad get a few hits in to save face? It was a puzzle playing on all our minds, of that I'm sure. Tallack leaned forward on his seat, concentrating hard on Kitto's moves.

That kind of swagger only comes when you've seen all there is to witness in battle, but did he also have the temperament to handle the men when they were weak and injured or in need of support. A good clansman should be almost a parent to those young green warriors and respectful of the limits of the elderly. Was Kitto a good fit for all those roles?

Ren called the start of the bout and moved closer to the young man. Kitto postured for a short while, examining his hazel pole intently. Every now and then he peeked up at the lad, as though he was waiting for him to act. Sure enough, the poor boy took Kitto's ruse as a sign that he could attack him while he was off his guard.

The young man hurled himself at the older warrior, taking a great swing at him with his stick. At the very last moment, Kitto blocked the strike with his own staff, pushing him backwards with such force, the lad's feet lifted off the ground. He toppled backwards and stumbled to keep his balance. Kitto bent his knees and prepared for the next assault. He'd chosen to let the boy tire himself out. All who looked on knew that the older man could kill him in a flash if he so chose. This was his way of girding the admiration of the tribe. His kindness towards the lad would stay in the memories of young and old alike. He was shrewder than I'd predicted.

Time and time again, the young fighter launched his skinny mass at Kitto, sometimes with an upwards thrust of the pole end to his gut, other times with a leap and downward strike, but all were deflected without much effort expended. Kitto was not even panting in the arid heat of the late afternoon. Just when the crowd were growing tired of the same moves, Kitto saw his chance. The young lad altered his grip and the pole slipped to the ground. Before he could stoop to retrieve it, Kitto was on him.

With a single manoeuvre, he grappled the boy's wrist and twisted it up his spine until he was squealing in agony. A swift kick to the back of the knees had him slumped to the ground. It was all over in an instant.

"Do you submit?" Kitto roared above the clamour. The lad closed his eyes and squirmed. As soon as he nodded, Kitto released him, ruffled his hair and offered his hand to pull the boy to his feet. It was a masterful show. The tribe's folk lapped it up, chanting his name in unison as he took his victory stroll around the ring.

I couldn't stop looking at my nephew. His expression was one of deep concern, and rightly so. This man was everything Tallack was not. It would take an act of the Gods to make Kitto fall from favour now. The slaves and womenfolk poured him water and offered him what little meat there was to spare, while his defeated opponent slunk off to lick his wounds. I was amazed that the first round of fights was complete without the need for my services.

Ren repeated the selection process with the stones again to decide the pairings for the second round, and after a short rest, the bouts began again. My interest waned shortly after they started. I scanned the crowd looking for signs of Cryda and her babe. She was not near to Tallack where I expected her to be, nor was she among the elders' wives or homesteaders. I thought perhaps that she had taken my advice on board and was packing her belongings ready to escape, but she appeared a short time later with Delen slung over her shoulder bawling her little eyes out.

She approached Tallack's tall chair from behind and whispered something into his ear, but I was too far away to hear. Whatever she said to him, he turned his gaze upon me and shot me a withering look. Moments later, he rose from his chair and raised his arms to silence the crowd. The tribe listened to their leader with a mixture of contempt and amusement plastered across their faces.

"I was considering leaving the final fights until tomorrow when everyone is fresh and full of vigour. Now I see that you're all having so much fun, let us conclude the trials tonight. As soon as you are down to one final victor, we shall rest and eat together and then I will enter the ring when the moon is at its highest. We will fight by torchlight under the gaze of the gods."

The tribe's folk stamped and thudded their approval. I was relieved my nephew had the common sense to fight Kitto while he was most weary, until I caught sight of the worrisome brute winking it his clansmen. What had they in store for my foolish young nephew?

# CHAPTER ELEVEN

Sure enough, the bouts continued until only Kitto remained. Whether that was because he was genuinely the better fighter or because the Head Hunters had planned it so I could not say, but my gut told me that there was some devious plot afoot. With scant resources at our disposal, only those who fought valiantly in the trials were permitted to drink the last of Tallack's ale. Everyone else made do with water or milk from the few goats that had not yet been put to the knife.

Endelyn took the opportunity to steal the attention of most elders and their wives, asking their advice on the preparations for her binding ritual set for mid-summer's eve. She gambolled and strutted as though there was no question of her authority over the tribe. Even Cryda appeared to be taken with the priestess, something I couldn't have imagined only a moon or so ago.

With no sign of rain and a gentle breeze coming from the direction of the moors, the smell of burning was strong. The fires were still raging on the heath, sending all the wild horses across the borderlands into the Durotriges' territory along with the herds of deer, hares, geese, and birds that we relied on for food.

Treeve eked out the precious ale reserves among the men, while Ren and I chewed over our options if Tallack should fall. Our choices were few indeed and as the night wore on, my roiling belly refused to accept either food or drink.

"I know you are loyal to Tallack, Meliora," Ren said, "but there is no need for you to lay down your life too. Please heed my advice. Take Cryda, the babe, and Kewri, and go now. Kitto won't have me killed while I can teach the men how to navigate, but your healing skills won't be enough to spare you from his axe. I'll leave it a day or two and then come and find you. We still have friends in the east. Make your way to Cryda's people. You know that they will assure your safety."

I rested my hand on his. "You are a good and honourable friend, Ren, and I thank you, but I have already tried to plead with Cryda. She will not leave."

He looked crestfallen. "I hope I am more than a friend to you, Mel." He placed his hands on both sides of mine and squeezed gently. I thought my heart would swell until it burst from my chest. Struggling with a lump in my throat, I found myself unable to respond. The best I could manage was a teary nod and a smile. Why would the gods send me such a fine fellow just as my life was nearing its end?

"At the very least, have your new girl prepare your horses at the edge of the forest to the north. If things go ill this evening, I'll distract Kitto and the Hunters to give you time to get away." He'd turned my own plan around to favour me in his stead.

It was only then that I remembered Vina. Where had that girl been all day? She'd taken Tallack's dagger and a bag to search for herbs and not returned. My curiosity descended into alarm when I recalled that the new

Chieftain of the Duros was her uncle. If any foul deed had put the girl in harm's way, the peace treaty with our neighbours would collapse.

Excusing myself from Ren, I walked among the revellers to find Kewri. He was sitting with the Sea Warriors, sulking with a bowl of uneaten stew congealing in his lap. He acknowledged my presence with a nod and returned his gaze to his cold food.

I had no time to listen to his women troubles. He was big enough to sort out his own messes. "Do you know where Vina is?"

He shook his head without the courtesy of looking me in the eye.

"Did you at least notice if she came back from foraging earlier today?"

Another shake of the head was all I could get from him. I had a growing sense of unease gnawing away at my insides. Leaving the congenial atmosphere of the training grounds, I took a burning torch and walked back across the trickling waters of the tributary into the western gate. The compound was so still and quiet, it was almost eerie. Not a bleat came from my goats, tucked away in Kewri's shelter as I passed them. Their demonic eyes glowed as some kind of phantasm when I shoved the torch closer to do a quick head count, but not one made a sound. I supposed that they knew the fate of their kin after the homesteaders had made off with them.

I knew that Vina was back when I heard the crackles and logs falling from my fire. "By the gods, girl. Where have you been all this time?" I said it long before I was through the door. The wall of heat inside was intolerable. What on earth possessed her to light a fire? I stuck the torch into a hole in the ground and looked about for my apprentice. I expected her to be penitent and eager to explain. Instead, I found her lounging like a Ruvane across my bed, dressed in my finest tunic. It was tight about the middle and far too short for her, revealing more thigh than was decent. I could hardly contain my anger. My huffing and blowing should have given her the impetus to jump up and rectify this gross invasion of my hospitality. Even fixing her with a potent scowl did nothing to provoke a reaction.

"Get your cheeky arse out of my clothes and off my bed. If you expect to gain my favour, you'll wash my tunic this instant and make amends for your impudence." I practically screamed it at her, my wrath bubbling inside along with the build-up of nervous bile in my gut. A quick glance about my work table told me that she'd not brought back a single herb, nor bark shavings and the place was still a mess.

It took all my strength to stop myself from grabbing up my besom and whacking her from here to the Underworld. "Did you hear me, girl. Move yourself!" I stomped towards the broom and shot her a glare that told her I meant business.

She swung her legs down to the floor and shrugged as she stood up, but I could tell from her eyes that I'd rattled her. She noticed my shock at the lack of herbs. "It was too hot to gather anything today. I'll try again in the morning." She made no attempt to remove my best tunic as she wandered over to her own bunk and slumped inelegantly onto her furs.

"You'll do no such thing. Those chores won't do themselves." As soon as I'd said it, I knew that there was a possibility that I wouldn't live long enough to see those chores completed. Neither was it an option to trust the girl with my horse, and what few belongings I had left, to wait for me at the edge of the forest as Ren had suggested. "How are you expected to learn if you won't do as I ask?"

"You haven't taught me anything yet. What am I to learn by slicing off a bit of willow bark every now and then?"

"*You offered* to go out foraging. Where have you been all day?" She shrugged in the same infuriating manner that Kewri had in response to my questions. These young people were determined to vex me. "Change back into your old gear and come out to the west training grounds where I can keep an eye on you. The Chief and another warrior will fight soon." I so wanted to cuff her about the back of the head, but I stayed my hand. If she was plotting her escape back to Duro lands, I didn't want Vina to tell Fane that we'd abused her in any way.

"I'm not going." She yawned, rolled onto her back and turned her face away from me.

"You'll do as you're told, Vina or find another healer to train you." I thought the threat would be enough to shock her into line but I was wrong.

She buried her face in her furs until her words were muffled and feint. "Send me back to my wretched family if you will. I didn't ask to come."

I opened my mouth to scream at her, but something stopped me. She called them her *wretched family*. Was she no longer pining for their company? Did her jaunt out alone take her to the borderlands to meet up with scouts from her own tribe? She had been cooperating and almost helpful in the previous few days, I wondered what had occurred to make her glower return with a vengeance.

Despite sweating from the heat of the fire, I tarried a while, thinking. Scooping up scattered dried herbs and seeds back into their respective pots, I gave the girl's plight some thought. If she felt that her own tribe had abandoned her, and our people despised the ground on which she walked, I could see why she would be so melancholic. Our young spat at her feet wherever she walked about camp; an insult the Duros reserved for their enemies. Reining in my temper, I moved to her bunk and sat on the edge. She jerked her feet away, as though my touch was more deadly than a black ague. "What ails you, Vina? I can be less severe if you'll help me to understand."

She shifted about restlessly, taking a deep breath and releasing it while she contemplated my words. I waited, hoping that she would not take long to confide her troubles. I needed to be back with my nephew, before it was too late.

She sighed, tutted, and did all manner of annoying gestures. Still, I waited.

"It's just… oh, never mind. You wouldn't understand, and even if you did, you'd care even less."

I was about to question her reasoning, but then I hadn't really given her much of a welcome. It was hardly her fault that she was forced to become my apprentice. Like so many women of Chieftain blood, her life was little more than a commodity or bargaining tool. At least her uncle had no intention of marrying her to a great tribal leader. That was the future ahead of Vina's cousin, poor girl. The moon was full and round in the evening sky; the perfect time to prearrange a meeting.

"Did you see your kin in the borderlands today?"

Her head snapped around at me, her eyes staring wide as if I was some mystical prophet.

"I was young once you know. That was a long walk to make in a day." I held her steady gaze for some time before looking away. "Who did you meet at the crossing, your mother or a young man?"

To this she sat fully upright, slack jawed at my guesswork. At length she muttered. "My mother."

"You pleaded with her to take you home, but she sent you back here anyway?"

Vina nodded, her eyelids welling with tears. So, this was the reason for her changeable mood. "The way I see it, child, you have two options; either come up with a better plan of escape or decide to make a good life for yourself among us."

She snorted her contempt. "Your people spit at me."

"Then show our foolish tribe's folk that they are wrong about you Duros. Make them see what I see; a clever young woman who can be relied on, someone who understands family duty and honour, or am I wrong?" I gave her a firm glare, making her squirm under the pressure. How could she gainsay such lavish flattery of her character?

Her chin dropped to her chest and her eyes closed, but she didn't answer. There was nothing else for me to say that could rouse her from her sadness. I got to my feet, clicking and crunching my joints to straighten my back. Before I reached the door, Vina called after me.

"I'm sorry that I let you down, Fur Benyn. It won't happen again."

I waved my hand about, dismissing her apology without facing her. Whether she chose to flee or remain, it was out of my hands. There were no secret tin deposits, nor jewels for her to steal. At worst, I'd lose my best tunic and my nephew's knife, but if that allowed her safe passage to a happier life, she was welcome to both.

There were more important tribal matters to deal with than the fate of one ill-tempered Duro girl. When I got back to the fighting ring, Ren was lighting more torches around the edge of the circle, while the womenfolk cleared away the cups and bowls. The Head Hunters were all gathered on one side of the training grounds, while Tallack's Sea Warriors were on the other side, offering him words of wisdom and support.

Endelyn and Cryda fussed about Tallack, straightening his clothing and hair in between their nervous chattering and fawning. Why couldn't they see that this was the most idiotic scheme that our Chief could have ever concocted? They billed and cooed about the place as if it was a midsummer gathering wrestling match between two brothers. I doubted that anyone surrounding this fighting ring would bet on Tallack winning the bout. Kitto was stronger, faster and more experienced than my nephew by a large margin.

Tallack grew impatient with the fussy women and batted them aside. Just as well that he did, for the Hunters were already smirking and whispering their scorn amongst themselves. Far from gaining the men's respect, he was rapidly becoming a figure of fun. I edged closer for a while, hoping to catch him on his own. If there was a chance to put an end to the folly, I had to try. The priestess and Cryda took their seats and Tallack chose a hazel pole from the stack. It was too late to back out now. I'd missed my chance.

The crowd hollered and bayed for blood. All I could do was to find my bench at the head of the elders and watch my kin get torn limb from limb. Kitto strolled into the circle, keen to start the bout. He swilled the dregs of his ale down and threw the empty cup to Ren. They roared and stamped their feet in anticipation. Despite the nip in the night air, Kitto's bronzed torso shone with the sweat of the day. He flexed his muscles and winked at the group of maidens who'd sneaked away from their families for a closer look.

He was everything a Dumnonii warrior should be; charming, intelligent, fierce and ambitious. By comparison, Tallack looked like a bumbling child, taking his time in selecting a pole that would inevitably break under the force of one swipe from his opponent. I tried to focus over the clamour from the tribe's folk and the pounding thrum of my heart in my ears.

Kitto was growing impatient with Tallack's indecision. "Are you ready to begin, Chief?" It sounded more like a command than a question. Tallack dropped two of the hazel rods to the ground and hurried into the ring with a third. I looked the pair up and down. A part of me was relieved to see that there was no way Kitto could be hiding a blade on his person. His chest and feet were bare and his leggings were tight, leaving nothing to the imagination. That only eased my fear for a single beat of the musician's drum. The moment Ren blew the horn to start, Kitto launched himself at my nephew with such force, Tallack was thrown backwards out of the ring. It was only thanks to the quick reactions of his Sea Warriors that he stayed on his feet. They cushioned his fall and shoved him towards the mighty warrior.

Tallack was not prepared for such a rapid response. He readied himself for the serious task ahead, planting his feet firmly and adjusting his grip on the staff. From the expression on Kitto's face, I could see that he thought it would all be over in moments. To him, Tallack was simply an obstacle in his path to the Chieftaincy. My nephew took the initiative, stepping closer and striking out at Kitto's head. The larger man used his staff and blocked with ease, before kicking out at Tallack's legs to unbalance him once again.

The Chief was ready for him this time, jumping over the clumsy move before jabbing the end of the pole into Kitto's chest. Rather than knock the wind from him, it provoked his anger. What had started as a friendly trial, descended into a venomous clash.

With sheer brute strength, Kitto dropped his own staff and grasped the hazel rod of the Chief's, raising it and my nephew at the same time. He shook Tallack loose until he dropped down to the sandy ground. The Chief stepped out of his opponent's reach, scrambling for a replacement weapon.

Before he could seize a spare pole, Kitto was on him again. He grabbed the bunched fabric of Tallack's tunic and yanked him away from the edge of the circle, sending the Chief tumbling in a backwards roll. Kitto thundered across the circle to finish the task. His eyes twitched and he slowed for just a moment, before shaking his head. I thought that a fly had blurred his vision, but he was soon to recover. He threw down Tallack's hazel rod and towered over my nephew, pounding him to the ground in a rain of mighty fists.

There was a sickening squelch of gristle as it separated from bone, sending a spray of blood skyward from Tallack's nose. A second punch closed a swollen eye, the third and fourth looked set to cave in his cheek bones. I held my breath, as the warrior took my nephew ever closer to the Summerlands, one forceful blow at a time.

# CHAPTER TWELVE

Cryda stood up, clasping her hands to her mouth. "Fight back, son." Her despair was moving, her cry muted and pained. She was right to plead for him to act. The Chief's arms were loose at his side, his body limp and unresisting. Why hadn't he rolled away from the pounding fists of our most fearsome warrior? Tallack was nimble and fleet of foot. Surely, he could out manoeuvre such a beast? My own breathing quickened as our worst fears played out before us all. There was no way my nephew could withstand such a beating for any longer. He must have had his wits knocked right out of him.

I could see Ren's look of abject horror, unable to intervene to save the life of our young Chieftain. He was the judge and adjudicator and as such, he had to remain fair and impartial. It was never supposed to be a fight to the death, but events played right into Kitto's hands. The mean brute could see that Tallack was all but spent. He slowed his assault and took in the glory of the crowd's cheers. The Head Hunters frenzy of admiration manifested in wild foot stamping and roars of support.

Kitto straightened up and gave them a beaming grin. He had more than respect, this was adoration. He was everything my nephew was not. All that was missing for his immediate elevation to leadership was his lack of Chieftain blood running through his veins. Instead, he was spattered in the congealing stuff. Tallack roused a little while Kitto strutted, playing up to his men. The huge man thrust his arms high into the air and faced us elders. This should have been the time when I made my excuses. I should have gathered my things and scuttled off into the forest and away. Watching my nephew meet his end would be a memory to haunt my nights forever more.

Ren did all he could to gain my attention, gesturing towards me from across the fighting ring. He wanted me to save myself; to Grab Cryda and the babe and run for our lives. Instead, I sat dumbstruck and immobile. How ignoble our end would be.

Tallack struggled to his knees, spitting out blood and tooth fragments but keeping a weather eye on his opponent. Kitto had his back to the Chief. He stood tall, punching the air in time with his men as they chanted his name over and over. Surely Ren would call it a definitive win and end the bout. I signalled as much to my friend, who stood and entered the edge of the circle. Tallack was on his feet, closing in on the unsuspecting warrior. I wanted to call out to him, warn him against angering Kitto further, but the crowds were too loud. He wouldn't have heard me.

When the warrior turned to face the Chief, his eyes widened and he swayed from side to side. He thrust his arms out to regain his balance, but I could tell his head was spinning. Kitto blinked rapidly, shaking his head and rubbing at his eyes. He staggered about as though he'd drunk a skinful of ale rather than a cup or two.

When Tallack landed his first punch, Kitto tried to side step out of his way but failed. The burly man's legs buckled beneath him. Tallack barely connected fist to chin before the warrior fell to his knees. The Head Hunters fell silent as their champion slid without grace or dignity to the dusty ground.

This was not a knock out, nor was it a fair fight. I glanced at Ren who was staring into the empty cup that Kitto had thrown before the bout. When he looked up, we exchanged a knowing nod. My suspicions were confirmed when I turned to see Endelyn and Treeve grinning at one another, congratulating themselves on the success of their devious plot.

It was all too clear to me now; Endelyn's need for valerian and the missing poppy resin, the mess left behind in my hut to conceal what had been taken, the sneaking around with jugs of ale, Treeve's insistence that he should take charge of sharing out the last of the beer to the fighters, a job meant for slaves. They assured Tallack's victory with my potent medicines. If this became common knowledge, Tallack would lose more than the respect of the men. Every tribe south of the River Trent would hear about how he won.

I shot Treeve a shrivelling look. He ignored me, sticking his nose into the air and hugging Endelyn. How could I have been so foolish? Far from being a potential threat to the priestess, the pair were plotting together all along.

Before I could wrap my brain around how Endelyn persuaded the crewman to abandon hopes of becoming the first male Ruvane and support her instead, I was distracted by my nephew's grunts. Rather than ending the bout and claiming his victory, our Chief had decided to pound Kitto's face into the same bloody mess as his own. Talk about make matters worse. The warrior was unconscious, addled into a resin filled haze.

Ren dashed into the ring and grabbed Tallack's wrist, holding it high and proclaiming him the winner of the bout. At least that put an end to the whole farce. I couldn't decide whether I was pleased at the outcome or furious. My family were still leaders of the tribe, our lives spared for another day, but at what price? Would the Head Hunters be as suspicious as Ren and I or had Treeve dosed them too? I slumped back down on the bench and rubbed my forehead.

Cryda wandered closer, with a smug grin plastered across her face. "See, Meliora. I told you he would win. My son is the best warrior in all the lands."

I scanned her face, judging her level of sincerity. The poor woman believed every misguided word escaping her mouth. How could she not see what had happened before her very eyes? Tallack leaned on Ren in front of the crowd. Only a faint show of foot stamping came from the Sea Warriors, none from the homesteaders nor Head Hunters. Far from uniting our clans, the trials had broken them beyond repair.

Now who would lead the Head Hunters? If we were to take back control over our mines, we needed every able-bodied man fighting as one, not bickering amongst themselves or second guessing Tallack's orders. Worse still, what would Kitto do once he'd recovered? Would he take his revenge on Tallack when he least expected attack or wait until he could gain the favour of our whole tribe?

I sidled past the elders' benches to sneak a quiet word with the sulking Kewri. Leading him to a thicket near to the stream, I spoke in earnest to my giant of a friend. "I know I have no right to order you to do anything for me, but what I ask of you now is of the utmost importance."

He looked at me with wide and frightened eyes and nodded his consent.

"You must protect the Chief's life as though it were your own. Do you understand? You cannot let him out of your sight for a single moment."

For such a brooding dolt, there were times when he was often quite shrewd. He flicked his gaze over to the Chief and then at the Head Hunters, who were lolling about on the parched grass at the far side of the circle. They were all a potential threat to Tallack's safety, and although it would be impossible for one man to protect him against every single warrior, I knew that he would try. Kewri lowered his stare to the floor and nodded again. It was, perhaps, unfair of me to ask it of him but there was no one else I could trust.

Ren blew the horn and announced that Tallack would inform the elders of his decisions in the morning. That gave us a chance to patch him up and talk some sense into him. The most immediate crisis may have been averted, but we were all far from secure in our positions.

Endelyn looked positively put out when the elders joined us in shooing everyone to their respective huts. The homesteaders were bawdy and boisterous, having had few opportunities to gather in such large crowds for similar events before. The novelty was beguiling, tipping them towards bickering and infighting themselves. For once, the Sea Warriors were the only sobering influence in the entire tribe. They took their cues from Massen and kept order in our place.

When, at last, I was able to battle my way through the stragglers to my nephew, he could hardly stand with the pain. His poor face was a ragged mess of cuts and bruises, his nose misshapen and bleeding. He clutched his middle with a tenderness that gave me some insight into his level of agony, but to give him his due, he did not murmur once.

Kewri and Ren walked either side of the Chief to the western gate just in case he collapsed, sparing him the indignity of being carried. We left Kitto on the ground where he fell. His clan would see to him when they came down from their addled state. Treeve fell in behind them, alongside me and Endelyn, all of us instinctively closing rank to protect my nephew. The Chief's hut was closer than mine. Kewri stood guard in the doorway while Ren scurried off to collect my healing kit.

The priestess stayed for mere moments before excusing herself. "I must give an offering to the gods to speed his recovery." She was almost back out of the door as she spoke, such was her haste to leave. Perhaps that was part of her deal with Treeve to garner his support, that when it came to something as personal as nursing Tallack back to health, only he could stay at the Chief's side. Whatever the situation may have been, we saw nothing more from her all that night.

I stitched and bathed, pasted and wrapped what parts of my nephew I could, but he was in a bad way. That made two of my most favourite men in the world laid low. Poor Ren looked gaunter than ever. His strength failed him when the moon was at its peak, but still, he wouldn't leave. Treeve laid his furs down on the rushes for Ren to rest on, while the young crewman and I kept Tallack's bindings cool with fresh water from the spring.

Cryda alternated between dashing to her hut to feed the babe before leaving her with the slave so that she could check on her other child. "Oh, Meliora. His beautiful face is ruined." She sobbed, when she caught sight of the wounds as I changed the dressings.

"Looks worse than it is. Don't fret so. He'll have a scar or two, but that'll make him all the more mysterious and worldly. I dare say we won't love him any less." I winked at Treeve, who suppressed a giggle. Perhaps I have misjudged that young crewman. For all his manipulations, his love for my nephew is steadfast. In the middle of a balmy summer's night, at that very moment in time, I felt mightily ashamed of my assumptions. I can't condone his and Endelyn's foolish scheme, but given the stubbornness of my nephew, what else could they do? I redressed the gashes absently, deep in my own thoughts.

Ren touched my arm. "What do you think he'll do with Kitto in the morning?"

I shrugged. "It's a puzzle, that's for sure." We sat in silence for a time, ruminating over the issue. "We should have talked him out of the trials."

"Like that was an option." Ren snapped, pulling a face. He was right. Ever since his twin's death, no one had attempted to contradict my nephew's bizarre decisions. Blydh had always been the voice of reason when Tallack's head was filled with adventure and bold ideas, at least up until the end. Perhaps Tallack was rudderless without his brother. I knew how close they'd been, even when they were at each other's throats. Now he was surrounded by people who had their own ambitions prioritised above those of the tribe's. The more Endelyn and Treeve sank their hooks into him, the less he listened to the advice of elders such as me.

Ren laid back in the furs and beckoned me closer. He seemed to think that his frustrations had hurt my feelings. I sighed and joined him on the rushes, letting him envelop his bony arms around me.

"We should have let Tallack kill Kitto while we had the chance. It's the only way out of this mess." I whispered, making sure that neither my nephew nor his slumbering crewman could hear me. Ren didn't answer. He just clung tightly until we were both fast asleep. As weak as he was, I still felt safe with him by my side, and with Kewri laying in front of the door, there was no way that Kitto nor the Head Hunters would be able to sneak in and slaughter us while we slept.

It was long past dawn when we stirred. Kewri woke us, coughing loudly from the doorway to warn us that Tallack had left the hut. By the time Ren and I had shaken off the confusion of awaking in a strange room, my nephew and friend were already far across the compound. My poor bladder was fit to burst, but I had to know what Tallack planned to do.

"Where's he going?" I muttered, more to myself than anyone in particular. Ren and I watched Tallack and Kewri stomp down the boardwalks to the Head Hunter tents; stopping every little while so that the Chief could shoo the giant away. May the gods bless that lad, he would not be dissuaded from the mission I had laid before him. Kewri stuck to him like birch tar on a fletcher's thumb. When they reached the largest tent of the last row next to the freshest end of the tributary, they disappeared inside.

"He's going to speak with Kitto." Ren said, grabbing my hand to speed my progress. He almost yanked my arm off, hurrying me along until my feet were practically airborne. It was fortuitous that the morning was so warm. The tent flaps were pinned wide open to allow a gentle breeze to funnel through.

By the time we were level with the doorway, Tallack was standing in front of Kitto while he sat on the stool bucket. The stench was inescapable, the noises almost comedic. Kewri stifled a snort of mirth, clapping his hand over his mouth and nose to avoid the brunt of the smell.

Tallack maintained a dignified frown. "You are not well, my friend." My nephew nodded towards the profusion of liquids gushing from the warriors back end. "I came to commend you on a trial well fought and lost, but I see you need time to recover. It explains why I was victorious in yesterday's bout. You are the superior warrior."

Was I hearing him correctly? Tallack was admitting that Kitto should have won the fight? I opened my mouth and started forward but Ren pulled me back.

Before I could struggle free from his grasp, Kitto peered up at the Chief and smiled. "You won, Chief. I bow to your grace." His cheeks flushed. Whether that was from the vile humours flowing from his bowels, his blooming facial bruises or embarrassment, I could not say, but he seemed to be placated by Tallack's high praise.

"I won because you were not at full fitness. I'll send my aunt to give you one of her tinctures. When you are rested and well, we'll announce your elevation to clan leadership together."

The two warriors regarded one another for a moment, both sporting swollen eyes, blackened cheeks and bent noses. At length, Kitto nodded. "It would be my honour."

Ren reached over and pushed my chin upwards, closing my gaping mouth. Was that it? No brawling, or arguments, no calling Tallack out as a cheat or charlatan, just an amicable settling of differences? The Chief and Kewri stepped outside to find us lurking.

"Ah, there you are, Aunt. Were you listening to my private conversation in there?" He squinted at me and sighed. "Honestly, Aunt Mel, you have got to stop treating me like a child." He stormed off down the boardwalk with poor Kewri spinning about not knowing whether he was coming or going. "And call off your dog! I don't need protecting." Tallack yelled, halting the giant in his tracks. Ren and I wandered back towards my hut with Kewri dragging his heels behind us.

"Was Kitto genuinely sick after all?" Ren whispered.

I thought about the missing poppy resin and my scattered herbs. It was a fair assumption that Endelyn had taken more than valerian when she distracted Vina in my hut. The dried blackthorn flowers were strewn everywhere. They are known to loosen the bowels to an unwelcome extent. "No, Ren. I think the warrior was given a special concoction mixed just for him alone."

"Do you think he knows that he was dosed? He could be biding his time and planning revenge."

"I guess I shall find out later when I take him some medicine to staunch the flux."

# CHAPTER THIRTEEN

The sensible thing to do would have been to send Vina with the tonic to Kitto's tent. She would be received as nothing more than my messenger, fulfilling the Chief's request to treat his ailment. Ren offered to accompany me, but he was not fit enough to fight against a warrior of Kitto's strength, even one who could barely get up from the bucket.

"Go, get some food down you and rest." I said, dismissing Ren's kindness with the flick of my wrist. "Kitto is not likely to attack a weakling elder like me. There's no honour in that. Besides, I want him to let his guard down. I might learn something of value." In truth, I was still giddy from relief having avoided catastrophe the night before. That kind of turnabout in events tends to embolden your senses.

Ren puffed and postured for a while, grunting and muttering with frustration. "There is just no arguing with you, is there?"

"Better get used to that." I said, before I'd even thought the implications through. My presumption that we would become a couple was obvious to all. Vina and Kewri's eyebrows rose on their foreheads, both smirking and giggling. I couldn't take it back. It was already spoken. Ren said nothing, but his grin brought a rosy glow to my cheeks.

I scooped up my bag and the blackthorn bark tea and scuttled off as though I'd been scalded. The irony was not lost on me as I walked back towards the Head Hunter's tents. It was blackthorn flowers that had scoured his innards and it would be blackthorn bark that would soothe them. Endelyn knew far more about my craft than she'd ever let on. I would have to watch her more closely from now on. The question remained though; had Kitto realised that his ailment was not some ague but a deliberate affliction?

I stood outside his tent and took a breath of fresh air before entering. The stench was so overpowering, it made my eyes water. Holding out the cup of steaming tea at arm's length I spoke through the sleeve of my tunic. "The Chief sent me. This should calm things down for you."

He was in a shocking state. His taut, bruised skin shone with perspiration; his shoulders slumped as he tilted his head up to see me. "Thank you, Fur Benyn. That was kind of you." Where I'd seen a braggart and bully the night before, I now saw a pale and broken man.

My defences softened and I chose my words carefully to avoid suspicion. "If you're in pain, I can fix you some willow tea in just a moment…" I took out a handful of bark from my pocket and presented it to him.

Kitto shook his head. "I can handle pain, Fur Benyn." He took the tonic and peered up at me with sorrowful eyes. It was then I realised the extent of his dilemma. He'd worked hard on building a reputation within his clan; a respected elder statesman and warrior, feared by all who crossed his path. The previous night's events saw him staggering about after drinking only a couple of cups of ale. If that was not enough of an embarrassment, he had passed out after taking a beating from a man half his age and size.

If he was aware of the priestess's plan, he would've been beyond angry. No bout of the squits would stop him from wreaking his revenge. I saw no sign of fury or belligerence. Endelyn and Treeve appeared to have scraped through undetected.

A gash on his brow oozed with pus. I gestured towards it, shame bursting in my chest. "Will you at least let me see to that cut? It'll fester if it's not cleaned and stitched."

"I'll stop by your hut later, if that's acceptable. You can't be expected to tend my wounds while I'm like this."

My stomach lurched. Despite all that Endelyn and Treeve had put him through, and the respect he'd lost, he still showed me more respect than my own kin. For just a moment, I almost believed that our tribe would be better off having Kitto as our leader, were it not for the possibility of him taking off my head in the process.

I dithered for a while, wondering whether to hold my breath and treat his wounds there and then, but my nose made my decision for me. I left the warrior alone with his woes and headed north towards home.

Before I had left the Head Hunter's camp, I spotted Tallack leaving another tent further along the row. He wore a wide smile as he bounded along the boardwalk in front of me. I walked on the dry earth, keeping my footsteps light and unheard, curious as to his carefree manner.

The entire area was packed with displaced homesteaders, idle crewmen and gossiping elders' wives. We were out of grain, with no tin or jewels to trade for more and we had lost control of our mines. Even the fishermen returned from the bay with empty boats. What was there to smile about? After all young Treeve had done for my nephew, I hoped to the gods that he'd not found another young warrior to warm his bed. It was the only explanation for Tallack's jovial mood.

I followed him right up to the Long Hut, but broke off my pursuit when I saw him aiming for his mother's house. Still, the thought of him betraying the young sailor, right under his nose prayed on my mind for the rest of the morning. That nephew of mine is simply incapable of being true to one love. It must be a trait from his mother's side. Her flights of fancy have left her in hot water many a time.

Vina and Kewri were screaming at one another across my hut when I returned. Groaning, I spun about and walked straight back out before they could invent a reason for me to stay. Scanning the island made my head spin. Everywhere you looked, people bickered and argued over space, or livestock. Shelters and fences sprouted in the few gaps between houses until the compound was bursting at the seams.

I stuck my head through the doorway of Kewri's shelter and sighed. My herd had dwindled to just three goats, two of which no longer gave milk. It was like holding back a flood with your hands. No matter what measures I put in place to protect them, the homesteader's need for food was greater than respecting another's property.

With an ever-growing clamour in camp, I needed to get away and clear my head. I collected my old pony from the enclosure and trotted out of the western gate heading north. A half day of foraging would put me straight and replenish my stocks. I took the narrow path through the woods alongside the main course of the River Exe. Other than the snorts and whickers of my pony, the forest was curiously silent. I saw a few tiny birds, but other than those, the entire area was deserted. Had our Hunters killed most of the creatures and driven the rest away?

The track was riven with huge cracks and the tufted grasses were sun-scorched and dry. I did find a few useful herbs along the bank side but not all that I needed. This dry spell was proving more of a challenge than I'd anticipated. As I broke the cover of the woodland on my way to the crossing, I saw a group of compound slaves carrying huge baskets laden with curling sections of bark. Behind them, a row of alder trees was stripped bare of bark, twigs and all lower leaves; their naked trunks left pale and vulnerable.

My heart sank. They had taken too much. Those poor young trees would never survive the next winter. "Ho there!" I called to them. Dutifully, they dropped their baskets, expecting me to give them more orders. "Who asked you to take all this bark?" I knew the answer as soon as the question left my mouth, but I needed confirmation.

"The new Ruvane, Endelyn sent us, Fur Benyn." One called out across the expanse of the river.

I shook my head at the priestess's stupidity. These saplings were the closest source of alder for my medicines. With the latest infestation of lice, I was in need of a fair amount of bark myself, not to mention the sticky, sap coated leaves to trap the fleas from the floor rushes. "What about the trees yonder?" I gestured upstream where another such bank of mature trees grew.

The slaves shook their heads. "We harvested those this morning." One shouted back.

It was my own stupid fault. I'd recommended the deep ochre colour for Endelyn's bridal gown, but how was I to know that she would take enough bark to dye the clothes of the entire tribe? I left them to carry their plunder back to the compound and chided myself for speaking before thinking. There was half our tribe scratching about to find enough to eat and the priestess was wasting the slaves' time making dyes. They should all be out gathering roots, mending fishing nets or collecting shellfish for the pot.

I wandered further upstream for some time without finding anything of use before turning my pony and heading home. We would have to endure the fleas and lice for the time being it seemed. My slow trot back through the forest put me in the path of a team of warriors. As far as I could tell, they were a mixture of Head Hunters and Sea Warriors, all hard at work felling trees and weaving hurdles. Most were young and looked ill equipped to swing an axe. Their spindly arms and narrow shoulders had not the strength for the task. At the furthest end of the group stood the young Hunter from the clan trials, Skentel.

Stopping to admire their determination, the man approached me. "You shouldn't be out alone, Fur Benyn." He said, clutching the reins of my pony. "There are some desperate folk about. Chased a couple off myself earlier."

I tittered. "I have nothing left of value for them to steal."

"You have a horse, good linen, and I dare say a blade or two tucked about your person. That's more than enough to get your throat slit."

I looked him up and down, frowning. There was a calm confidence about him, not a swagger like Kitto, but an authoritative air that was seldom seen in one so young. He took my lack of response as a plea for help. "I'll walk back with you to the island. At least I'll rest easy knowing you got home safely." I turned and looked at the group of youngsters hacking lumps out of the trees. He seemed to comprehend my thoughts without the need to voice them. "I'm not slacking off, Fur Benyn. The Chief put me in charge of them. We are to remain behind, keep order and oversee the new buildings." Skentel yelled at the youths, informing them of his intentions.

"Won't they down tools the moment your back is turned?" I asked, astounded at their compliance.

"Nah. They're good men. I told them that if they built their muscles quickly enough, the Chief might change his mind and allow them to go with him to the mines."

"And how long do they have to reach peak fitness?"

"Chief Tallack told me that he intends to leave on the morning tide." His grin was delicious. Had I been a number of summers younger, I would have relished a night or two beneath his furs. We shared a conspiratorial chuckle together as he walked alongside my pony, avoiding the worst of the dry fissures in the fractured earth. How had I missed the presence of such a sharp-witted lad in the compound for all this time? I knew him by sight, but to my recollection I'd never treated him for sickness or wounds in all his days amongst us.

"What else did my nephew tell you?" It stung that I knew nothing of Tallack's plans. I'd spent my entire life wishing that I could be rid of the burden of having Chieftain blood, be away from the constant turmoil and strife, but when my wish was granted without warning, it upset me. I was no longer in the Chief's inner circle of advisers. Endelyn and Treeve had taken my place. Breathing steadily, I managed to hold back my emotions at this revelation, keen to hear this clever man's take on my nephew's plan.

"We're to return at nightfall for a bowl of stew in the Long Hut. I gather the Chief wants to make an announcement, but I think we've all guessed what that will be." He glanced up at me and sneered.

"Kitto?"

"Yeah. It makes sense. He's taken more heads than the rest of us combined, although some might say through the luck of the gods more than skill. There will come a day when he can no longer cut through enemies with sheer force."

I smiled to myself. Skentel was perceptive enough to wait for that day before challenging the mighty warrior. He was in possession of some admirable traits, being both patient and strategic. There were now two potential threats to Tallack's leadership and I didn't envy my nephew's chances for long-term success.

We chatted amiably all the way back to the compound, stopping every once in a while, to gather what hardy plants I could from the side of the track. He told me that Tallack and his crewmen planned to sail to Bentewyn, where the largest of our tin mines were located, while the Head Hunters rode across land. With that many warriors at his back, Skentel claimed that Tallack was confident of overthrowing the Alchemists within a quarter moon.

I held my gaze steady, lest he should detect my doubt. Was this the entirety of my nephew's plan? He was simply going to charge in and ask Kenver for our mines back. Had he forgotten the trouble his half-sister, Wenna had attacking the same valley just one summer ago? The entire settlement was deeply embedded in the woodlands, the access points narrow and sheltered. It was a perfect spot to slaughter all invaders before they could get within fifty boat lengths of the mines.

If this was what Tallack had in store for his men, Skentel and his little crew of spindly boys would be the only warriors left by the next full moon. How could I make my nephew understand my misgivings if he no longer sought my counsel?

I thanked Skentel for his protection and rode through camp to Ren's hut. He was asleep inside, wearing little more than a loin cloth. His ribs were still too prominent, but there was some colour in his face. More than anything, the poor man needed good food and lots of rest, but neither were possible.

What food remained in camp was cooked at the Long Hut fire pits and distributed evenly to all the tribe. Only the homesteaders failed to abide by our sense of fair play. They hoarded and stole and kept whatever they could scavenge for themselves. I couldn't blame them. They'd spent a lifetime around the moors or along the borderlands fending off attack from the Duros. Their will to survive in such harsh conditions left little room for community customs such as sharing.

"Ren?" I spoke softly, trying not to startle him from his nap. Creeping closer, I could see the sweat shining on his skin, his heart beat pulsed between his ribs. He was skinnier than the camp dogs. I touched his shoulder and he awoke with a start. His taut frown relaxed when he saw it was me.

"What is it? Has something happened?" He sat up and pawed at my arm.

"No, not yet, but I fear it will if we can't talk some sense into my nephew." I sat on the edge of his bunk as he lay back down and rubbed at his eyes.

"What's he done now? It's not another pointless contest is it?"

I screwed up my face, bewildered. "You mean he hasn't told you that he's leaving on the morning tide?" This was worse than I feared. Tallack relied on Ren's superior navigation skills, not to mention his talent for diplomacy in tricky situations. If he'd cut Ren out of his circle of advisers too, we were all in grave danger. I started explaining all that I'd learned from Skentel while my friend splashed cold water on his face, slipped on a pair of leggings and a loose tunic, and prepared himself to approach the Long Hut with me.

It was dusk when we arrived at the main door and the place was already packed with warriors and elders. The sticky heat amplified the musky stink of so many men crammed into the room. We pushed past the warriors standing at the back until we could see those sitting at the top table. Tallack's mother teetered on the very edge of the platform, cradling her babe while sitting on a tiny stool. In her former place, at her son's side sat Treeve with a self-satisfied grin fixed across his plump face. The priestess sat on a fur cushion in the tall wolf's head chair where my dead nephew once sat. Her eyes stayed firmly on the fierce shield maiden to her left, Senara.

So, this is how it would be, our Metern and new Ruvane of the Dumnonii, shunning their family and advisers before the binding ceremony could make it official. I stood on tip-toe to see over the heads of the elders in front of me. The central Ruvane chair was gone. In its place lay a wooden crib, bedecked in ochre coloured bedding. As if any of us needed reminding that

Endelyn carried the heir to the tribe. These four duplicitous youngsters, held all our lives in their hands.

# CHAPTER FOURTEEN

Ren and I struggled towards the top table, stepping over young and old who were gathered to hear Tallack's announcement. The heat was beyond oppressive, yet my nephew thought it sensible to make the slaves serve the food before he spoke. They passed bowls of thin stew through the back door from the cooking huts and slid them down the tables until every man had their allotted portion. The top table dined on roasted birds. From the smell, I would say it was goose.

Endelyn picked on a few morsels while the rest tucked in as though they hadn't eaten in a quarter moon. Can't say that I blame them, their platters looked delicious; tender meats and juicy roots all bathed in a rich gravy. My small table in front of them, did not receive the same lavish meal.

As my stew cooled, a film of grease hardened at the edges of the bowl. I ate it nonetheless and was grateful. My wasted day of foraging had given me an appetite. When Skentel and his young warriors arrived from the woods, those sitting near to the back made room for them at one of the tables. There was just enough food left to fill their bowls as Tallack stood to address the crowd.

His face was still raw from his encounter with Kitto, but I admit to being proud of the neat little line of stitches crossing his eyebrow. Considering the battering he'd taken; he was remarkably cheery. "I called you all here tonight to hear my decision with regard to clan leadership. You already know that I've appointed Massen as my successor within the Sea Warriors. As we sit here, he and his crewmen are making my fine ship and the other remaining vessel, ready for the next voyage, but more on that later." He coughed, breaking his concentration. Endelyn leaned forward in the wolf's head chair. Tallack caught the movement in the corner of his eye, turning to gaze into her pale blue eyes. He was transfixed. She gave him a little nod of encouragement, which prompted him to face us once again and continue.

"The Head Hunter trials were fought valiantly and they proved beyond doubt that we Dumnonii have the best warriors in the whole land. Kitto certainly gave me a tough time…" He grinned touching the bruises to his jaw and making everyone chuckle. "But it was not a fair bout. By all rights, Kitto should have won." I held my breath. Was the idiotic man going to admit to Endelyn's treachery? What could possibly be achieved by revealing the truth to our whole tribe? Kitto glared from the side benches. His men peered around them waiting for the Chief to explain.

"No, Kitto was not at his best. An ague of the gut gave me an unfair advantage. He is a formidable warrior and one I am honoured to have at my side helping me to defend our lands and our people from those who would attack or betray us." The men roared and cheered, thumping their fists down on the table and stamping their feet on the hard floor. Tallack raised his hands to quieten the rabble. "With Kitto leading the Hunters and Massen taking charge of the seas, let this be a time when we fight together as one people and one tribe, against all who threaten our existence."

The Chief wafted his hand towards Kitto, inviting him to stand and take his share of the praise. This he did with an exaggerated flourish, tutting and waving coyly, but there was a flush to his cheeks above his wry smile. For the life of me, I couldn't figure out his expression. Had he learned of the priestess's mischief or was he genuinely pleased to remain subordinate to my nephew? Ren and I exchange knowing looks, both fearing the worst.

I noticed as the warrior passed me, that his wounds were clean and stitched, though not by my hand. He must have asked one of the weaver women to tend them.

Tallack turned to me. "Aunt Mel, I need the dagger I lent you."

I should have remembered where I'd seen it before. As it happened, I carried the knife with me after Skentel's warning about desperate folk who might slice open my throat. Now I would be wholly without protection. I stood and passed the blade to my nephew.

He snatched it from me and turned back to Kitto. "This was the oath blade given to me by my father, the great Aebba the Wild. By rights, you should have my brother's dagger, but its whereabouts following Blydh's death remains a mystery." He turned the knife in his hand until the bone handle was directed at the warrior. They locked eyes for a moment. The whole room fell silent, wondering if Kitto would accept the binding oath of clan leadership. Had Tallack done enough to assure Kitto's loyalty or had he handed him a blade with which to cut him down?

My temples pulsed with the tension and the overbearing heat. The tip of the blade was directly opposite Tallack's heart. Ren clenched his fists until his knuckles were white, preparing himself to act. Just when I was beginning to think that it would mark our downfall, Kitto reached out and took the knife. Without pausing, he ran the sharp edge across the width of his palm until it oozed with blood. Spinning the dripping blade about, he returned the knife to our Chief. Tallack did the same. When they raised their palms together, I began to relax, at least for now.

"Do you swear to lead the Hunter Clan with wisdom, honesty and courage, to follow my orders, defend our people, our land and our ways until your dying breath?" Tallack pushed hard against Kitto's palm, making him counter the pressure with his own. Their hands leaked with the mingled red humours.

"I swear. You have my blood oath, Chief."

The elders and warriors renewed their cheering and stamping. Tallack grinned and passed the bloodied dagger back to Kitto. As the warrior wiped the knife clean and tucked it into his belt, I wondered just how seriously he'd taken the part about following Tallack's orders. They were riding into battle of one sort or another and accidents do happen. I've lost count how many men I have stitched over the seasons from wounds inflicted by one of our own, deliberate or otherwise.

When the racket calmed to a dull roar, Kitto sat down. Tallack took a sip of something from his cup. If it was ale, then he had more stashed away than I'd thought.

Tallack remained on his feet. "Whether it is common knowledge or not, one of our clans has deceived us." The Chief waited for the elders to react. Some nodded having already heard the news, others flicked their heads about assessing who among them were in possession of this volatile information. "You heard right, my friends. The Alchemists have turned against us. They have denied us all access to our tin and killed those messengers sent to make peace with them." The elders gasped, the warriors mumbled, shuffling about as though they were expected to fight there and then.

It wasn't strictly true, of course. Not all our messengers were killed or we should never have heard about their rebellion. I understood why Tallack garnished the facts though. We needed all the support of the tribe to retake the tin mines.

"This summer's drought and the raging heath fires are a warning that the gods are angry with us." Tallack glanced backwards and held out his hand to the priestess. She used his sign of affection as an excuse to stand by his side and cling to his arm. What was he doing blaming the gods? The moors were parched, just like everywhere else in this wretched heat. Fires were only a matter of time.

"This is their way of telling us that we have been too lenient… complacent even, with our mining clan. Our grain stores are empty, the deer and boar have fled, the crops are burned, and we have no tin to trade. None of us will survive the winter unless we act now. The gods are telling us to retake our land by force and punish those who have broken their vow of allegiance. Now who among you will stand with me and rid us of these treacherous foes?"

The men were now so accustomed to cheering, they were barely listening. They all sprang to their feet and yelled their support, punching the air and waving short swords and cups about in the cramped space.

"Hunters ride out with Kitto; sailors join Massen in the estuary, elders send your boys to the forge. We'll need all our men in this fight." As soon as Tallack had finished speaking, the warriors jostled and barged their way out into the night air to make their preparations.

Ren got up from the bench and faced my nephew "I assume you want Meliora and me to sail with you, Chief?"

Before Tallack could reply, Endelyn piped up. "There won't be room for you. Senara and I will be travelling on his ship."

This was news to Tallack. He stepped away from her and frowned. "We're going into battle. It's no place for a woman like you." I knew what he meant. She was untrained, frail and ill-equipped to deal with the rough conditions ahead.

The priestess pouted, glowering in my direction. "How come she gets to go and not me?"

Tallack inhaled slowly and let out a noisy sigh. "I need you and mother to stay behind to prepare for the binding ceremony. Someone has to greet the Duro girl when she arrives, make her feel welcome."

Senara snickered with laughter, clamping her hand over her mouth. I could only imagine what opinions those two women had formed about the poor girl in the privacy of their hut.

Tallack looked over at Ren and me. "You don't have to come. I'll have it sorted within a few days. I thought Ren was still recovering from his time in captivity."

I couldn't believe what I was hearing. Tallack had relied on Ren and I since way before his father's death. Had he declared us unfit or unworthy of his time? Was our counsel dismissed so easily?

Ren moved closer to the Chief, lowering his voice. “I’m fully recovered.” He lied. “And I think it best if we came along. You’ll need Mel to heal your men and I can help Massen learn the ropes.”

Tallack shrugged before turning his back to us. “Just as you like. It’s your choice, but I’m sure we can manage without you.”

What had triggered this inflated arrogance? Was he stupid enough to believe that a quick mingling of blood was all it took to secure Kitto’s allegiance? We watched him step down from the top table’s raised platform and disappear through the back door with Treeve darting behind him. We had but half a night to gather our things and pack all we needed. My medicine stocks were at an all-time low; my poppy resin dwindling, my cattle gut was down to a few dried lengths and still I was without a new set of knives. How could I treat the sick and injured without fresh supplies?

Endelyn continued to scowl at us until Senara held her shoulders in both hands.

“I think I should go with them.” The shield maiden said, keeping her eyes fixed on the priestess’s. “They’ll need a reliable scout, someone who can move about the area unheard and unseen. Plus, my aim is better than most of the men put together.”

“You can’t leave me alone.” Endelyn wailed.

“You won’t be. You have the pup, and um…” Senara nodded her head towards Cryda, nursing her babe at the end of the platform. “You’ll have her for company.” The wry smile prompted Endelyn to scoff, before the pair of them started to titter. I could tell who the Chief was in their relationship. “You’ll be busy with the preparations for your binding ceremony, not to mention all the new homesteaders who will need the benefit of your priestly advice." Senara gave her a knowing smile. I knew it too. There were times when those of her sect do little more than exploit the ignorant. The homesteaders had already lost their homes, livestock and crops, now they were expected to appease Endelyn's gods with tributes and sacrifices. Within a couple of moons, she'll be the wealthiest person in the tribe.

When the Long Hut was almost cleared, Ren and I left to pack our gear. I told him about my lack of equipment and the dear man gave me one of his knives. The blade was the sharpest I'd ever known. He must have spent a great deal of time smoothing the edges with a whetstone. He's such a thoughtful man.

Clutching the sheathed knife to my chest, I hurried back to my hut to rouse the others. Vina looked excited at the prospects of travelling to the mining settlement at Bentewyn, until I told her that she was to remain behind.

"But why? How am I supposed to learn anything if you keep leaving me alone all the time?"

"You'll have to learn through trial and error. There's nothing you can't handle. Go further afield to gather alder for the lice infested homesteaders, blackthorn bark to stop the squits, the flowers to make them go, and if the loud red head from the weaver women goes into labour, fetch Cryda or the priestess. They'll know what to do." I bundled the last of my plantain paste and the poppy resin into my bag, along with my bone needles and Ren's blade. When I looked up, Vina was pulling a face.

"There'll be no arguments, my girl. You have to stay here, especially since your cousin will arrive soon and she'll need a friend." I thought that would appease her, but her frown deepened until her face was fully screwed up. "I don't care if you like her or not, she'll need your help to settle into our ways."

"You mean the camp kids will spit at her too." Vina sulked.

"I mean that you have a chance to win favour with someone who will have great power in the tribe. If I were you, I'd take all the opportunities I could."

She was relentless. Her hands flew to her hips in a defiant posture. "What about him?" She nodded at Kewri lying on his bunk. "I suppose he gets to go?"

"You do realise that we are going into a blind battle here, don't you? Either one of us, or all of us could end up dead. This is not some happy pilgrimage to a sacred spot, there'll be no feasting nor carousing, just blood and death and maybe worse." It wasn't what she wanted to hear, but it did shut her up for the rest of the night. By dawn, Kewri, Ren and I stood at the southern gates, waiting for Massen to direct us into the row boats, and from there to the ships in the estuary.

Some of the Sea Warriors volunteered to ride with the Hunters, giving us more room for provisions and weapons in the two remaining ships. With all the tribal turmoil over the last few moons, there had been no time to build new vessels to replace those smaller crafts lost in our fight against the Novantae.

As soon as we were out in the bay, the cool sea air revived us. Ren urged me to cover my skin as the mid-morning sun burnt off the haze and beat down on us from high. Despite my reluctance, I did so, knowing that his experience of sailing spanned more summers than could be counted. For most of our journey along the coastline to the west, I stayed beneath the shade of a canopy at the stern. Kewri paid no heed to the warning, and my mid-afternoon, his nose and cheeks were crimson and sore.

Sometimes I forgot how fortunate we were that Tallack was in a position to trade tin for this fine Phoenician craft. It was far beyond anything that our tribe could create, indeed it was superior to any other vessel in the land. We sped through the choppy waves all afternoon, leaving the crew on the second boat trailing in our wake.

Ren was at his usual post, steering a true course while exploiting the prevailing winds to the fullest. "Not long now." He said, when I woke from a much-needed snooze. It all seemed like a relaxing day out on the sea, rather than the solemn purpose that lay at our journey's end. None of the warriors were fired up for battle. They sat smoking and chatting, sharpening blades or checking the birch tar and twine holding their arrow heads and feathers to the shafts had not melted in the heat.

The sun was low in the sky when we drew close to land. The youngest among us hung over the side, straining their eyes to see if we'd be met by angry miners. No scouts were spotted on the cliff path, nor fishermen on the beaches. All looked to be safe to land. With only one row boat towed behind us, most men proclaimed their intention to swim to shore.

"Do you think it safe?" Ren muttered to Tallack. "Perhaps we ought to wait on board until the other ship catches up with us. We'd be better able to defend ourselves if we landed together." We waited for our Chief to give us some indication of his thoughts. After a protracted silence, he simply shrugged.

Ren tied off the tiller. "Meliora should stay here, at least until we can determine whether we face a few or many warriors."

"I will not. None of us are safe while we are this close to land. One sharp shooter could fell each of us right here and now." I struggled to my feet and gathered up my belongings. I'd be grateful of a seat in the row boat though, my swims are reserved for disasters and crises only." Ren smirked at my attempt to lighten the moment. It failed to rouse Tallack from his sullenness.

The men dithered and delayed for some while before showing any signs of disembarking. It riled me more than I could say. If they intended to surprise the Alchemists, they were failing spectacularly. As the sky turned a deep pink, the sails of the second boat appeared on the horizon.

Tallack watched the men coiling rope and stowing the oiled cloths before addressing us all. "Their scouts will have warned Kenver that we're here. Make ready men. We will land together. Kewri, row my aunt and Ren ashore with the heavier weaponry and stay on the beach until we can reach you."

It was only then that I noticed the small purple pennant missing from my nephew's ship. It was usually flown in a prominent position at the top of the mast as a signal to all that we Dumnonii bore unusual and expensive colours. The ship needed no identifying banners. As far as I was aware, it was the only one of its type among any of the tribes. We'd always been wealthy people, having the only sources of tin in the land. Now, Kenver and the Alchemists threatened to ruin our standing and starve our people.

The low tide made the swim a short one. Some of the men, including Treeve, reached the beach as I lowered myself into the row boat. They crept up the shoreline with blades and daggers in hand, spreading out along its length in search of Alchemists. I almost wished that

Kewri's rowing arms would weaken. My stomach knotted inside. Every shadow at the high-water mark caught my eye, every sound made me jump the closer we got to landing.

Ren walked in front of me, Kewri to my side, protecting me from any potential archers hiding on the cliff top above us. The men ran silently in the failing light between the huts and shelters, ready to flush out the wives and families from the mining settlement. One by one our men reappeared, having checked the immediate vicinity. All shook their heads and shrugged.

Tallack strode right through the main cluster of houses. "Where the kyjya is everyone?"

The settlement was deserted.

# CHAPTER FIFTEEN

I stayed next to the river mouth with Ren and Kewri, hardly registering what was happening. Our warriors had completed their sweep of the area and found not a single man, woman, child or beast in the place. The huts were stripped bare of personal items, bedding, cooking pots and implements, yet they were in perfect condition. The thatches were sound, the bunks intact and serviceable, there was even a few cut logs outside some of the huts. Where had the whole mining community gone?

It felt peculiar walking along the main track between the larger of the roundhouses. The drought had browned much of the low-level plants and grasses, but the wooded valley was still lush and green from the two adjoining rivers and their tributaries. I peered up towards the highest point of the gorge.

Out of us all, only I had entered the mine tunnels, treating those injured in rock falls or burned by their torches. Tallack and his brother had spent a night in an abandoned shaft on the seaward side of the cliffs, but not in the valley. I knew how deeply they'd gouged into the rocks, how disorientating the tunnels became the moment the light was extinguished.

When we reached the edge of the wooded area, Tallack stopped the men from proceeding. “It’s too dark to see clearly.” He said to Massen. “We’ll camp on the beach tonight with a heavy guard rotation. Send eight men in pairs up the cliff path to keep watch over us.”

It was the first sensible thing he’d said since we’d left the compound on the River Exe, although I was anxious to be so exposed. At least I was able to get some sleep during our journey on the boat. Poor Ren looked shattered.

“Chief?” Ren said, “Do I have your permission to take Meliora back to the ship for the night?”

He was always trying to keep me out of harm’s way. It was a lovely suggestion, but I was famished. There’d be no food on board. “It’s fine. I’m sure it’s safe enough among so many worthy warriors. I’ll make myself useful and collect some seaweed and shellfish for supper before the light fails entirely.” I started to walk away from them. Kewri lumbered after me, unsheathing his dagger and flicking his head in all directions looking for danger.

I knew all the best spots to forage. We’d spent much of the winter in the same area, but it felt like a totally different place now, so barren and hostile. I headed towards the rock pools at the end of the bay, but other than a little tough weed and a few limpets, there was nothing left to eat. If we had a little pork fat or leftover gristle, we may have had a chance to catch a crab or two from the shallow beds of the tidal streams. As it was, Kewri and I returned to the river mouth empty-handed.

Fires lit up the whole central part of the beach, our men patrolled the outskirts while others went in search of food. It’d be another couple of days before Kitto arrived with the rest of the warriors. Until then, we were vulnerable to surprise attacks. I sat next to my nephew and Treeve on the sand and peeled off a layer or two of clothes. It was a sultry evening before they lit the fires, but I was glad of their light. The watchmen could raise the alarm should people approach from the shadows.

"I'm sorry that I couldn't get your replacement knives forged, Aunt Mel. I know I promised you but…"

"I understand. Weapons and food come first. There simply wasn't enough tin or copper left. Besides, Ren has given me his knife for now. I'll manage." It was the first kind words he'd spoken to me in some time. Where once I was a favourite of his, now I was just a useful healer in the tribe. His fickle attentions were easily swayed. While he was away from Endelyn and Senara, perhaps there was a chance for me to regain his favour.

By the time the moon was high in the cloudless sky, some of the men returned from their first watch on the top of the cliffs with a few pigeons. Ren found some roots along the steep path up to the top of the cliffs and all went in the pot to stew. Meagre portions for such stout and hungry men, but there was nothing more that could be done until dawn.

We slept in rows on the beach with guards keeping watch over us for protection. There was no need for shelter. We were glad of the gentle cooling breeze across our skin as the waves lapped the shore in a rhythmic swish. I nestled in the sand next to Ren and Kewri and drifted off into a dreamless slumber.

At the sound of men shouting Tallack's name, I awoke groggy and trembling. Spinning my head about, I remembered where I was and panicked. Why were the men rushing about, unsheathing short swords and gathering up their spears? "What is it? What's happened?" It took me a little while to get to my feet and wander over to the group surrounding Tallack. As I pushed through them, I saw the dead man lying on the sand at their feet. Two of the guards sent to relieve him at his post on the cliff path, carried his body down. His throat was slashed with such ferocity, I could see his back bone through the dried clots of blood.

"Well, that proves that we're not alone. They are hiding from us." The Chief said, pursing his lips and holding in his anger.

None of the men spoke. They kept their heads bowed to the young corpse, probably thanking Cernonnus that it was not them.

The Chief scored his heel through the sand. His jaw clenched. "No one stands watch alone. Double the guards in rotation. It'll be tough on us all until Kitto arrives with the rest of the men. With any luck, we can flush them out of their hiding place during daylight." That was when the men glanced up and around at each other. I'm sure we were all thinking the same thing; that we should wait for reinforcements before attempting to find the Alchemists. This was their home land. No one knew its ways better. Ordering our Sea Warriors to go in search of them needlessly risked their lives.

Tallack did not notice the restlessness of his men. "We can send out scouts to the edges of the territory while the rest of us comb the forests in the two valleys here. Once we have their location, we'll forge a plan for when the Hunters arrive."

Ren looked up at me and almost imperceptibly shook his head. I took that to mean that he wanted me to keep quiet. Maybe I had been too vocal in the past few moons. Young men never like to hear common sense from their elders, especially from women.

"Just a suggestion, Chief." Ren began. "We should go through the huts again now it's light to see if they've left any clues to their location. Might even find some food."

I tried not to scoff. Kenver and his clan were too shrewd for that. You could be certain that whatever the Alchemists were up to, it would be well thought out and prepared in advance. They knew we would come for them. Those tunnels and the mine on the northern coast were the source of all our prosperity, our trading power and dominance in all of the land. Our family would be nothing without them and Kenver knew that.

If only Tallack had not killed Kerensa in such an underhanded way. She should have been accused publicly and given the chance to defend herself to the elders. Maybe then Kenver and his wife could have accepted her disloyalty and any forthcoming punishment without resorting to an all-out revolt.

Tallack nodded his consent to Ren and Massen. They organised the search parties and sent them in different directions. Their main focus was the larger of the two wooded valleys. My understanding was that there were no mine shafts in that area. Ren was crafty sending the warriors along that route. It was an unlikely hiding place for Kenver and the miners, but there was a good chance of us finding food and materials for more weapons. He was stalling the Chief until the Hunters could get to our location.

I went into each of the huts closest to the beach. As I predicted, there was nothing to be gleaned nor salvaged from any of the existing huts or shelters. Wandering into the largest of them all, I recalled the tense moments from sharing Kenver's home with Cryda and my old slave, Jago. It was where he helped to deliver the babe, Delen all those moons ago, before the fateful trip to the top of the world where those cruel men took his life. Bitter-sweet emotions distracted me from my task, until I realised that all the men had moved on and left me behind.

They hurried along the river bank, diving into the undergrowth and cutting straight lengths of wood for arrows. Ren was nowhere to be seen, which usually meant that he was hot on the trail of something worthy of roasting for supper. I filled my bag with moss and useful herbs, a little sorrel and burdock root, and then hurried after them along the bank.

Tallack cut through the trees and began scaling the steep incline towards the ridge. I slowed down, hoping that the youngest among them would complete their sweep of the area before I reached the top, thus saving my old knees the bother. He was about three-quarters of the way up the side of the valley when an arrow whistled past Tallack's ear and thudded into a tree trunk. Massen yelled to take cover, as a second bolt scored a path through the skin of his shoulder, knocking him to the floor. I crouched low behind a large rock, peeping out from its edge.

A third bolt flew and stuck in the ground, but no more. With so few arrows in flight, it was probably just one scout on the trail. That seemed to be my nephew's assessment too, as he called out from behind the tree.

"Tell Kenver that I'm prepared to talk. Let us speak together like men. This can all be resolved over ale around the fire. We will be waiting for him at the beach." He yelled it loud enough to be heard in the next valley. We waited for more arrows, but none were fired. After a short time, the sound of snapping twigs and rustling leaves told us that the scout was moving fast. With caution, we moved from our cover and hurried back down the slope to the water's edge. The men caught up with me in no time at all.

"They must be encamped at the top of the ridge." Massen exclaimed, picking at his shoulder wound. "Why else would they be defending that trail?"

Ren approached with a number of trout suspended from the end of a pole. "What did I miss?"

"A single archer trying to pick a few of us off." Tallack said, scratching his chin. "What would they be defending up there? Are there any mine shafts in this valley?" He looked at Ren and Massen who both shrugged, and then at me. "Aunt Mel? You spent more time here last winter than any of us. What's so special about this region?"

I thought about his question for a few moments. I couldn't recall any signs of tunnels at all. This was the area of the forest where the best timber for props was felled. "Do you think the scout was sent to deliberately misdirect you? If you spend all your time searching here, you are ignoring whatever they are doing in the next valley."

Ren sucked in his lips to stifle a smile. I probably should have worded it better than that, but I was a bit shaken and keen to be back on the beach.

Tallack nodded slowly. "Go on, Aunt Mel. Tell us where you think they'll be."

"Where the tin is, of course, at the top of the next valley where the smelters live. There are a number of shelters not far from the mine entrances. There's a good water supply and access to the cliff tops." If I had overstepped my boundaries again, I didn't care. We were standing in a clearing between the trees. It was not particularly sensible to give the Alchemists another chance to fill us with arrows.

I'd said all I had planned to say. Without waiting for my nephew to make a decision, I turned on my heels and trudged back the way we came. Ren tramped after me, grinning with pride. I wasn't sure whether it was because of my stand against Tallack, or from his skill at fishing. At least we would eat well.

Sometime in the afternoon, Tallack announced that we would make use of the empty huts rather than camp out on the beach. I wasn't sure how happy I was about this declaration. I felt safer on the beach surrounded by guards and fires, but I knew that it was a temporary arrangement. I also knew that there would be little room to spare at full tide when Kitto arrived with all the men and horses. We'd have no choice but to move further inland for water and grazing. How long would this standoff take to resolve?

If Tallack could get to speak directly with Kenver, and a deal struck to avoid conflict, then Kitto could turn about and ride home to the island compound on the River Exe. If not, then who knew how long we would have to stay?

On our way back through the huts, I found Kewri wandering out of the bushes, tying the fastenings of his leggings. How is it that he always needs to move his bowels at the worst possible time? I thrust my water bladder into his arms. "Make yourself useful. Fill up as many bladders as you can carry from the spring just beyond the bridge on the opposite side of the river. The track is well worn so you should find it without trouble."

"But…" He curled his lip in confusion, pointing to the fresh water tributary flowing into the main river.

"No buts, my lad. We need water straight from the rocks. I'm not falling for the whole tainted water supply again." As I said it, Tallack walked by, chucking his water bladder to Kewri.

"Fill mine too." The Chief said, encouraging all his men to copy him. I had to chuckle, watching the giant juggling slippery bladders in his arms as he lumbered over the bridge. It was the only sensible thing to do. The winter ague carried off so many people from both Kenver's clan and our own before we found the source of the contamination.

It was also how Tallack and his brother came to part ways with the Priest Sect. He'd banished them to the moors after killing their clan leader for tying festering goat carcasses in the water upstream. I recalled how I'd thought we'd seen the back of the priests. Now Tallack was all set to bind himself to one.

Ren descaled and gutted the fish, while the men chopped wood to keep the fires burning. Massen persuaded Tallack to spend one more night on the beach before moving the camp into the huts. His reasoning was to allow Kenver the chance to take up the Chief's offer to talk. None of us believed that the Alchemist would do so after all his effort to prevent us from retaking control of the mines. I offered to patch up Massen's shoulder but he declined saying that it was only a scratch. A little splash with sea water and he was content to let it air out.

The body of our young watchman was more of an immediate problem. The flies were gathering in large numbers and there were few places to keep the corpse cool. It wouldn't be long before it'd stink up the place. The men were reluctant to go near it, in case the Morrighan should mark them as next in line to fall. I must admit, it did give me pause to think that the longer we stayed, the greater the likelihood that Kenver's men would kill us all by stealth.

The fish was cooked in no time at all, and wolfed down by the men even quicker. With their bellies silenced for a while, Tallack was keen to approach the narrower valley before nightfall. Ren tried to talk him out of it, but he was determined.

"We have no idea whether their entire clan is up there or only some of them." Ren kept his voice low so that only a few of us could hear. "For all we know, we could be utterly surrounded."

My gut twisted into a knot. Perhaps I should have stayed on the ship. What use was I at times like this? I didn't want the men to put themselves in further danger just to protect me.

"That's why we need to walk up the ravine." Tallack hissed back. "Let's see for ourselves where that traitorous kyjyan and his men are hiding so that we may rest in our furs more easily." The Chief had a point. Without further exploration to get an idea of what we were up against, we were sitting ducks.

# CHAPTER SIXTEEN

Tallack was in no mood to listen to our opinions. Neither Ren nor I were in his circle of advisers. If only Senara had sailed with us instead of riding over land with Kitto. She was exactly what the situation required. I'd never known a better scout than her. I looked about me at the men. They were without doubt brilliant sailors and loyal to a fault but they were clumsy on land. None could match her for stealth.

What surprised me the most, was Tallack's solution to the problem. In Senara's absence, he chose young Treeve to take her place.

"You're small and wily, Treeve." The Chief said. "Creep up the gorge as far as you're able. Count their watchers, take note of their positions, and what defences are in our way. Can you do that for me?" He stood close to his lover and smiled down on the lad. I didn't know whether to be horrified at Tallack's lack of regard for the crewman's life or proud that he would put someone he loved in harm's way to protect the tribe's best interests. After all this time of distrusting the lad, I suddenly feared for him.

Treeve squeezed the Chief's arm and smiled. "You can count on me." He scooped up his weapons, took his water bladder from Kewri, and then ran off beyond the headland into the valley.

The waiting was the hard part, especially knowing that at any moment, we could be overrun by angry miners with their sinewy strength and tenacity. These folks were hardier than any other in our tribe. They toiled come rain or shine, deep underground, hammering, scraping, choking, and dying. It wasn't hard to see why they resented us.

We profited and lived a bountiful life based on their labour, although my time with Kenver during the winter made me see that he was indifferent to their rough treatment. Our Chief's laid down a minimum age for the younger miners. Their laws ensured that those youngsters who were required to support their families stayed above ground, breaking and sorting rocks, assisting the smelters and so on, but I saw children no more than six summers underground.

Kenver had no intention of protecting the young, unless they were his kin. Their little hands were raw and bloody from picking at the seams with antlers and dragging the ore to the surface. We had no idea what promises their leader had made to gain their support in the rebellion. If there was a slim possibility of a better life, I don't blame them for taking the chance.

I stayed close to the fires on the beach, searching for razor clams or buried crabs, anything to add to the pot. Ren and Kewri loitered close by. I was always under their watchful eyes. To be honest, I was glad that they cared. At nightfall, I returned to the most central fire and sat opposite Tallack. I could see that he was fretting about Treeve but doing his best not to let it show. He chewed at the sides of his nails, stood up and paced for a while, and then sat back in the same sandy depression as before.

The three whistles sounded from the cliff tops, indicating a change in the guards. Those whose turn it was to replace them, hurried off to the path at the edge of the headland. A short time later, those who had finished their watch, returned to the beach. There was still no sign of Treeve.

When the moon rose, the tide went fully out exposing a large tract of wet sand. I needed time away from the men. They were offensive in many respects, from their bawdy tales of the marshland women to their smell.

You'd think being so close to the sea that they'd rinse themselves down after a long day of sweating. "Kewri, can you come and hold a torch for me? I want to see if I can't rake some cockles down there." I jabbed my thumb over my shoulder, indicating my intention to forage at the low water mark in the dark. He slipped in the loose sand as he attempted to stand up, falling on his backside with a thump.

Ren tapped his shoulder. "I'll go lad. You get some sleep before your watch." I had a feeling Ren would volunteer to help me. It was like we were the only two elders in the world, looking out for one another in this harsh land.

I held the torch close to the ground, searching for bumps and bubbles in the smooth shoreline where the shellfish pumped out waste water but it was almost impossible to see. Ren dug about with a spear in the hope of hitting something edible but there was not much to be had. I suspected that Kenver had already stripped the beach of food before we arrived.

The night wore on and with another watchman change, Treeve still had not returned. Tallack sat gazing at the dancing flames, picking his calloused hands in silence. Every now and then, he strolled along the guarded section of the dunes before settling back down by the fires.

I too found it hard to sleep despite the cooler temperature and the gentle breeze. Late into the night, I did manage to drop off, but it wasn't enough to revive my spirits. Ren was already plucking a couple of wildfowl from the wetlands further along the bay when I awoke.

"Treeve?" I asked him. Ren shook his head. "He's not…?"

"Not that we know of, just hasn't returned." Ren's face dropped into sadness. "But we did lose two more men last night."

"Is Kewri safe?" I shot up from my sandy bed in a panic.

Ren looked up and pointed to my giant friend wandering back from the dunes. It took quite some time for my heart to stop racing in my chest. He smiled at me as if to say, *always fussing*. "It was a couple of our youngest crewmen, both shot through the back with arrows." Ren took out his anger on the dead bird, ripping great handfuls of feathers from its corpse in rapid strokes and plunging them into a sack.

"Where's the Chief?" I got to my feet and dusted myself down.

"Arranging for the funeral pyre. Doesn't look like this mess will be resolved for a while, so we can't take the bodies back to their families."

I understood why he was so upset. These were sailors who looked up to Ren, learned from him and took their values from his actions. One day, they would have taken his place in the Sea Warriors as navigators and wily traders. Our numbers were declining at an alarming rate.

"I did manage to persuade Tallack to wait until Kitto and the Hunters arrive before we venture into the woods again."

That was something for which to be grateful. This headstrong and arrogant side of my nephew was hard to stomach, especially when his decisions led to loss of lives. With a great many more men, Kenver might just agree to talks instead of this bloody uprising. When Tallack wandered back to the fireside he approached me.

"Aunt Mel, how well do you remember the position of the mine shafts in the gorge?"

"Fairly well, I'd say, although some were new and shallow, whilst others looked to be much older and deeper, with many interconnecting branches. I only went inside a couple, and not far at that. Kenver usually had the injured person carried closer to the entrance for me to treat."

The Chief unsheathed the huge greying sword from its scabbard and passed it to me. "Can you draw it in the sand?"

It was a tall order, considering I could barely wield the heavy weapon and my memory of the tunnels was patchy at best. Most mines ran next to each other from a single external path, with one man gouging out the rock, and a small boy or girl shovelling out the ore. The deepest cuts were on the left side of the tributary and low in the valley. I suggested that as the ore became scarce, new tunnels were created further up the ravine on both sides. I did my best to score a rudimentary map into the wet sand, but it was hardly accurate.

Tallack pulled at his whiskers, frowning. "So how are they able to fetch clean water or food without coming down to the river?"

"The whole area is riddled with fresh water streams that pop up from the rock face. I wouldn't imagine it difficult for them to store dried meat strips, grain, and roots, especially since they've had unlimited access to tin for trade with passing ships."

No one liked what I had to say. They all scoffed and moaned, kicking at the sand and spitting, before walking away. Did they really think that someone as bright and knowledgeable as Kenver would hide in the tunnels without fresh water or provisions?

Tallack gave the men orders. Some were to secure a boundary around the huts at the foot of the headland, others were sent out to hunt for and gather food. More warriors were tasked with fletching new arrows or building the pyre. With all the warriors occupied, there was little for me to do.

My nephew instructed me to stay by the fires until I could move into one of the huts. Left alone with my thoughts, I started to imagine all sorts of unpleasant fates for young Treeve. If he'd been injured, it was unlikely that we would find him in the dense woodland of the gorge since calling out would make him a target for the Alchemists. If, however, he'd been killed or worse still, captured, I was convinced my nephew would not recover from the loss.

It was late afternoon when Kitto arrived with Senara and the Head Hunters. They must have ridden the horses hard to cover that distance in less than three days. I first saw a glimmer of them on the top of the cliffs, when the guards whistled down to gain our attention. Not long after that, they dismounted and walked the horses down the steep path and around the headland.

Both the warriors and their ponies glistened with sweat. A few of them made straight for the river. Many of the younger ones were not aware of the brackish water. I watched them stoop low and cup their hands in the water before slurping it into their mouths. It was hard not to laugh, as each of them blew out the salty liquid, spraying one another in the process.

Ren directed them to a fresh water source, just beyond the settlement, where the Sea Warriors took it in turns to stand guard. I was relieved to see so many of our people, ready to fight for what was ours. Tallack made a point of welcoming Kitto, grabbing his forearm tightly and pulling him into a manly hug. Both men had healed well from their fight and seemed keen to deal with Kenver's clan.

I loitered outside the hut that Tallack had selected for himself, watching Kitto enter before the Chief. Tallack looked about at those of us gathered, considering which of us he would consult. After a short time, he called on Massen to join them. The three leaders requested the presence of no others, which I found to be most disheartening. Massen had a sound head on his shoulders, but my concerns about Kitto's ambition had not abated. Whatever suggestions he made, would be in order to benefit himself more than the tribe.

Try as I might, I was not able to hear their discussion and all my attempts to get close to the door were for nought. Kitto's men stood guard outside preventing my entry. Slinking back the way I'd walked, Ren and Kewri met me outside the largest of the huts. It was the same one that I'd stayed in before with Tallack's mother.

Ren pulled back the door drapes and gestured for me to go inside. I looked up at Kewri.

"I'll um…" The giant muttered. "I'll stay in that one over there with the men." He seemed almost embarrassed. There was more than enough room for us all. I don't know why he should want to share with those stinking warriors. When I got inside, Ren had collected bedstraw for the bunks and logs for the fire. Not that we needed one with the heat funnelling in up the valley. The waterfowl were plucked and gutted and ready for the pot. He'd even found some green linden twigs for me to clean my teeth and a solitary clay pot filled with cool water from the spring. It was a proper home from home.

We built a fire outside the house on which to cook. I suggested another stew to eke out the birds, but Ren said he could find more. A little roasted fowl would brighten our spirits no end. While I took care of the cooking, Ren stood outside Tallack's hut with some of the other men, waiting to hear their plans. At nightfall, Ren returned.

"We are to gather at the far end of the beach tonight for the pyre." He said, more solemn than ever.

"And what was decided about the miners?"

"From what I can make out, Kitto has convinced Tallack that our actions since we arrived, have only served to give the Alchemists the upper hand."

I shook my head, sighing.

Ren turned the spit roast. "He intends on riding right up the ravine at day break, smashing through any defences and killing anyone on sight."

"But that's…"

"Foolish? Yes, I agree, but Massen was in no position to gainsay the mighty Kitto. Our Chief hangs on his every word. He might just as well hand over leadership of the tribe now."

This news was most disturbing. In his bid to curry favour with the man, Tallack weakened his position even further. I thought back to the incident the summer before where we were in a similar situation as Kenver. Tallack and his brother ordered their men to build paling walls and archers traps all the way up to the mines. For the life of me, I couldn't remember if Kitto was among them. If he was, surely, he hadn't forgotten the impenetrable defences the Duro raiders were up against?

I didn't need to state this obvious flaw in Kitto's plan. Ren was fully aware of the perils. We cooked the birds, shared them with Kewri and a few others and then walked the length of the beach to await the lighting of the pyre. Senara made a point of seeking me out as we stood around the bodies of our fallen. The raised platform was rough but serviceable, stuffed with dry grasses and weed. None of the dead were washed nor wrapped. That was the job of the womenfolk. Maybe I should have offered, but I hardly knew the men and there was no cloth in which to wrap them.

Senara jogged my elbow. "Do you want to say the words over them, Fur Benyn? Endelyn would normally do that but, you know?"

My brow wrinkled up in confusion. "I'm not of the Priest Sect, Senara. It's not my place." She looked affronted, but I would not be swayed. "If you want to speak to the gods on their behalf, be my guest. I don't think they're listening anyway." I made sure that those standing closest to us heard me, including Tallack. I hadn't realised just how much her relationship with Endelyn had elevated her in the tribe. She was bolder than I ever thought possible. Senara did have some admirable qualities, but I wasn't used to being ordered about by anyone other than Chiefs. My nephew glared at me, but he didn't offer to speak either.

In the end, it was down to Massen. He spoke from the heart, listing their qualities and begging the gods to find them an honourable place in the Summerlands. When it came down to it, there was not much to be said about those poor young men. Their accomplishments during skirmishes and battles amounted to the events from the last few moons at most.

Tallack lit the pyre with a torch, throwing it into the dry brush beneath the wooden platform. We stood and watched as the fire spread quickly, the flesh from their young bodies charring and sizzling in the engulfing flames. All three were of the Sea Warrior Clan, whose numbers had taken a beating during the last cycle. Kitto stood next to Tallack for a few moments, just long enough for the blaze to take hold, before ordering the Head Hunters back to their posts. He didn't even wait for Tallack to realise that he'd been usurped in the line of command.

Ren gave a bag of plucked feathers to Senara for fletching and joined me on the slow walk back to the hut. The Sea Warriors remained at the pyre, sharing stories and lamenting the loss of their friends. The shield maiden stood at the river mouth, clutching the bag and looking back along the beach. Most of the Hunters were either at their watch posts or bedding down at the high water mark next to roaring fires. I could see that she was struggling to decide where to camp for the night.

Chewing on her lip, Senara skipped into a slow jog to catch up with Ren and me. "You don't mind if I bunk down with you two tonight, do you?"

Ren gave her a sharp look. "I thought you'd be keen to share stories with the Head Hunters. Aren't you one of them now?" He didn't even attempt to mask his annoyance.

She glanced down at her feet as she flicked the sand with a toe. "I don't belong anywhere." She wouldn't make eye contact with either of us. When Ren said nothing in response, she swallowed hard.

"I'm neither sailor nor Hunter, Alchemist nor priest. I have no clan and no clan wants me." She sniffed. I was fairly sure that she was sincere. Three days riding with the Hunters had diminished her confidence. The show at the pyre was all an act. It made me wonder whether they had done something to her, some bizarre initiation or ritual to test her worth. As much as I was looking forward to spending a quiet night alone with Ren, I pitied the girl. She was just trying to find her place in the world, and that was no easy feat for a woman.

I held out my hand towards her. "Come with us. You can tell us about your ride down here."

Ignoring Ren's perpetual scowl, she threaded her arm through mine and together we sauntered to our hut. Senara rolled out her furs on a smaller bunk that was once occupied by one of Kenver's children. Ren and I shared the largest, but it was still too humid to stay close to one another for long. With no fire inside the hut and the door skins pinned back, we made the most of what little breeze we could to keep cool.

As my eyes adjusted to the dark shadows, Ren began to snore. That was when I heard her little voice from across the hut. "Fur Benyn, Kitto is going to kill the Chief."

# CHAPTER SEVENTEEN

There was not much chance of me sleeping with Senara's proclamation spinning around my head all night. It had confirmed what Ren and I already suspected. Becoming clan leader was not enough for the warrior, Kitto wanted power over our whole tribe. The question remained, would he wait until we had regained control of the mines or strike before more men were killed and negotiate a new deal with the Alchemists?

I rose before dawn with the aim of speaking to Senara. She was more likely to reveal what she knew to me without Ren about, making her feel unwelcome. I drank a little water from the jug and squatted outside in the grasses. There was no meat or fish left, nor grain to boil up for porridge. It was too early in the season for most berries and too dry for fresh shoots and leaves. I returned to the hut with my stomach growling and nothing to offer to Ren and Senara. She was awake and sitting up on her bunk as I entered.

"Did you mean what you said last night?" I leaned closer to her, narrowing my eyes and watching her reactions.

She stretched and slung her legs down to the ground. "I did. I overheard Kitto talking to some of his men. They had no idea that I was so close to them."

"But are you certain that it wasn't just men bragging and making ridiculous claims, like they do?" I practically hissed at the girl so that Ren would not wake. Senara nodded. Blowing out air over my teeth, I sat on the edge of her bunk. "Have you spoken to the Chief about this?"

"And say what? You've seen how he is with Kitto. The man could murder every one of us and Tallack would dismiss it as necessary. He's untouchable. Not to mention the fact that the men would gut me for betraying their new clan leader." She was certainly in a difficult situation. I looked over at my slumbering friend. Perhaps my nephew still held enough respect for Ren to pay heed to his advice.

While Senara went to prepare her horse for the attack, I woke Ren and updated him on Senara's news that Kitto had announced his intentions to kill Tallack. He wasn't at all surprised. Splashing water on his face and hair, he stared out at the horses grazing on the river banks in the distance. Many of the Hunters were already fastening reins and leading the ponies towards the mouth of the adjoining gorge.

"I'd better try and catch Tallack before it's too late." Ren said, slipping his leggings and shoes on and heading for the open door.

"Wait, I'll come too." It was hard to keep up with his long strides. Ren was a man on a mission and nothing would stand in his way, not even the dozens of warriors loading up their ponies with shields and spears, scabbards and blades. For so many people milling about, the valley was ominously quiet. This would normally be the time when someone from the Priest Sect would take a moment to give an offering to the gods and ask for their support, but I saw no such devotional rituals among the Head Hunters. The Sea Warriors were guarding the perimeter and looked set to stay where they were. What orders had Tallack given them? Were they not a part of the planned stampede on the miners?

Every one of the warriors we passed wore a grim stare of defiance as we walked between them on our way to the Chief's hut. Tallack was alone when we reached the doorway, the coverings pinned back just as we had done. Poking my head inside, my eyes adjusted to the gloom to see my nephew struggling to fasten the leather straps securing his wrist guards. Without invitation, I wandered over to assist him. He let me, turning his gaze to Ren.

"You've come to talk me out of the attack." He picked up the second wrist guard and passed it to me, raising his other forearm so that I could repeat the process.

Ren held the Chief's stare. "I have. We've heard about a plot against you."

I expected Tallack to be shocked, to demand details or get angry over our interference. Instead, he merely nodded and then checked my handiwork. "I know you both have my best interests at heart, you are loyal to a fault, but you should not concern yourself with Chieftain matters. I have everything under control."

"We think Kitto..." Ren began, but his protestations were met with the Chief shushing him and steering my friend and I back towards the door.

"If you want to make yourselves useful, find food, prepare medicines and make the camp more secure. I'm leaving my best men to defend you while we're gone." That was all we could get from my deeply altered nephew. I had attributed most of his mood changes to the loss of his twin brother but this was a whole new level of arrogance. It began when the priestess declared herself Ruvane of our tribe.

With a little shove, we were expelled from his presence and sent packing. More and more warriors gathered at the foot of the headland, close to our hut. Senara was among them, waiting for her friend to return with fresh drinking water from the springs. I took a few moments to check the contents of my healing kit and went in search of Kewri. He too was preparing for the attack, looking for a spare horse that could carry his hulking great weight.

Even I could tell him that no such pony existed in this neck of the woods. When I pointed this fact out to him, he pouted, and then announced his intention to run up the gorge track after the warriors. Either way, I could not dissuade him.

"You have Ren to protect you now, Fur Benyn. You don't need me anymore." There was a sadness in his eyes that crushed my heart. My growing fondness for Renowden had displaced the giant in my household. Now the poor lad didn't know where he belonged. I wondered if my nephew had given him different orders to follow, dismissing him from the duty of protecting me. When I enquired if this was the case, Kewri shook his head.

"Chief Tallack hasn't spoken to me." His bottom lip trembled. "Now that Vina's your apprentice, I just assumed…" His shoulders scrunched up around his ears. How hadn't I seen this sooner? He was elated when I welcomed him into my home. I'd lost track how many times he'd saved my life or helped me when no one else could. With all the turmoil on the island compound, I'd overlooked the giant.

Grabbing his wrist, I stopped him and spun him about until he was facing me. "Kewri, you are my friend. I cannot ever repay your kindness towards me. You'll always have a place at my fireside and under my roof until such time you ever wish to leave. Do not think me ungrateful or that I don't need you, because I do. My home and my heart are large enough for us all."

The corners of his mouth edged upwards and his cheeks flushed with a rosy glow.

"You are part of the family now, lad. You can't get rid of me that easily." I winked at him, making him chuckle. Together, we hurried back across the bridge to where Kitto sat on his huge black stallion calling his men around.

Senara led her pale horse past our hut where Ren was standing. He flicked his hand at her, beckoning her closer. She leaned down the side of her pony's neck until she was level with Ren's head.

Whatever he said to her made the shield maiden dismount and hand the reins to him. With a curt nod, she loaded herself up with her weapons and water and shot off into the undergrowth behind our house. I was out of breath by the time we reached him but I had enough in my lungs to demand to know what he'd done.

Ren passed the reins to Kewri and ducked back inside the hut. He returned moments later, strapping his weapons to Senara's horse. "I've sent her along the cliff top path to scout the far end of the gorge. I shall ride alongside Tallack and make sure that he comes to no harm." As he mounted the bay mare, he addressed Kewri. "Stay here. Make sure Fur Benyn is protected at all times. Got that?"

The giant nodded, grinning with pride. His mission restored; he was happy to be useful once again.

I was less than pleased with this turn of events. While everyone galloped off to battle the miners, I was to stay behind as a prisoner. "But if there are injuries, I won't be able to treat them. You can't carry more than a couple of men down the valley at once." I was almost smug with my quick thinking. Ren sucked in his lips. He knew that I was right. I needed to be there too.

Kitto was bellowing at the warriors. He praised their courage and fortitude, inciting a cheer that drowned out all other noises. If the Alchemists didn't know they were coming, they did now. I shook my head in disbelief, but on Kitto went.

"We will show them which is the mightier clan within our tribe, those who are loyal to our people." He took a breath while the hollering and whooping grew louder. "We'll show them what happens to kyjyan traitors. We'll ride hard and fast up that valley and show them what courage looks like. When we've finished with them, they'll be grateful of the open arms of Cernonnus to carry them into the Underworld. They love hiding so much, let's see how they like spending eternity with the shameful dead." The roaring made the ponies skittish. They jostled and whinnied, adding to the general clamour.

Kitto unsheathed the dagger bestowed upon him as leader of the Head Hunters and held it aloft. "Ride now and take as many heads as you can carry. Let's make them wish they'd never been born." He yanked the reins of the stallion until it reared up and squealed. The beast's mane swished across the warrior's chest, its front legs kicking out in fury. Kitto held on tightly, drinking in the glory of his men's admiration.

Lowering the oath blade, Kitto used it to point up the gorge, before jabbing his heels into the horse's flanks and riding away. The Head Hunter's followed the galloping stallion into battle.

"Where's Tallack?" I said, snapping my head about in search of my nephew.

"We'll find him. Come on, old girl." Ren linked his arm about mine and pulled me up onto the back of Senara's horse behind him. I pulled my healing kit strap until the bag rested on my hip and then clung to Ren's middle as we set off at a canter. Glancing back over my shoulder, I saw poor Kewri break into a slow run after us. We should have told him to stay in the camp, but I knew he'd do all in his power to keep his word.

When we'd passed the first small incline in the track, we hit a thicket of dense shrubs. The warriors ahead of us fell in line, riding in single file and making it impossible to see whether Tallack was among them.

Undeterred, we rode on, passing some of the heavier men on struggling horses. I knew the tracks well, but Ren held the reins. Senara's bay mare was sure footed and bright. As the trail hit a steep stretch, we cantered on while others fell back. Mists hung between the trees, being shaded from the rising sun. It made it harder to see to the head of the clan.

"The trail splits up ahead." I warned Ren, unsure whether he was familiar with the area. As far as I knew, he'd spent much of his time on Tallack's ship during the early winter, or on their trip over to Iwerdon. He pulled on the reins to slow our horse. Clambering up to the large patch of gravel where the path diverged, I spotted Tallack just ahead of us.

Kitto halted, taking the opportunity to turn his horse around to speak with the men. He seemed to have some sort of hierarchy set out among them, as though some were raised in status above others. He barked out his orders and half of the men branched off to take the low path alongside the river. The hooves rumbled on the hard baked earth, their ponies taking the brunt of twig and branch lashings as they powered through the overhanging shrubs.

Sweeping his arm over his head as though he was about to launch a rock, he signalled the remaining men to follow him. Ren waited, pulling back on the reins until we could see which direction our Chief would take. To my shock and surprise, Tallack chose to follow Kitto along the high track carved into the side of the valley.

On we pushed, through narrow and steep embankments and over wider and flatter areas until we were spread out among mature trees. The leaf litter and scree slowed our progression, forcing the ponies to pick through the undergrowth to avoid a misstep. Kitto drove on relentlessly, determined to have possession of the mines before the sun was high.

When we reached a flat area of woodland, a rockfall ahead of us narrowed the track substantially. It looked only wide enough to accommodate two horses to pass at a time. The broken rocks looked fresh, as if someone had deliberately caused the fall to halt our progress. Everyone could see that it was an ideal spot for an ambush. Kitto held his arm aloft, slowing all those behind him to a trot.

Drenched in sweat and spitting out gnats and dust, we lingered behind the Head Hunters at the rear. Tallack spun about in his saddle and caught sight of Ren and me. His opened mouth of shock transformed into a seething pucker.

"What is she doing here? Ren you had no right to put my aunt in danger." Tallack hissed.

"I couldn't stop her, Chief. She worries about you," he half-whispered, half-shouted back.

It was comforting to know that he cared about me enough to be angry with his old friend. I had wondered just how far I'd fallen from his grace. The admonishment didn't last long, there were more pressing concerns for us all. We were deep in enemy territory with warriors who were unfamiliar with the terrain. If ever there was a good time to knock us all off the side of the gorge with a sizable rockfall, now would be the time.

I kept a weather eye on the overhanging cliffs, the canopies of the trees and shrubs ahead, looking for shifting shadows and rustling bushes, anything to indicate that we were riding into a trap. Tallack must have sensed it too, for he yanked on his horse's reins until he'd fallen back in line with us.

"I don't like this, Ren." My nephew declared. We were surrounded by warriors, yet I had never felt as vulnerable as I did then. Kitto sent one man through the gap in the fallen rocks ahead. He galloped through and disappeared into the trees beyond. A single whistle came from the other side, indicating that all was well. The scout had passed without danger or challenge.

That was when we heard the screams from below us; a mixture of howls from our men and the agonised squeals from the horses. Those sent on the lower path were under attack. The men looked to Kitto for guidance, halting their ponies and exchanging looks of panic.

"We go on!" Kitto bellowed. "There's nothing we can do to help them. By the time we double back to reach them, they could all be slaughtered." I understood his decision, even if the men balked at his callous disregard of the men's welfare. The gorge was simply too steep to ride down to the lower path and we couldn't go back.

The great man saw that they were losing their confidence in him. "Send your prayers to the Morrighan, men. She will choose the worthy among us to sit with the gods in the Summerlands, but not before we have that kyjyan, Kenver's head on a spike first." He roared, unsheathing his short sword and waving it about as he kicked the ribs of his horse into a gallop.

I peered over the edge of the path, down to the dark and misty valley floor. Our young men faced almost certain death down there, or worse still, maimed and captured. Their cries and moans echoed across the gorge, until it was all we could hear. A haunting wail of death surrounded us and turned my stomach. Blydh would never have let his men go on such a dangerous path alone, but then he would never have insisted on this foolish raid into unknown territory. Why hadn't Tallack taken over control? He was the Chief when all was said and done. All our people were at his command, and yet, he hung back to allow Kitto's lead. Was this part of his plan? I couldn't see that it was working terribly well if it was.

Two by two, we slipped through the narrow gap and out into a wider section lined with sturdy oak and ash. The thick layer of leaves blocked out most of the light. It took a few moments for my eyes to adjust. When they did, I realised why Tallack gasped at my side. Ahead of us, suspended from a thick overhanging branch, hung a blood drenched body.

# CHAPTER EIGHTEEN

It wasn't hard to figure out which of our men was hanging from the tree above us. Treeve's body showed all the signs of vicious and unnecessary torture; his skin flayed on his chest, arms and legs, his fingertips and manhood severed and missing. Flies swarmed about the open flesh, laying their eggs in the warmth of the morning and feasting on his open eyes. Kenver had placed all blame for his daughter's death on the boy, taking out his vengeance without any proof to back up the claim. I knew for a fact, that Treeve was only responsible for disposing of Kerensa's body at Tallack's request. It was my nephew who had taken her life; that I heard from his own mouth.

Tallack buckled in the middle. His shock kept him silent and struggling for breath. I reached out and grabbed his arm, stopping him from sliding from the saddle onto the ground. Ren steered us close enough to clamp his leg between the sides of our ponies.

"Steady on, Chief. Keep your head." I muttered, trying to rouse him from the spiral of despair he'd begun. "We will make Kenver suffer, you can be sure of that. There will be a time to grieve, but that time is not now." I patted his shoulder, then gave it a good shake.

The tears welled in his reddening eyelids and looked set to spill down his cheeks. I couldn't have him fall apart now. This was exactly what Kenver wanted. All the men could see him losing his composure. Young Treeve may not have been popular with the Hunters, but he was still one of us. My nephew's partiality for the lad was common knowledge. That alone made him a target for ridicule and cruelty.

"Tallack!" I snapped. "You have to lead."

He snorted, his breathing was laboured and fast. He shot me a pained look before coming to his senses. Winding the reins around his clenched fists, he kicked his horse and galloped off at speed. Ren took chase, but the bay mare was no match for the horse he rode. The dusty track plumed up behind him as he and Kitto were neck and neck on the trail, the men in pursuit just a fraction behind.

They were too far ahead for us to see, let alone be of use to the Chief. He was angry and careless, and that spelled disaster. Ren kicked our pony into the fastest canter she could manage through the trees towards another steep section of the trail. The men were farther ahead. Kitto had the stronger horse of the two leaders, out pacing Tallack by just one length of a pony. I could imagine the sneer on the warrior's face, grinning over his shoulder at Tallack as he raged through the pain of his loss. There was one last patch of tall trees in their path before the scree sloped track to the mines. All the men pushed their ponies hard, cantering side by side, hollering their signature cries and waving their weapons about to scare the hiding miners.

Before they reached the edge of the forested glade, Tallack suddenly pulled up on the reins. His horse groaned, skidding to a halt while all those around him galloped by. "No, Stop!" He yelled, but it was too late. He had spotted what they had not. A taut rope snapped with a twang between the thick trunks of two oaks, decapitating the warrior leading the charge. The gut churning sound of breaking bone marked the moment two more lives were taken; their necks snapped in an instant. Kitto, a larger man all round, took the force from the rope across his collar bone and chest. It flipped him backwards until he was face down on the earth. His horse rode off without him, leaving the rest of his men to screech to a halt or crush into the fray. Those of us at the back managed to stop in time, but many didn't.

Shrieking and bucking, the horses kicked out, throwing some off their backs and trampling others. Kitto took the full weight of one pony and his rider as it slammed down on his spine from rearing up high. All we could do was to sit and watch the Head Hunters smashing and flailing into one another in a melee of crushed limbs and shattered bones.

"Do something!" I cried, but I knew that nothing could be done. Those who were less injured scrambled to regain control of their mounts and ride to a safer distance. I fidgeted on the back of the bay mare, preparing to slide down with my healing kit. Before I could throw my leg over, an arrow whistled past my ear and thudded into a tree. A second scored a direct hit, straight into the neck of a warrior in front. Ren took evasive action, yanking the reins to the side and turning us back the way we came. Before long, the air was filled with the evil darts, each aiming for our softest parts.

Tallack called the retreat. He slipped off his horse and, risking life and limb, struggled to load Kitto across his pony's back. I screamed in Ren's ear to stop and help, but we were already through the narrow gap in the rocks. Clinging onto my friend, I watched over my shoulder as our Chief mounted the laden beast and urged it away from danger. Some followed but many could not, their horses injured or dead, they were sitting ducks for Kenver's archers.

We did not slow down until we were more than half way back to camp. Survivors from the low trail were few in number and all were injured, shot through with arrows or wounded when their horses threw them from their backs.

They too, encountered a similar trap, with the rope low in the undergrowth, set to cripple their horses, thus proving us right all along. It was an unbelievably foolish plan from start to finish. My anger bubbled inside like molten tin. So many men lost, so many horses suffering or killed.

Kewri had tried to catch up with us but stopped to rest on a rock by the river. When we rode past him, he began the run back to the huts. I held my fury inside until we were all back within the boundaries of the camp. Ren helped the Chief carry Kitto into one of the empty shelters, expecting me to summon the gods to cure him.

The massive warrior made no sound as they hooked his arms over their shoulders and dragged him inside. It was as though he had no sense of pain despite the terrible injuries he'd suffered. From the stains on his leggings, he'd pissed himself too. That was all the confirmation I needed. Kitto had not lost control of his bladder through fear. His back was broken.

I looked at Tallack and shrugged. "There is nothing I can do to fix him. His fate lies in the arms of the Morrighan." I wasn't sure whether the warrior could even hear me. He neither spoke nor showed any indications that he understood my words.

Tallack's face remained impassive, calm. He scratched his face, nodded, and left the hut. At first, I thought it was all too much for him to process, the brutal death of his lover, the number of men killed in such a short space of time, plus the news that Kitto would never recover, but he surprised me. He went straight to where the wounded had gathered to lend a hand.

We left Kitto with one of the able-bodied Hunters and joined my nephew outside on the grass. Here the injured lay. Most were shot through with arrows, others with simple gashes and cuts or dislocations.

The worst was a young lad who was thrown by his horse onto rocks. His thigh bone was splintered into sharp spikes erupting through his skin. Even though the warrior was unconscious, I could see from the spurts of fresh blood that his heart still pounded in his chest.

One look was all it took to know that it could not be mended. It had to come off entirely. The problem with leg amputations is that they often bleed to death before you can cut through the limb. I stroked the fair curls away from the lad's forehead. He was no more than sixteen, maybe seventeen summers in age. I had to at least try to save him.

My anger had to wait. This was not the time to vent, I had work to do. For once, none of the men argued with me when I directed an orderly line of minor injuries to wait in front of Kewri and Ren. Together, they took charge of stitches and relocating dislodged joints. My task was more critical and destined to fail. I glanced about me to see who among the uninjured could assist me with my operation. That was when Tallack stepped up.

"Tell me what you need, Aunt Mel. I'll do my best to help."

I thought he'd be distraught, unable to function effectively, but he was dry eyed and composed. It took me a moment to think of all my requirements. When I finally listed them, instead of ordering his men to fetch and carry on my behalf, he gathered the items himself. Nothing was too much trouble for him, in the attempt to save this lad's life. Kneeling on the hard ground, I arranged the pull saw from the carpentry tools, Ren's sharp knife, and a pile of clean rags in an arc around me. Once I begun, there would be no time to dally.

"What do you need me to do?" Tallack said, crouching at my side.

"Give me your belt and hold his shoulders down. If he wakes, pour some of this poppy resin water in his mouth until he passes out again."

"That I can do. Anything else?"

I glanced up at the cloudless sky and closed my eyes. "Yes, ask the gods to guide my hands. If I can't saw through his bone fast enough, he won't be with us for long." I sent a silent prayer to the Summerlands too. You never know if they will answer.

Rolling up my sleeves, I took Tallack's belt and fastened it around the top of the lad's thigh, pulling tight until the gushing blood reduced. With Ren's knife, I sliced at the muscles and flesh until I could see the white of the bone. My haste left the raw meat ragged, but I couldn't afford the time to make it neat.

I wiped the blade and rested it in the fire to heat up while I finished the job. In the time it took for me to position the pull saw inside the cut and against the bone, the warrior came to his senses. He thrashed about screaming in agony until he managed to loosen the belt, allowing the blood to pump out of him at an alarming rate.

"Hold him down." I commanded, struggling to cinch the belt tighter. I'd done my fair share of amputations, but I wasn't getting any younger and my strength was failing. Speed was critical if I was to save this lad's life.

Tallack called to another warrior and together they clamped him down so that I could work. They tried to get the lad to take some of the resin, but he cried out and squirmed too much to swallow the mixture.

Putting my back into the task, I wrenched the saw through bone towards me, then the warrior on the opposite side wrenched it back again. The young lad's lashes fluttered, his eyes disappeared into the back of his head, and he passed out again. It was better that way. The less he wriggled, the cleaner the cut.

With a searing hot blade, I pressed it against the open flesh until it sizzled like roasting pork. Memories of cauterising my brother's severed arm came rushing back to me from all those summers past. In that instance, I knew Cador the Cruel would survive. This time, I wasn't so sure. I'd never had to cut at the top end of the thigh before. It was a massive wound. The pain and shock of the procedure could still carry him into the Underworld.

I left the stump unbound to dry off for a while. When I looked up, Tallack was smiling at me.

"What?" I asked, wiping my hands on the rags.

"You are truly masterful at that, Aunt Mel."

"You kyjyan fools give me plenty of practice." I bit my lip, but it was too late. My anger could not be suppressed any longer. "Why didn't you stop the warriors charging ahead? Surely you knew the Alchemists would set traps and defences in the gorge?"

His smile disappeared as quickly as it had blossomed. He lowered the boy's head to the ground and got to his feet, dusting the dried earth from his bloodied leggings. "I'll see if Ren needs help." He wandered away from me without answering. I should have known that he wouldn't be keen to hear my opinion after banishing me from all talks and decisions. He was eager to put me in my place.

As I watched him checking on the wounded, I suddenly saw his game plan. Each of the Hunters smiled through their pain, genuinely moved by Tallack's concern for them. It had cost far too many lives, but by allowing Kitto free rein to fail, the Chief had secured the respect of the Hunter Clan. In one fell swoop, Tallack had restored order in the tribe.

We were a sombre group that evening. What little food we could scrape together was shared among us all. A few wanted to speak of the dead, but most did not. Their grief was too raw, too new to share. Every time I closed my eyes, I relived the crunching sound of necks snapping in the gorge. Those poor young men lay there still, alongside the warriors felled by the eagle-eyed archers. It was too risky to retrieve them for the customary pyre. A couple of the horses that had made it back to camp almost lame, were put out of their misery and drained ready to butcher for meat. Our survivors would not go hungry for some time yet.

At nightfall, I indicated my intention to retire to our hut. I needed to sleep. Ren stood to follow me, leaving Kewri and Tallack at the fireside. As we walked away, I heard Kewri volunteer to take a double shift on guard duty. Bless that lad. He was feeling guilty at having missed the foray into the gorge.

In truth, I was looking forward to spending some time with Ren alone. I may be adept at holding in my emotions in times of crisis, but it doesn't mean that I feel them less than others. My heart was heavy with sorrow.

Ren didn't expect me to talk. The moment we were inside our hut, he unpinned the door skins, giving us our privacy, and surrounded me with his sinewy arms. I lay my head on his chest and sobbed. How many more young men would have to lay down their lives for our family? The sight of Treeve's flayed body and pecked eyes wouldn't leave me. Just when I was starting to understand the boy, to like him even, he was sent to his death writhing in agony, forever to walk the plains of the Underworld without his fingers or his manhood. What a wicked message to send to Tallack.

My thoughts flickered to Senara. She was still out there, watching the Alchemists just as Treeve had tried to do. This was not her home territory and as such, put her at a distinct disadvantage. Even a good scout would struggle to outwit Kenver and his devious clan.

My nephew's reaction was even more puzzling. His initial anger which fuelled the charge towards the mines had faded already. Was he hiding his grief or was his partiality for the crewman not as strong as we'd all thought? Between him and his brother, Tallack was always the more sensitive and caring. Was that too just an act to win favour when the occasion suited? My misery and confusion fused inside my mind. Ren didn't try to coax me from my tears. Instead, he led me over to the bunk and lay down at my side, all the while holding me close.

Neither of us slept much for a long time. When my tears subsided, and the sticky heat of the night over powered us, we undressed in the darkness. It'd been a long time since I'd been intimate with a man, but it was something you never forgot; the skin against skin, the ripple of pleasure tingling inside, the ecstasy of muting all the troubles in the world for just a short time. Without caring for what the morning might bring, I set my worries down and my emotions loose until I had nothing left to give.

Dawn broke early, reminding us all how close it was to midsummer. Endelyn and Cryda would be making their way to the stone circle on the moors for her binding ceremony any day now. They would have to wait until this whole mess was resolved, one way or another. I dressed, took a drink from the jug and washed in the river. The cool water was enough to revive my sense of duty.

Trudging across camp, I checked on the amputee warrior first, keen to see if my handiwork had been sufficient to save his life. When I walked into the crowded hut, the men thanked me for my efforts, and for the resin Tallack had left for them. The lad's breathing was steady, his friends had bound his stump with care, and given him enough poppy juice to knock him back out, but he lived. That was one less thing to worry over.

My next call was to Kitto's hut. Here I found one of his trusted warriors watching over him and Tallack standing by the door. Kitto was alive. His eyes followed me as I drew closer, but other than that, he did not move.

Tallack faced the worried man at Kitto's side. "Can you leave us alone with him, just for a bit?" The Chief gestured for the Head Hunter to leave, holding the door drapes back to ease his path. Tallack lowered his voice. "What are Kitto's chances for recovery, Aunt Mel?"

I gazed at my nephew, unable to ascertain his feelings on the subject. He'd become so tricky to read of late. "Difficult to say really. He might last a few days, maybe longer. From the smell of him, I'd say he's lost control of everything from the shoulders down. He's lucky he can still breathe." As soon as I'd said it, I realised how cruel I was being. Kitto's eyes widened, his breaths were ragged and fast. I should have waited to say those things when the great warrior could not hear.

Tallack nodded, and kicked his shoes against the dirty floor rushes. "I see." His voice was quiet and authoritative. "I think you should go now, Aunt. I'll sit with him for a while and then make an offering to the gods."

I smiled, giving the Chief's arm a little squeeze as I passed him. Hurrying outside, I let the door skins fall behind me. That's when I heard the unmistakable sound of cracking bone.

# CHAPTER NINETEEN

It took all my will power not to run back inside the hut. I knew what Tallack had done, but I struggled to reconcile myself with his decision. Kitto looked set to live, but for how long and in what state was a mystery. I didn't need confirmation of his death.

Had Tallack snapped his neck to rid himself of a rival, or to spare the great warrior the shame of living a life where others had to wipe his arse and feed him with a spoon? I told myself that it was no different to putting the lame horses out of their misery, but that was a lie. Kitto was no animal. Would he be assured a place in the Summerlands, or would his murder be considered a humiliating way to die? Only the gods knew the answer.

I loitered outside our house for a while, waiting to see how Tallack behaved when he left Kitto's hut. It wasn't long before the Chief called out to the men, bringing them all to his side. He stood in the doorway as brazen as you like and made the announcement.

"Men, the mighty Kitto lays in the arms of Cernonnus. May he carry him into the Summerlands to sit with my father and all our brave ancestors." There was not a hint of emotion to betray him. He was so different to the boy I used to know, so cold and calculating. "Tonight, we will give him an honourable send off, along with the rest of the fallen. Gather the wood and build us a pyre of which we can be proud." There were no cheers nor foot stamping, just a group of grieving warriors with their heads bowed in reverence.

Ren pulled on his leggings and joined me on the dusty path outside. "What did I miss?"

I couldn't tear my eyes away from my heartless nephew. "Tallack killed Kitto." Neither of us spoke as we absorbed the ramifications. This was another family secret that would have to be taken to our graves.

The pair of us stood watching the group of Head Hunters rally to their Chief's orders, darting about camp to collect their blades and axes for the long day of wood cutting and stacking ahead of them. They were without a clan leader once again, but this time happy to comply with the young Chief's wishes. Kitto's insidious influence was gone. Tallack held sway over two warrior clans. He just needed to bring the Alchemists and the few followers of the Priest Sect to heel.

After a while, Ren finished dressing and went to help with the pyre building. I should have offered to wash and bind the dead ready for the pyre, but I couldn't face such a grim task. Since I was under no obligation, and Tallack did not give me a specific order, I slipped away to the beach and spent the afternoon in the dunes and salt marshes. There were a few useful plants to harvest, but mostly I just sat in what shade I could find to come to terms with all that had occurred.

There was a certain comfort to be had watching the men toil. Hunkered down in a cool hollow of the dunes, I sat still as they passed by carrying the split logs and brushwood to the pyre at the end of the beach. Our tribe was not as large as many, and our menfolk were diminishing fast. If we were to keep hold of our lands, Tallack would need to begin training the womenfolk with axe and spear as well as archery. That would mean a new supply of forged bronze weapons, something we could not achieve without tin. Everything depended on us retaking control of the mines, and for the life of me, I had no idea how to bring that about.

I had hoped that my afternoon in hiding would oust the fog inside my head. My aim was to return to camp with a fresh outlook and renewed vigour, but my spirits were lower than ever before. I met up with Ren at the side of the river, hoping that he would have an answer to our problems. He nodded and handed me a soaked cloth, then presented his bare back for me to scrub. "Where have you been? I was about to fetch Kewri to help me search for you." He tried to sound light-hearted but I heard the worry in his voice.

Scrubbing the dirt and sand from his back, I drifted into a daze.

He faced me, taking the cloth from my hand. "What is it? What's wrong?" His brow wrinkled; his stare was intense.

"I can't see a way out of this. I sat in the dunes just thinking, hoping for a solution, but drew a blank."

Ren smiled, dipping the rag in the water and wringing out the excess. "We'll find a way. We always do. Even if we just wait them out, they'll eventually run out of food, then we've got them."

I frowned at him. "By that time, Kenver's men will have shot all our watchmen through with arrows. They'll be no one left!"

"Ah, you're just tired and grieving. It'll all seem better in the morning."

I left him to finish washing, slightly annoyed by his condescension. It wasn't like him to dismiss my opinions so lightly. Had I lost his respect as well as that of my nephew's? Being the only woman in camp was certainly not ideal. How did Senara cope with them on her own among such bawdy men? The more I thought about her, the more I worried that she too might be suspended from a tree with her skin shredded and bits lopped off her poor body. That was another one of Ren's ideas, neither asked for nor sanctioned by our leader.

When I got back to our hut, Kewri was helping to butcher the horse carcasses ready for drying. Blood pooled beneath the benches attracting flies in their thousands. A quick glance up the gorge was enough to tell me that the crows had found the bodies of our men. They made such a racket, flapping and bickering over the tenderest portions of flesh. How the mothers of the fallen would quail if they knew we'd left them in the ravine to be scavenged while they rotted in the heat.

When it came time to light the pyre, Tallack ordered a few of the Sea Warriors and Kewri to stay behind in camp to watch over the cooking pots and protect the boundaries while we all filed down to the beach. Tallack was prepared this time, having a full speech memorised in praise of the men's bravery. He paid particular tribute to Treeve, as was expected, and to Kitto for his courage in surviving the rope trick for so long after the event. His performance was immaculate, even managing to make his voice break in the middle of his eulogy. For all his feigned emotion, his eyes were dry. Perhaps I was being too harsh on him. People deal with sorrow in such different ways.

I scrutinised the faces of the men in search of any signs of disbelief. Not one of them suspected my nephew of foul play. Aebba the Wild would be ashamed of his son if he were still alive. He may have been idle and dissolute but he was honest until his last breath. Tallack stepped forward and lit the kindling at the farthest end of the pyre, before retreating from the high flames as they licked the greased poles to the top platform of swaddled bodies. The heat was fierce, driving us all backwards until the sea breeze cooled our backs.

Ren and Tallack kicked a comfy depression in the sand and sat, encouraging others to join them. I watched the men gather, wondering if the invitation extended to me. I loitered for a time, but this was a place of mourning and remembrance traditionally held for men alone.

Tallack looked up at me and patted the sand at his side. My heart almost thumped out of my chest in surprise. It was a long time since he'd graced me with his favour, apart from false praise over my skill with a hot blade. All anger over his dishonesty vanished; such was my elation. As I struggled to fold my legs and lower myself down, he put his arm about my shoulders and hugged me close.

"Shall we stay here to eat, Aunt? I'll send someone to fetch the food down from the camp."

I'm ashamed to admit that I beamed up at him and nodded, my eyes filling with grateful tears. This was how he always won. His charm was more deadly than any blade. Before long, we were all tucking into the roasted horse and a bowl of the stewed roots and leaves I'd harvested in the afternoon. It was not my favourite meat, though it was tender, almost sweet, it tasted too much like venison for my liking. Since the priestess sacrificed the white hart, my preferences had shifted somewhat. Still, I was hungry and food was in short supply.

Ren licked the juices from his fingers. "Bet old Kenver wishes he could have some of this." He tore another chunk off the communal joint and crammed it into his mouth.

"He's welcome to come out of hiding and join us." Tallack grinned. "I'll permit him a couple of mouthfuls before I run him through with a spear."

The men chuckled and grunted their amusement. They seemed uneasy, laughing alongside the blazing pyre. Was it better to disrespect the fallen and titter at their leader or offend Tallack by remaining silent? The Chief sensed their apprehension and changed the topic. "The Alchemists should be running low on food by now. Another couple of days and they'll be chewing on their shoe leather. If we leave the horses behind, we can sneak up the gorge on foot and capture them as they leave the tunnels for supplies."

The warriors made agreeable noises in support of Tallack's plan, but we could all see how it was flawed. Kenver would have enough food stored to last them for a number of moons. He had access to all our tin. The Alchemists could have signalled any passing foreign ship with which to trade grain, wines, and even exotic goods.

We were more likely to starve than his men. As the night wore on, I couldn't stop myself wondering about the children and womenfolk. Surely Kenver did not have them tucked away in the tunnels all this time too, and if not, where were they?

It bothered me for the rest of the night. When the pyre burned low, Ren and I walked back to the huts. Some of the torches marking the path back to camp sputtered and fizzled out, leaving us to step cautiously for fear of falling into the river. Our hut was the easiest to spot in the dark. It was far larger than the others, having once belonged to Kenver and his whole family at one point.

I looked at the perfect thatch in the moonlight. "Why do you suppose the miners left this entire camp in pristine condition? If you were Kenver, wouldn't you trash the place before retreating to the mines?"

Ren scratched his chin thinking. His gaze followed mine, taking in the state of the huts and shelters all around us. "Hmm."

"What?"

He shrugged. "I don't know. Maybe they didn't have time. Perhaps their scouts saw our sails and they had to make a run for it at the last moment." He ducked under the door frame and started flinging off his clothes. That was a lame excuse but the more I pressed him, the more determined he was to shut me up, clamping his lips over mine until I could hardly breathe.

I was still thinking about it in the morning when we woke. I took the water jug and began the walk to the spring up the adjoining valley. Senara was waiting for Tallack outside his hut, out of breath and eager to divulge information. I was so pleased to see her, I dropped the jug to the grass and embraced her.

"Thank the gods you are alive. I've been out of my wits with worry."

Senara blushed, but being the good-natured woman I know her to be, she hugged me back. "You know me, Fur Benyn. Slippery as an eel in pork fat and twice as cunning." She grinned, tucking my head under her chin.

Tallack heard us and came outside. "What news do you bring?" He pushed us both through the door, away from the warriors' hearing.

Senara cuffed her nose and looked at each of us in turn. "I um… saw the ambush yesterday, and I'm sorry for what happened. I wasn't able to stop them." Her gaze fell to the floor as she adjusted the straps of a wrist guard on her arm.

Tallack moved closer and put his palm on her shoulder. "No one could have, Senara. I cast no blame on you. Were you able to find out precisely where they are holed up?"

Nodding she said, "Yes, and no. There are several tunnel entrances from what I could see and many that are blocked. From waiting and watching, I could tell that they are all connected together somehow. Even if you could get close, they can escape through alternative routes."

"So, attacking from the gorge is pointless?"

Again, she nodded. "There is a small clearing at one of the larger entrances, where they've erected defences, but it's well guarded. They came out of the mines when you had all gone and strung up the rest of our men next to Treeve for the crows. It was a gruesome sight." She faltered for a moment, trying to hold herself together. "I did creep along the coastal path on the top of the cliffs towards the east though. There's a small creek that leads down to the gorge from the opposite side. It's densely forested at the bottom end as far as I could tell, with a track leading from the cliffs that is obviously well used."

"You think that this is how they are able to sneak out of the mines at night and pick off our watchmen?" I said, desperately searching my memories. It's possible that there were hidden pathways on the cliffs, although I saw none while I was watching my nephews complete their warrior quest. "I don't remember there being such a path…"

"It's there, Fur Benyn. I promise you."

Tallack rounded on her. "Could you see if there were any ropes across the trees, maybe low down near to the base of the trunks?"

She was already shaking her head. The path is lined either side with rocks at the top. There are no trees until much further down."

Tallack's frown smoothed out and a smile reappeared. "Then that's how we'll catch them. They won't be expecting us from that direction."

"Begging your pardon, Chief, but Kenver will defend all approaches to the mines." I said, before I could stop myself. "He grew up here, he knows every blade of grass and rock. He will have set traps; you can bet on that." He wasn't best pleased with my outburst. The scowl he threw in my direction leeched the heat from my bones.

Just when I thought I'd undone all the good will between us, he chewed his bottom lip and rested his fists on his hips. "You could be right. We can't risk the rest of the men, until we know for sure." He said no more. Instead, he grabbed his mysterious grey sword and his water bladder, and charged out of the hut with Senara and I stumbling after him.

Calling out to the men, he picked six of his crewmen out of the crowd and told them to follow him. They were all young and lithe, some having seen fewer summers than our Chief. They were no match for the brute strength of the miners if they should stumble into their hideout. He hadn't thought anything through. Tallack the Fearless, seemed determined to live up to his name.

"Tallack!" I cried out, but I clamped my mouth shut quickly. He was the Chief and he'd made his decision to go with them. I had no right to undermine him in front of the men.

Senara looked at me and sucked in her lips. She understood my concerns as well as anyone. "Should I catch them up, Fur Benyn? I know the path better than any of those boys." As soon as she'd said it, I had visions of another ambush, more entrails spilling from guts, broken bones and smashed heads and much worse besides. Without thinking, I clutched the sleeve of her tunic. "We both have to go. Will you help me, child?"

There was a moment's hesitation from her lips. I could see she thought me irrational and she was right. How could I even begin to keep up with their speed and agility. I set my face to stern, glaring until she nodded. We hurried back to fetch my healing kit and then straight along the start of the gorge to the cliff path beyond. Thank the gods that Ren was not in the hut or he would have stopped us from going.

It was certainly steeper than I remembered. Either I was less fit than during the winter season, or the hot breeze was taking its toll on my strength. Senara led the way, taking me along a lesser used path that came out further along the cliffs. Panting heavily through the pain in my joints, I heaved myself up the last chalky scree slope to the top. The bright sun was almost blinding. Shielding my eyes against the light, I could see across the grassy strip of land where the miners used to graze their goats. It was empty now, save for a shadowy mass of moving figures at the far end of the cliff.

"They're over there, Fur Benyn." Senara gasped, pointing to the blurry visage ahead of us. I too was shocked that we'd caught them up so easily. I stood still, squinting until I could see Tallack and the boys laying down on the grass. One was running towards us. We met him half way between the path and the lounging crewmen.

"Why has the Chief stopped?" Senara grumbled at the young man.

Puffing and blowing, the lad caught his breath before answering. "He sent me back to fetch you. We can't find the creek that you mentioned. You're to come and lead the way." It wasn't long before we were all standing on the edge of the cliff overlooking the bay.

Senara pointed to the ridge top behind us. "It's not here, but further inland. We need to climb up there."

I might have known that the route would be awkward to reach. Course grasses and gorse grew thickly between the thin loam and scree. Every step sent pebbles and loose gravel skittering down towards the cliff. I lost my footing a number of times, until my heart thumped in my chest.

Senara tightened her belt and shifted her bow across her body. "Give me your hand, Fur Benyn." I didn't need her to ask twice. She hovered no more than a step away from me, ever ready to act should my balance fail. Straining every muscle and sinew, we followed the men to the highest point of the crest, before creeping along in a north-westerly direction for a short distance, until we were looking down on the gorge beneath.

The breeze was stronger here, funnelling through the valley to cool the sweat from our skin. I took a moment to catch my breath, bending over and rubbing at the pain throbbing in my knees.

Tallack turned to the shield maiden and frowned. "Are you leading us on a merry dance? Where in the name of the gods is this path you speak of?"

Finally letting me go, Senara moved to the head of the line. "Not far now, Chief. It's just over that rocky outcrop." She scuttled off before he could stop her. The men hurried after the scout, keen to keep up or lose face. By the time I'd caught them up, the men were stock still and pale as snow at what lay ahead.

I leaned around the boulders and looked in the direction of Senara's outstretched arm. There was a tiny ledge carved out of the leeward side of the ridge, not more than the width of my foot, leading down to the creek. It was filled with trees and jagged rocks. My stomach lurched.

# CHAPTER TWENTY

It was all I could do to stop myself from trembling. The sheer drop was more boat lengths than could be measured, assuring anyone who fell a swift but painful death on the rocks and treetops below.

Tallack pursed his lips and growled. “You shouldn’t have come, Aunt Mel. You know the dangers we face.” He took a length of rope from Senara, tying us together around our waists. “But I can’t leave you behind for the miners to find either.”

Before he could change his mind and send me back through enemy territory, he helped to lower me down onto the ledge to where Senara was waiting. I closed my eyes and asked the gods to protect me. Within moments, I was clinging to the rock face more terrified than ever. The first section was the steepest, taking us on a faltering path along one side of the slope, past the scree and shallow soils to the base of the gorge.

Every step had the potential to send us tumbling, but I felt a little safer being tethered to my nephew. He seemed confident in his ability to cling to the rocks by his fingertips while edging closer to his men. Perhaps his time at sea had trained his body in the art of balance. Mine was ill equipped for such mountain goat antics. I found myself giddy with nervous panting. Each time I looked over my shoulder, the valley spun until bile erupted in my gullet.

Just as I was regretting my insistence at tagging along, the path widened until we could walk quite naturally down the remainder of the incline to where water gushed naturally from beneath the ground. Slowing my breaths, my wobbling knees stopped quaking when Tallack released the knot tying us together.

"Well, I can't imagine this being any use for our attack. If all our men clambered over that ridge at once, Kenver's scouts would have no trouble at all filling them all with arrows." Tallack announced, winding the lengths of rope into a neat loop.

"True, but that means it's not likely to be protected with lookouts or traps." Senara replied, taking her cord back and attaching it to her belt. "We could get the men to sneak over the top under the cover of darkness in smaller groups."

The men continued to trudge down the narrow creek between two giant rocks, shaped like massive gateposts on the trail, while Senara and my nephew discussed tactics. Picking my way through the sharp gravel and boulders behind them, I bit my lip every time my ankle turned on the uneven surface. I spent so much time watching my step that I failed to see what was ahead. It turns out, the men had done the same.

Where the ground levelled out and widened between the fast flow of the river and the hillside, our only route through was between the giant rocks. It was the ideal spot for another ambush. Tallack hissed at the men to keep alert for scouts, archers, and missiles. Those at the front drew their weapons. One man primed his bow and pulled back on the string, moving closer to the rocks.

With everyone craning their necks in search of Alchemist attackers, they failed to see what lay underfoot.

A quiet crack sounded beneath the archer, his weight shifting downwards by a fraction. Before he realised what was happening, the ground under our men gave way, sending them crashing into a deep pit. As the rest of the wooden poles and leaves gave way, some managed to jump clear of the opening, flailing their arms to grab at anything to prevent them from slipping into the hole. The shrieks of the three men at the bottom of the pit were blood-curdling, but fleeting.

One lad teetered on the edge of the pit; his arms flung out to the sides, his feet dancing on the moving earth. Senara dropped her blade and grabbed out at his tunic, yanking him back to safety. He clung to her for a few moments, before thanking her for her speedy reactions.

It took a short time for us all to figure out what had occurred. In our zeal to avoid incoming arrows from above, none of us had spotted the thinly covered pit of spikes between the rocks.

The archer was impaled in several places; narrow poles protruded from his neck and torso. Blood streamed down the stakes and pooled around him. A second man took a post right through his gut, splitting him open like a hazelnut, until his entrails spilled out of the opening in his back. Their agony was over in mere moments.

The third man was less fortunate. Somehow, he'd managed to slide between most of the spikes until he was wedged. One narrow rod had sliced his side, severing a large blood vessel on its way. The life-giving fluid spurted with each beat of his weakening heart. Every attempt to wriggle free, opened his wound further, until he was almost unconscious from the blood loss.

His muted whimpers were woeful. They clawed at my heart in sympathy for his plight.

The stench of kawgh and innards from their loosened bowels wafted up to hit me full in the face. To my trained eye, I knew the poor man wouldn't last for long. Even I cannot stitch fast enough to staunch a gusher like that.

Tallack rallied his men, lowering Senara's rope to the stricken man and yelling at him to tie it off around his middle, but despite positioning the end close to the warrior's hand, we lost him before he could be rescued.

Another three men were denied the chance to sit next to the gods in the Summerlands. They would not even receive a fitting send off with pyre and ceremony for all their courage and bravery. Their trip to the Underworld would be marked by no grand gestures nor ritual, just a passing lament from those they knew best.

"What now, Chief?" Senara asked, when it was apparent that none of the men would speak.

We stood in a circle around Tallack, waiting for his command. Our path ahead was blocked, short of wading through fast flowing water to reach the opposite side of the creek. There was also no way of knowing whether Kenver's men were watching our every move as we closed in on the upper edges of the mines.

"We go back. Where there is one trap, there will be more. We can't afford to lose any more men." He didn't wait for them to acknowledge his order, nor did they offer to be lowered down to retrieve the dead men. They simply turned tails and hurried back the way we had come.

It was a gruelling climb back to the ridge top, but surprisingly easier to navigate. We knew the way now and the men were keen to be away from the unknown peril and stink of death. It was hard for me to keep up at times, but I managed to make it to the ridge without injury. The men hung their heads, clenched their jaws and marched back to camp in silent mourning. Senara waited with me at the top of the cliff path while I caught my breath, and then descended into the valley at a more leisurely pace.

Renowden was spitting with fury when he saw us walking towards the back of our hut. "Where the kyjya have you been? Kewri and I searched everywhere for you." He rushed to meet me, grabbing my shoulders and shaking them with such vigour, I thought my head might fall off. "Don't ever go off like that again without telling us. You hear me?"

That was a surprise. I'd spent so long doing what I wanted, whenever I wanted, it hadn't entered my head that he would worry. A part of me was annoyed that he was intent on shackling my freedom, but another part was touched that he cared. It was a fine line to tread, especially since I was of Chieftain blood, and as such enjoyed greater privileges than most women of the tribe. It irked me that Ren now believed himself to be my keeper. Kewri was the only one tasked with my protection, but he could not make any demands of me.

I chose to make light of his distress rather than build it up into an argument for later. "Don't fuss so. Senara and Tallack were with me. I was in no danger." I lied, shooting a glare at the shield maiden to back my claims. "We went in search of a different route to the mines but lost three more warriors."

That diffused his anger. His frown of consternation slumped into sadness. When Senara gave him the names of the crewman in the pit, his eyes glistened with sorrow. Two were his particular friends. The thought of them spending eternity in a blood-soaked pit at the top of a gorge was the worst ending for such noble Sea Warriors. Ren wandered away in the direction of the beach. We let him go on alone to speak the words of mourning unto the Goddess of Lakes and the Sea.

Our clans were so depleted that we were in danger of the Alchemists outnumbering us. It was a pity that Tallack left the shield maidens and women archers back at the island compound on the Exe. Senara followed me into our hut. Kewri had caught and left us a couple of flatfish, suspending them by their gill slits from the roof joists. While I strapped my sore ankle with bindings, Senara scaled, gutted and prepared them for our supper.

We took them along to the fire outside the hut Kewri was staying in and roasted them over the flames. It didn't take long before the flesh was soft and flaky and ready to eat. I was glad of the food, but it somehow felt wrong that we hadn't given an offering to Cernonnus.

It was our duty to pay for their passage into the Underworld. We had no effigies nor priests with us to incant the words, nor could we spare any of the meagre supplies of food in camp. Despite the fact that I was ravenous and the fish delicious, it stuck in my throat with guilt.

We'd seen so much death and destruction and we were still no closer to regaining control over the mines. The longer we stayed, the greater the opportunity Kenver had to pick us off one by one.

Ren didn't come back to the hut until the following morning. I didn't go looking for him since I'd guessed where he'd spent the night. The Sea Warriors had customs of their own whenever they lost good men. Women were not welcome. From the stories I'd heard over the course of my long life, their rituals involved a night on the beach around a fire, singing dead men's tales to the Goddess of the Sea.

When the moon was at its peak, they would wade out into the ocean until their faces were all but submerged. Some say that they would float offerings of figures woven from marram grass to trick the goddess into releasing the bodies of the fallen from the waves.

Others said that in the darkness, no one could see the salty tears of the men mixing with the brine of the sea. Whichever account was true, the passing of their clan's folk was a private affair and those who were dead did not drown. Perhaps their customs were different under these circumstances, but I was unlikely to ever find out for sure. The clans were guarded about their practices, their secrets binding them together as kin.

Tallack stayed on the beach for much longer. Perhaps he had more to say to the goddess than the rest. It was, after all, his decision that got them killed. For all his recent stoic detachment, I refused to believe that he'd lost all compassion.

In accordance with Ren's admonishment, I informed him of my need to walk the long valley adjacent to the gorge in search of food, herbs and bark.

He nodded at me and climbed into our bunk. "Don't go alone. Take Kewri with you." He demanded, before turning his back to me as I stood in the doorway. I could have argued, or ignored him, but I could see that he was beaten. The night of mourning had knocked the spirit right out of him.

"I'll fill the water bladders up on the way back." I muttered, grabbing both his and mine as I left.

It was good to get away from the odour of men in the camp. They cared not about washing, and had a habit of emptying their bladders and bowels wherever they fancied. Tallack did little about enforcing the use of middens or making them walk into the wooded areas to keep the main camp clean. The more the warriors were left without the influence of their women, the more squalid they became.

The valley where the Alchemists harvested their wood, was shallow and bright. This provided all the timber needed for processing the raw rocks into tin and for structural support for the mines. The mature trees were well spaced, giving us dappled shade as we walked next to the river.

It certainly looked more inviting than the last time I saw it back in the winter. The trails were even starting to overgrow despite the dry spell. The one thing that struck me most, was that the entire valley, which had been bustling with activity before, was now completely deserted. There were no washer women pounding grubby linen on the rocks, no children swinging on the overhanging trees and splashing into the water, no leather scrapers or smoke huts, nothing.

Kewri held open my bag as I cut some willow bark, picked a little sorrel and found a marshy area where fresh watercress grew.

"Are there any mines in this valley, Fur Benyn, or are they all in the gorge?" Kewri asked, keeping a weather eye on our surroundings as he spoke.

I straightened up, clicking my spine and neck before trimming off the soggy roots from the cress. "I believe all the working tunnels are in the gorge, but you can never tell where the old passages are. Kenver's ancestors have mined these parts for generations. Seams play out and they block up tunnels, then go in search of new ones to dig. Only his family knows them all."

Kewri looked down at me, those huge dark eyes of his full of fear. "There's just him and his young son left now. He could be the only one who knows all the tunnels and how they connect."

I pondered on the age and abilities of the Alchemist leader's youngest child and decided that he'd be too young to pose us any problems. My mind strayed to Kenver's family and how happy they'd been just two seasons ago. How quickly things can change in the span of a few moons. I glanced back downstream and sighed. Where were the children and womenfolk? There was no sign of them in the gorge when we were under attack. I couldn't imagine them tolerating conditions underground for all this time.

For a while, we walked further upstream following the sweeping meander in the river. Kewri managed to hit a couple of ducks with arrows, although one he had to get wet to retrieve. At least we could return to our huts with something for supper. By late afternoon, we'd harvested all we could find and began the slow walk to the freshwater spring on our way home.

The sweat poured down my back, soaking through my tunic and cloak. I stopped for a moment, handing my healing kit and gathering bag to Kewri while I stripped off a layer or two. Grunting with effort, I knelt on the bank side and dipped my hand into the cool water. It was so soothing, I pulled out a cloth from my pocket, dunked it into the river and wiped it all about my face and neck. After a quick rinse, I offered to do the same for my giant friend.

He declined my gesture. "Thanks anyway. It'll only make me want to jump in the river for the rest of the day. Better to sweat it out till we get back."

I shrugged, wringing out my cloth and giving my face another going over. When I took back the strap of my kit bag, I noticed the shrubs moving in the undergrowth behind Kewri. It was a breathless day, so I knew it could not have been from a breeze. I nudged the giant and whispered. "Over there. Might be a deer or something."

With excitement brimming on his sweet face, he dropped the foraging bag and pulled his bow from across his chest. Nocking an arrow from his quill, he crept closer to the bushes, treading as lightly as the huge man could manage. I stayed still and quiet not wanting to spook the beast unduly.

When Kewri was level with the rear of the bushes, his expression changed. His eyes grew wide, he dropped his bow to the ground and paced vast and deliberate steps backwards. That was when Kenver and his men came into view. There was a half dozen men, all aiming their deadly bronze tipped weapons at Kewri's chest.

# CHAPTER TWENTY-ONE

Some held spears, others aimed their nocked arrows and all were close enough to kill Kewri in an instant. The Alchemist leader and his men must have watched us for the entire time that we were in the valley. My giant friend stepped back until his great body was directly in front of mine. This loyal and brave protector was willing to die for me. If I hadn't been so scared, I would have cried with pride and gratitude.

"Step aside, giant. I need to speak with Fur Benyn." Kenver roared with an authority that startled me. For such a mild and placid man, I never imagined him capable of such power. Kewri didn't move. He planted his feet firmly on the soft mud of the river bank and folded his arms across his chest. I couldn't have him die for sheer stubbornness.

I peered around my friend's middle. "Kenver. I've always known you to be a good and reasonable man. Why would you turn on us like this?" I tried to sound calm and imploring but in truth my fear made me tremble until my voice wobbled too.

"You know full well, Meliora. How could you stand by and let them butcher my children?" His chest was heaving with the strain of holding in his anger. This was my chance to put the record straight, even if it meant angering him further. Maybe his men would talk him around after hearing the truth.

"None of us killed your son. He fought bravely against the Belgae in protection of our people, me included. He sits with the gods in the Summerlands a proud warrior with his head held high." I judged the Alchemist leader to be receptive to my explanation and gingerly stepped further into view. "Neither was Kerensa butchered. She was caught conspiring with our enemies. The Durotriges bribed her with false promises to spy on us. It almost led to our ruin. You know the penalty for betrayal." I chose not to finish the account of events, thus avoiding the explanation of how her corpse was hidden. It was a shameful way to handle affairs. It made Tallack look guilty and worse still, gave the impression that Kenver was right.

"I saw her body, Fur Benyn. Her face was smashed in. I wouldn't have recognised her if it were not for the tunic she wore, stitched by my wife's fair hand." He was panting his indignation, his breaths whistling through the bushy growth in his nose. "Even if what you say is true, how is it that she did not receive a fair hearing in front of the elders? None that I spoke to had any idea how she died."

It was a fair point. Tallack accepted Treeve and Ren's word that she was a spy and acted immediately. There should have been no need to hide her body, or for the lie about her dying during the attack on our compound. I needed to think carefully, since Kenver's complexion was crimson and deepening in colour every moment. "There were reliable witnesses to her crime. The Chief had no time to summon the elders since we were preparing for imminent attack."

Kenver's fists balled at his side, turning them blotchy and pale. "That's not how the young sailor described it when I was peeling off his skin and slicing his manhood." He took a large pace forward. Spittle flew as he snarled at me.

I shuffled back behind Kewri, afraid that I too would be subjected to this grief-stricken and crazed leader. "I can assure you that she was not brutalised. Her face was disfigured after she had passed. Her body fell against a rock." It was a minor bending of the truth but I deemed it necessary. To recount all that Treeve did to his dead daughter would've only angered him further.

"Then by your own words you condemn yourself as a liar." His eyes narrowed to slits; his lips sucked in with contempt. "You told me that she was treated with dignity and respect and added to the pyre of the fallen."

He was right. I had lied to him to protect my nephew. There was nothing that I could say or do to rectify what had happened, no way to ease back tensions between our clans. I couldn't hold his gaze. My head bowed in defeat; we were wholly at his mercy. I could hear his noisy breaths slowing as he regained control over his emotions.

"Whether what you say about my daughter is true or not, the mines and the lands surrounding them belong to me now. Tell your nephew to pack up his things and take his men away from here or we'll kill every last one of them. You included, old woman."

It was futile to argue further. I'd lost Kenver's respect. If anything, all I had achieved was to make matters worse, despite confirming much of the story given to him by Treeve under extreme torture. I was lucky that he didn't subject us to the same punishment.

The miners waved their spears and bows towards the path back to camp, urging us to move with haste. Neither of us had any intention of hanging around in case they altered their minds and slaughtered us there and then. Kewri hooked his hand under my elbow to speed our return over the uneven ground. We didn't even stop to fill the water bladders for fear that they were still on our heels.

When we got back to our huts, Kewri slammed the ducks down on the work bench and muttered something about telling Tallack what had happened. He left me alone and frightened, sitting on the edge of my bunk wet with sweat and dry mouthed from exertion.

Within moments, Ren hurried inside and took my face in his hands. "Are you hurt? Are you alright? I should have come with you."

He meant well but his closeness was stifling. I couldn't breathe. Leaning back, I pushed his arms away. "I'm fine. Leave me be. Kenver just meant to scare us. Did a fine job of it too." I shouldn't have snapped at him.

He stepped away and swallowed hard. I could see how much I'd hurt his feelings. "Why would he do that? What's his game?"

"He wanted to send a message to Tallack that we can't win. He's the ruler of the mines, and if we're not careful, all of Dumnonia too."

Ren's mouth fell open. "You think he will take over the whole tribe? But he doesn't have the trade relationships or Tallack's ship."

I glared up at him. "It's sitting in the bay. Kenver only has to kill us off one at a time before taking everything; our ships, our people and all our land. Do you really think he hasn't planned this entire situation? You can bet your life that the pleasant and amenable side of him is just an act. He's probably been trading with foreign vessels right under our noses for dozens of cycles. No doubt he learnt that kind of deceit from his father. He was not a nice man." I added, allowing my vehemence to get the better of me. "We only have Kenver's word about the quantity of tin extracted and processed by his clan. How are we to prove him wrong?"

I leaned my elbows on my knees and rested my forehead in my palms. There was no solution to this mess. One way or another, the Alchemists were set to take over everything. It seemed too carefully considered to be a sudden reaction to the deaths of his children. I couldn't help thinking that he'd been waiting for the perfect time to strike, having simmered on the notion of becoming Chieftain of the Dumnonii all along.

Ren saw my distress and sat by my side, slipping his arm about me. Despite the feeling of being crowded, I let him hold me close. The last thing I wanted was to upset him further and I needed the comfort as much as he did. Kenver had secured the upper hand and neither of us could see a way out of this desperate situation. We stayed close and silent for some time, each of us mulling over all that had occurred since our arrival.

At length, I resigned myself to plucking the ducks for supper, if only to occupy my thoughts. It would've been so simple to have taken Ren up on his offer to flee the tribe when the chance arose and live for the rest of our days in obscurity.

With the benefit of hindsight, I should have left. These were problems fit for the young and strong, not the weary and cynical. I had given my life in duty to the health of our people, stayed by the side of each and every Chieftain since my birth. Surely, I had earned some respite in my dotage?

I looked at Ren as he rose from the bunk and began pacing the rushes on the floor. It was evident from his expression that he had not yet conceded defeat. His brow furrowed, his thumb and forefinger pinched his bottom lip. I watched him as he hunted through his memories in search of an answer. He was more determined than I to see an end to the conflict between our clans. For that alone, my heart swelled. There would be no escaping from our tribe now.

We talked and walked, ate and napped until our discussions began to circle back on themselves, every potential avenue explored and rejected in our quest for resolution. To make matters worse, a rider arrived at dusk to deliver a message from the Chief's mother. Most of us saw him skid his panting and skittish horse to a halt close to Tallack's hut and dismount. Those of us who dared, crowded around the doorway to listen to the news.

Tallack was in a foul mood. He stood with his hands resting on his hips and wearing an irritated scowl. The day's sweat trickled down his bare chest, gleaming in the final rays of the sun through the doorway. Two of his men lit the torches. The Chief gestured for the messenger to enter. Warriors crowded around, making it impossible for me to see.

"Mind out…shift yourself, man!" I bellowed, elbowing my way to the front until I could enter the hut. It was a risky move but Tallack was concentrating too hard on the rider to be annoyed by my presence.

The messenger was gaunt and burnt by the sun. He was as agitated and restless as his horse, unable to stand still and blinking rapidly. He fidgeted before my nephew until Tallack grew impatient.

"Speak. What news have you from my mother?"

"It's bad, Chief. She sent me to tell you that the men you left behind are overwhelmed. Skentel is doing his best to keep order, in between the building projects in camp, but the homesteaders are starving and fights break out daily. The elders have erected paling walls and tethered dogs around their huts to keep them out, such is the level of pilfering." He took a breath and hung his head, dropping his gaze from the puckered lips and furrowed brow of his Chieftain. Within a few moments, he plucked up the courage to continue. "The Lady Cryda tried to impose a system of rationing, but there was an outcry over the pooling of resources."

The messenger shuffled backwards, as though he was expecting Tallack to lash out. "If you'll forgive me for saying, Chief, there is a growing discontent with your intended, the priestess. Word's got round that she's hoarding a massive stash of offerings and won't share them, even though many of the new folk's kids are close to death with hunger."

This news shook me to the core. Endelyn had shown me nothing but generosity and kindness. It never occurred to me until then, that she might have singled me out for special treatment in the hope that I might ease her way into the bosom of my family. She had known hardship in her time, especially during the long winters at the Nine Maiden Circle on the moors, but to deliberately deny sustenance to the weak and sickly was low indeed.

Tallack turned away, rubbing at his eye absently. The messenger looked up at me for counsel, unsure if the Chief wished him to leave or stay.

I settled his quandary. "Has the Lady Cryda welcomed the Chief's new Duro bride to the island?" I asked, moving towards the centre of the hut.

The messenger nodded. "We only just got her roundhouse prepared in time for her arrival. She was given the best fabrics and furs, slaves and jewels from the elders." He looked shifty, stopping mid-sentence.

"And?" Tallack snapped, keeping his back to the poor exhausted fellow.

"And she complained that the slaves were too slow, that they didn't know how to cook and that her hut was too humid."

I thought Tallack might bark at the man, finding this to be his breaking point. Instead, he spun around and laughed. "If the foolish girl thinks that I have the power to influence the weather, she's in for a rude awakening."

I couldn't determine whether my nephew was gripped by a bout of hysteria or was just plain overwhelmed himself. Nothing seemed to be working out as planned. It was as though we'd lost the gods' favour entirely. Tallack's tittering spread to his men, who laughed from his doorway behind me. As far as I could see, there was nothing amusing about our situation. It called for a rational head and decisive action. Without waiting for the noise to die down, I moved closer to the messenger.

"How long did it take you to ride here?" I asked him, unconcerned about my nephew's reaction to my meddling.

"Three days. I changed horses twice. There aren't many homesteads left in our region where I could make an exchange, plus I had to take a longer route around the burning moors."

"They still burn?" I gasped. He nodded slowly, his eyes glazing with remembered fear. After all that had occurred with the Alchemists, the heath fires had slipped my mind. That put an end to the jollity.

Tallack was focused and listening once more. "Has my mother and the Duro girl set off for the midsummer binding rituals yet?"

"They were making their final preparations as I left, Chief."

Tallack stared at me; a long and knowing look in which we shared our collective concern for their welfare. "And who was tasked with accompanying them across the moors?"

There was a momentary pause, while the nervous messenger thought about his response. "Um, Skentel and that Duro girl of Fur Benyn's…" He peered at me for help with her name.

"Vina." I supplied.

"Yes, she and Skentel discussed the trip and decided that there would be too few men left to keep order in camp if they escorted your mother and the priestess to the stones."

Tallack sighed. "What did they decide to do about that, in…my…absence?" The last three words he positively yelled.

"They…um… arranged for some Duro warriors to ride alongside for protection."

Tallack spun away reeling from this revelation. His hands flew up to cover his face, his eyes closed in disbelief. I could see it all inside my mind. One foolish decision after another had put us in an impossible situation. The Alchemists held all our wealth and influence, our people were starving and angry, our territory was on fire, and now our most valuable womenfolk were under the protection of our former enemies; a tribe that revelled in holding hostages and overthrowing weaker foes.

I did not need to spell out our misfortunes to the Chief. He was sober enough to comprehend them fully. We exchanged glances for a few moments, but there was nothing more to be said. We had no way to stop our family's power within the tribe falling into ruin.

I'd heard enough and I had no solution to our predicament. With a dull ache in the pit of my gut, I turned to leave. Our men were ashen faced as they parted allowing me a clear path through the throng. The gentle breeze blowing along the valley was refreshing, but not sufficient to lift my mood. Suffering with aching joints, I wandered back towards my hut, and churned over all that I had to disclose to my friend.

In the twilight of the day, I watched Ren attaching strips of eel leather to a wooden panel, creating a hinge with the door frame.

"Got the skins from one of the men." He grinned. "Thought we deserved a bit of privacy for a change." Renowden welcomed me inside where he'd laid out a feast of roasted sea kale roots with toasted whelks and a huge, steaming pink crab. "After your scare with the Alchemists today, I thought you could do with a bit of spoiling."

How could I tell him that I would have preferred the hut open to take advantage of the cool air after all his troubles? Biting my tongue, I smiled at him as he secured the door behind us.

The meal was far more than I could have expected. He must have spent the whole day foraging out in the blazing sun. I toyed with the idea of keeping the messenger's news to myself so as not to dampen his happy disposition, but I knew that he'd wheedle it out of me eventually. We sat together and ate every last mouthful, teasing out the meat from the cracked claws with eager tongues. It was fit for the gods in every way.

When, at last, I relayed all that I'd learned in Tallack's hut, Ren sucked in air over his teeth and shook his head. "I have to admit." He said, moving over towards our bunk and smoothing out the furs. "I thought Skentel had more sense than to trust the Duros so soon after the peace treaty. I always took him to be a bright lad."

I stacked our bowls to wash in the morning and followed him over to the bed. "Aye, it's not like the lad to put Cryda and Endelyn in harm's way."

"Still, there's nothing we can do about it tonight." He stripped off his clothes and carried the torch over to the cold fire pit at the centre of the hut. The flame sputtered in the ashes and died.

Climbing on top of the furs, I said, "No, you're right, but I shall worry about them nonetheless." I snuggled down by his side and rested my head on his collarbone.

Ren kissed my forehead, slipped his arms about me and squeezed me tight. "Well, as things stand, they can't get any worse." His chuckling jogged my entire torso making me smile. He had a curious way of looking at things, ever hopeful, always calm.

Despite his attempts to pacify me, I could not sleep. I lay awake in the darkness until the moon was high and Ren was snoring. When I heard a dull thud, I elbowed him in the ribs. "What was that?"

He didn't even open his eyes. "Go back to sleep. Probably a bird dropped something on the thatch."

"In the middle of the night?" I sat up, but he was snoring once again. It was just a short time later that I caught a familiar smell, the acrid stench of smoke filling the upper roof space of our hut. The crackling noises grew louder until there was no doubt in my mind what was happening. Coughing, I shook my friend awake, just as the first clumps of smouldering reeds fell onto our bunk.

# CHAPTER TWENTY-TWO

"Get up! The hut's on fire!" I screamed, yanking Ren by the arm and pulling him free of the flaming patches of fallen material. My shoulder joint popped with the exertion; my heart raced in my chest. Every instinct told me to flee with all haste, but I had to make sure he was clear of danger. The sizzling timbers and roar of the flames pulsed with each gust of wind, spreading the embers across the width of the roof. The choking fumes swirled ever lower, prickling my scalp with the searing heat.

Ren rolled onto the ground and tried to rescue our furs but it was too late. The animal hair caught fire in an instant, filling the air with rancid vapours. Ren bundled our clothes into his arms while I grabbed my medicine bag and the precious blades. Together, we hurried outside calling for assistance.

I had no need to worry what the men would think of me wearing next to nothing. As soon as we were through the door, it was obvious that no one would come to our aid let alone notice my distress. The valley was thick with smoke, red hot sparks drifted as the wind fanned the flames over the roofs of every hut in our little community. Everywhere I looked, warriors spilled out of their shelters in blind panic, some with the presence of mind to grab their belongings, others shrieking in pain and dowsing their skin with water from the river. Horses broke free of their tethers and bolted upstream and away. A few of our ponies were slow enough for their owners to grab their reins and lead them to safety.

Through the wall of heat and charred reeds, I could see the remains of torches flung high onto the thatch of each hut. The Alchemists' patience had paid off. This was the first night since our arrival where the wind gusted, making the job of burning us alive in our sleep easy.

My first thoughts were of those I loved. I snapped my head this way and that, trying to peer through the smog and haze in search of my nephew. "Where's the Chief?" I wailed. "Has anyone seen Tallack?" Stumbling along the central path clutching my bag, I shielded my face from the scorching heat with a raised arm. The closer I ran towards his hut, the more Ren tried to push me back. He dropped our clothes and encircled me like a hunting dog, slamming the heels of his hands into my shoulders.

"Don't be stupid. You'll get yourself killed." He yelled.

"He might need me." I stopped dead in my tracks. Our Chief was standing in the clearing near to his hut at the heart of the chaos, shouting his orders to those who were unharmed to fetch water or dampen flames with earth and sand. It was just as well I'd spotted him in time, since the path narrowed a short way ahead and the houses on either side burned with ferocious intensity. Only a small gap existed through which I could see my nephew unharmed and coolly in charge, but my relief was short-lived.

A shadowy figure tumbled from the hut on the left, rolling on the singed grass to extinguish the flames licking his back and shoulders. His shape was unmistakable, his great hulking mass was like no other. Kewri stayed on the ground, curled into a ball. I could hear his whimpers above the shouting men, cracking wood and thundering hooves of the fleeing horses.

"He's not moving." I cried. "He needs to get away from there."

Ren turned to see of whom I was speaking. Without a thought for his own safety, my friend dashed into the narrow gap, bending low and dodging the forked tongues of flames snaking out from the huts either side. He pushed Kewri over until he could latch onto his wrists, tugging and heaving with all his might to drag the giant away from further harm. When they were beyond the narrowing, I took one arm from Ren and dug my heels into the earth, lending my meagre weight to the task.

We pulled him on to the soft sand near to the river mouth and flipped him over. Even in that dim light, I could see the damage done. It took all my strength to hold in the tears. His hair had shrivelled to a matted mass on his scalp, his shoulders were blistered with pus filled sacks, but worst of all was his lower back. The seared and charred skin had sloughed off as we dragged him free. All that remained was the bloodied and weeping soft flesh and rendered fat from beneath. A massive flap of skin hung from the open wound, caked in dirt and debris.

I could barely contain my emotions as he lay there panting and murmuring through the pain. Every one of my senses pricked me alert, the familiar scent of roasted meats and the revulsion at my stomach's response, the clamour of the turmoil filling my ears and the distraction from my duties, the cold breeze at my back and the warmth of the inferno on my face. I needed my mind to focus, yet I found myself spinning.

Ren sharpened my wits. "Shall I get river or sea water?" He shook me by the shoulder, as if he knew that I was struggling.

"What? Oh, sea water…and cloth, if you can find any." I rummaged in my medicine kit and took out what willow I could find, ramming it into Kewri's mouth and commanding him to chew. If ever there was a time for poppy resin this was it but my searches confirmed what I already knew. My stock was empty and there was no way to procure more.

Returning a short time later, Ren placed a pail of sea water at my side and offered up his own tunic for cloth. "Wouldn't it be easier to drag him down the beach to the sea?"

It was an option, but I feared that the surging waves would do him more damage. Added to the fact that more and more survivors had staggered from the blaze to seek my help, I knew it was not feasible to spread my patients over a wide distance. "No, we'll just have to make do right here." I said, emptying my bag onto the ground. I'd seen and treated burns before, but never on this scale. When small patches were damaged, I could cut away the dead bits and the healthy sections would grow to replace them. That's if it didn't rot first.

Senara rushed to help, dropping her quiver and bow, she took her lead from Ren. He carried my balms and ointments, bandages and willow bark and set about pasting and binding those in need.

Kewri was a mess. I knew my efforts would give him more pain, but there was no other option. Sloshing sea water over the whole area, I gently teased and stretched the skin over the exposed flesh. The edges were brittle, flaking off in my hand. It was unlikely that stitches would hold the skin in place, yet what other choice did I have?

While Ren and Senara tended to the less severe burns of the other warriors, I contemplated my approach. Accuracy and neatness were unimportant. I had to act fast if I was to prevent the rot setting in and finishing him off.

Taking a few moments to sharpen my best bone needle on a rock, I threaded the soaked lengths of gut from my bag and began my work, hushing and calming my patient with comforting words as I anchored his missing skin back in place. Kewri bore the pain better than any I've ever known. He neither flinched nor cried out, but I could see his clenched jaw and his fists tighten every time my needle pierced his sore body.

When my labours were over, I struggled to my feet. Tallack's men were laying out two more bodies by the side of the river. The first I could not recognise at all. His face was smashed in and charred, as though the roof timbers of his hut had fallen while he slept. I could tell from his clothing that he was one of the Head Hunter Clan.

The manner in which he died was a tragedy. It prevented him the honour of a place in the Summerlands with our Chieftains and warriors of old. Instead, he will pass through the earth and forever spend his days in the Underworld. At least it was a quick death and he would have not seen the end coming.

The second man was less fortunate. Most of his torso and limbs were blackened. Those carrying his body informed me that he'd run towards the river shrouded in flames, but failed to reach the water.

As the blaze raged along the valley, Tallack and his men were beaten back by the intense heat and futility of their efforts. Those who were able, lifted Kewri and carried him to the beach along with all that could be salvaged from camp. We were back where we had started but with many lives lost.

During the course of the night, the breeze dropped and the eerie glow in the sky lessened as the fires burned out. My back ached, my knees were bruised and my heart was heavy. I had all but exhausted my stocks of balms and pastes. Senara tried to forage for more herbs at dawn, but came back empty handed and desolate by mid-morning. In the end, the best I could offer to the wounded was damp sea weed wrappings and a rationed slice or two of willow.

Tallack sat facing the Phoenician vessel in the bay for a long time. His fine ship was all that he had left in terms of wealth or strategy, but he knew as well as I that Kenver could take it as his prize within days. All he had to do was to reduce our numbers until we could no longer defend ourselves. Maybe our Chief was thinking about jumping aboard and sailing away to far off lands, shirking all the responsibilities that were lumped upon his young shoulders.

Who could tell? I'd seen that look on my nephew's face before. It was the same hopeless gaze he wore when his brother was at the height of his ailment; that sinking feeling as he resigned himself to fate. We no longer had the gods favour and there was nothing we could do to turn things around.

Our options were slim to non-existent. If we stayed much longer, Kenver would wipe out the rest of our warriors and all hopes of our family retaining power. If we boarded Tallack's ship and collected his mother from the island on the Exe, we would spend our days fending off foreigners and pirates trying to take the vessel from us.

There was also a possibility that he was thinking about yielding to Kenver. It's not something his father, or brother would have ever considered, but Tallack had a softer heart than others in our family. He took an interest in the lives of his men, rewarded loyalty and praised them for their efforts. At least he used to, until this last bitter campaign with Kitto's attempts to oust him. For all I knew, our Chief was considering terms of surrender to save the lives of our remaining warriors in exchange for the Chieftaincy.

While Tallack languished in self-pity and despair, I had a job to do. Ren disappeared in search of food, Senara was fetching fresh water for the injured to drink, and Kewri's moans had dulled to a whimper. One glance at the expressions on my patients' faces told me that many were in great pain. I needed more goose grease, soothing herbs and willow bark. There was only one way to achieve that. I had to brave the wooded valley without my trusted giant.

I rinsed myself off in the sea, gathered my things and slipped away. After Kenver's threat of slaughtering us all, I didn't want to put anyone else in greater danger than they were already. Alone, I stood a chance that he would take pity on an old woman and make my ending a quick one should I be caught.

The soot and ashes stuck to my wet pattens in great sticky clods. An acrid stench of hot charcoal filled my senses as the slightest waft of breeze floated the pale flakes of burned wood around me. It was a terrible sight.

The hut where I'd found happiness after a lifetime of heartache was no more. What little remained of it, smouldered and crumbled when I passed by.

When I reached the worn track leading up the valley, I heard a shrill whistle coming from the marshy land on the opposite bank. I almost lost control over my bladder I was so startled. Spinning around, I squinted against the stark light of the morning. A slender figure was running towards me.

"Ho there! Where do you think you're going?" I recognised the voice before I could see him with any degree of clarity. Ren was hurtling along the opposite bank in pursuit. I watched him hurry towards a crossing point comprised of a few unstable boulders lined up across the width of the river. He hopped and stepped between them as sure footed as a goat, holding his long bow out for balance. Panting and doubling over, he clutched his sides as though they pained him. I hardly thought it was necessary to explain where I was headed. With my foraging bag and one of his knives in hand it should have been obvious.

He looked at me for an answer as though he had the right to make demands of me. When I failed to respond he said, "You're not going back up the valley after what happened last time." His tone suggested that it was meant as an order, not a question.

I tutted at him and started walking once again.

"For the sake of Cernonnus, woman. You'll get yourself killed."

I was frightened of Kenver making good on his promise, but this new attitude of Ren's irked me. Just because we shared a bunk for a few nights, did not give him the right to dictate what I could or couldn't do, even though he had my safety uppermost in his mind. I scoffed and stomped along the path faster.

"By the gods, you are stubborn." He snarled, traipsing after me.

I halted abruptly and turned on him, prodding his chest with a bony finger. "Why is it that when a man refuses to comply with a command, he is seen as someone with conviction, brave and forward thinking, whereas when a woman does the same thing, she is stubborn, idiotic and emotional?" My vehement glare bored into the black parts of his eyes until he glanced away. Maybe I am stubborn, but no one will alter me now. I am too long in the tooth to be shackled to the whims of a man, even one as honourable as Ren.

His mouth flapped but no words came out. I hurried away, determined to find all I needed to treat my patients. He had no other choice but to follow me, keeping his eyes trained on the shrubbery either side of the valley for signs of our foes.

"Don't go too far ahead." He moaned, hastening to catch up with me.

"Kenver will assume that we are all licking our wounds on the beach preparing to leave. If anything, now is the best time to forage." I said, changing my course and darting into the undergrowth. I sliced a few edible leaves into my bag for later and directed Ren to a patch of tall reeds where Kewri and I had caught ducks before. He looked askance at me, but he knew that good meat, feathers and rendered fat were all in short supply.

The more plantain and moss I gathered, the more I allowed my mind to wander. Before long, I'd drifted into a kind of trance, picking, cutting and slicing roots and shoots until my back reminded me of my age. In a small clearing further up the slope, I spotted the bright yellow of mullein flowers. They lifted my heart to think that I could give the men teas and ointments of this wondrous plant to ward off the rot and ease their pain.

Scrambling up the loose soils, I slung my bag behind my back, tucked Ren's knife into my belt and crawled on all fours closer to the luscious patch of this glorious herb. Rejoicing in my find, I set about plucking the tiny flowers from the tapered tip and then bent low to harvest the soft, downy leaves from the base.

That was when I heard Ren trying to get my attention from the valley floor with rasping noises. I glanced back over my shoulder to see him gesturing for me to stay low and hide. Dropping onto my belly, my pulse thumped in my ears until I was sweating with panic. Ren crept up alongside me, touched my shoulder and then pointed to a clump of bushes further up the slope. They were swaying and not from the mild breeze around us.

Ren moved his lips nearer to my head and whispered. "Stay here, we'll either have a feast this night, or a dead miner on our hands." With his bow held out and an arrow nocked, he sneaked closer to the source of movement. This time, no one could take us by surprise.

# CHAPTER TWENTY-THREE

Nausea swept bile into my gullet as I watched the man who meant the most to me in the world, creep towards danger. The rustling in the bushes ceased and within moments, a man appeared in the clearing. His eyes bulged with shock upon seeing the tip of an arrow so near to his face.

"Are you alone?" Ren growled at him, daring to pace even closer.

"Yes, yes, I am." The man raised his palms in supplication.

Ren flicked the end of the bolt to his left. "Move."

The pair of them scuffled and slipped on the loose earth until Ren was behind him and able to check the shrubbery.

"He's telling the truth." Ren said to me, while prodding his captive in the back. They scurried down the bank towards the valley floor. I followed with some caution, looking backwards every so often in case we'd missed more hiding Alchemists. When we were next to the river, Ren snatched the man's heavy leather bag and a small knife from his belt. I took both eagerly, tucking the blade in my belt before crouching on the ground to examine the contents of the satchel. As soon as I lifted the flap I gasped. It was filled with ingots of pure tin and strips of the finest dried venison.

"Well, well. This will take some explaining." Ren smiled.

"More importantly," I said. My nose crumpled in puzzlement. "How did you make it this far along the valley without us seeing you? There are no mines in this area. They're all in the gorge over yonder."

The man looked down and scuffed his feet on the dusty trail. "Working mines, no, but there are abandoned tunnels."

The smirk on the man's face was too much for Ren to bear. His clan had beaten us at every turn. They'd killed and maimed, burned and impaled more of our warriors than could be recalled in a single sitting. Ren sucked in a great lungful of air, his anger rising with each passing moment. He let out a long mournful growl and pulled the bowstring taut ready to release a bolt right through the man's chest. I couldn't let our only source of useful information die before my eyes.

Forgoing my own safety, I stepped between Ren and the Alchemist. "Wait! Don't kill him. I need to know more."

Ren's angry outburst wiped the grin from the man's features. "Hey, I have no quarrel with the Chief, nor his family. Take the tin if you want. There's plenty more where that came from."

Ren lowered his aim a fraction and frowned. "Why would you betray the Alchemists?"

The man kept his hands aloft. "The way I see it is that we're all Dumnonii, right?" He looked to me for confirmation. I nodded, encouraging him to continue. "As far as I can tell, your fight lies with Kenver and his kin or what's left of them. Never did like that Kerensa.

He won't tell us what happened, but I'd bet my best knife that she was to blame." He nodded towards the blade that I'd taken from him only moments before.

I had to hide a smirk of my own. Ren was less taken by this jolly fellow, thinking it all to be a distraction.

Softening to his earnest speech, I asked; "What name do you go by?"

"Nectan." He kept his eyes focused on Ren as he encircled him with the arrow still nocked in his bow.

I gave him my sternest look. "And how is it that you came to be in this valley with a bag full of tin and enough dried meat to last more than a quarter moon?"

He stared at me for a long while. "I know you. You fixed up my lad after that cave in last winter."

I couldn't tell from his expression whether he was pleased or angry. He was stalling for time. Perhaps he hoped that his clan would rescue him or he'd find a way to escape. With Ren protecting me, I decided to give him some leeway. "Did your son mend well? I can't recall seeing him afterward."

"He did, well enough. I thank the gods often for sending you to us that day. Kenver banished him to work the northern mine with my other lad. That was Kerensa's fault too, two-faced little kyjyan." His voice grew quieter, his thumb brushed against his bottom lip. I thought he was going to recount the event that caused his son to be sent away but he took a long breath and sighed instead. "I um, can help you resolve this entire situation, if you'll promise just two things."

"If you can end this whole siege, my nephew is likely to grant you almost anything." I blustered without thinking. After all my advice to the younger ones about holding your tongue and your nerve during negotiations, I had dropped my guard in an instant.

I caught Ren gently shaking his head in disbelief. "Let's hear what he has to say first. It might be another trap. Kenver is fond of those and this man seems far too willing for my liking." Ever the cautious one is my Ren.

Nectan stared at the bag of tin on the ground and then at Ren's perpetual glare. "I think you should take me to Chief Tallack. I'm more than happy to discuss my proposition with him."

Ren struck some threatening poses for a few moments but Nectan wouldn't be swayed. He was wise to use his solution as leverage. I had to admire that in him if nothing else. When no amount of cajoling would loosen his lips, we marched him back downstream to the beach.

Nectan slowed to a crawl when we reached the smouldering huts near the river mouth, taking in the devastation as he tiptoed through the ruins. He looked positively queasy after we passed the stretch of warriors tending to their burns and wounds. Senara was changing the wrappings on Kewri's back. The taut flesh and pus-filled blisters look set to burst at any moment. By all rights, I should have left Ren to take Nectan to our Chief and resumed my healing duties, but I was shamefully curious. How could this Alchemist resolve a situation as precarious as ours?

I dropped my kit bag containing the mullein and other herbs next to Senara and muttered that I would return shortly. Tallack was further along the beach, gazing absently at the horizon. Our captive raised his hands when we approached, more as a gesture of politeness than submission. Tallack was jolted from his reverie, hopping to his feet in short order.

"Who's this?" My nephew growled, his hand straying to the hilt of his sword.

"Calls himself, Nectan." Ren said, dumping the bag of clinking tin onto the sand. "We caught him in the valley upstream. Reckons he has a way to break the siege."

"Is that so?" Tallack did not seem convinced. Just as Ren had done, our Chief encircled the prisoner looking for evidence of trickery. Massen and a few other Sea Warriors crowded around, each of them snarling and preparing to strike Nectan down at the Chief's command. I'm not sure why, but I expected this Alchemist to be squirming with anxiety for his own safety. Instead, he watched with calm assurance while Tallack did his best to intimidate, puffing out his chest and flexing his muscles. The Alchemist's knowledge must have been worth a ransom to be so cool in the face of such hostility.

"Well? Speak, you kyjyan traitor, or we'll beat it out of you." Tallack was not master of his emotions. It was hardly surprising given all that had happened over the past few days. Here was a chance to repay Kenver's malice following the brutal torture of a beloved crewman. As much as I understood my nephew's need to assert his dominance, I couldn't let him squander our chance of resolution. His anger was too close to the surface for a reasonable negotiation.

Biting my lip, I edged forwards. "Chief Tallack, if I may?"

He spun on his heels in the sand and glowered at me. "Not now, Aunt Mel."

"But Nectan is offering us a way out of this mess. There's no need to threaten…"

"I said, not now!" His snarl was filled with such spite, I was shocked mute. His temper frightened me. Covering my mouth with my hand, I stepped backwards into the crowd of warriors. Emotions bubbled to the surface and would not be quelled. With his attention turned once again to Nectan, the young Chief moved in so close their noses almost touched. "You had better tell me all that you know, or by the gods, I'll skin every inch of you, just like you did my crewman."

"Ah, well, yes. That was a bad business all round. Many of our elders tried to stop him, but Kenver is a law unto himself. Poor lad was no more than a boy." Nectan bobbed his head about apologetically, but it only served to rile Tallack all the more.

He grabbed the prisoner by the neck and began to squeeze until the vessels in Nectan's face pulsed in great blue lines. Gobs of spittle flew from his mouth as the Chief's grip tightened. Tallack had chided me once already, I dared not interfere again.

Ren stepped closer to my nephew and rested his hand on his arm. "Chief, we need him alive." It was almost a whisper. For a single moment, Tallack increased the pressure, directing his rage into the man's throat, but even he could see that Ren was right. Nectan was our only hope to regain control over the mines.

As soon as Tallack let go, Nectan inhaled a vast gulp of air before doubling over and coughing up the contents of his lungs. With watering eyes and a bruised neck, he took a while to regain his strength. When at last he was able to speak, Nectan held up his palm. "I am not your enemy. I asked Fur Benyn to bring me here so that we could help each other end this situation. Many of us Alchemists are of the same mind. Kenver is not fit to lead our clan."

Tallack sneered and folded his arms across his chest. "So that's it. You want the leadership for yourself. You're willing to turn on Kenver in exchange for power over the clan. Why would I trust someone like that to oversee my mines?"

Nectan straightened up until he could look Tallack directly in the eye. "You really don't know him, do you? He's not the agreeable friend that he pretends to be. Oh, he can charm Fur Benyn and the ladies of the Chief, but down in those tunnels, he turns into a demon from the Underworld." He spat on the ground as though speaking of his leader put a foul taste on his tongue. "Your rule about keeping the young ones above ground?" His finger shot up, pointing at Tallack. "Ignored. I've seen him shove antler picks into the hands of children who've seen fewer than five summers. He sends them down tunnels from sun up till sun down. Some were kin of mine." Nectan's lip curled at one side. "The only ones to be spared were his own. The man is pure evil."

It was the Alchemist's turn to pant with fury. A blue vein in his forehead pulsed. "Frankly, I don't care whether you give me leadership in return for my help, just as long as you end Kenver's tyranny over my people." The two men stared at each other for a long time, Nectan still breathing noisily while Tallack's temper cooled. After all the posturing, I hoped to Cernonnus that whatever Nectan knew would prove useful.

Tallack raised his hand to his chin and stroked his whiskers. "Let's hear what you have to say. I'll decide what to do with you later."

Nectan was reluctant to open up at first but since he was surrounded by menacing warriors, he had little choice but to divulge all that he knew. The Chief and the most senior of his men stood together at the shore line as Nectan dug a stick into the wet sand and sketched the valley, its neighbouring gorge, and all the interconnected tunnels between them. The map was far more comprehensive than my early attempts.

When my nephew's fury had subsided, he allowed me to join them. Nectan showed Ren and I how he managed to evade us by using the disused shafts and hidden entrances leading to the western side of the region. Within a short while, Nectan had provided all the locations for Kenver's traps, where the lookouts were posted and which times of the day the guards swapped their duties.

It was invaluable information, but it only served to inform us of how impossible it would be to root them out. There were simply too few of our men left to attack such a vast area. From what we could tell, every entrance was either barred or guarded with armed men. They had enough stored food to stay underground for the rest of the season or more and fresh water from three different sources.

Tallack locked his fingers together behind his head and let out a massive sigh. We were no closer to a solution than before. For some time, the men pored over the soggy map, wearing intense frowns that served no purpose whatsoever. It did give them the appearance of contemplating our problem, even if none had the sense to find an answer.

When the sun tipped towards the horizon, I could no longer ignore the whimpers of pain coming from the wounded further along the beach. I left the warriors, my nephew and Ren to ponder over our dilemma, grabbed a few strips of venison from Nectan's bag and returned to my patients.

Senara was glad of the meat when I handed her and Kewri a strip each. The poor giant was still in a bad way. He nibbled on the salted deer meat but I could tell he'd lost his appetite. Pain can sometimes do that to a man. The more it gnaws at your body, the sicker you become, until food is the last thing on your mind.

As I made my way towards the central fire, I distributed what meat I had to the younger men. One was stacking more logs into a pile. "I need fresh boiling water to brew my herbs." The lad nodded to those idling on the sand. I flicked my head around and glanced at them.

"I'm all out." One of the lanky ones said. He was dour and had a dripping nose. It looked to me that he'd just swilled the last sip from his water bladder down his gullet and missed. I wrinkled my nose in disgust at their selfishness and trudged back towards Ren and Tallack.

They were still staring at the map as I approached. I held out my hand to Ren. "Can I borrow your water bladder? I'll have to walk back to the spring in the valley to fetch more."

He didn't think twice. "I'll go. It's quite some distance and you're needed here."

Nectan pulled a face. "You know that there's a closer spring on this side of the bay, don't you?"

There was a stunned moment of revelation all around us, as the Alchemist began to chuckle. "Come on, I can show you."

Tallack ordered two of his men to join us on the walk to the cliffs at the farthest end of the beach. Ren and I walked either side of the Alchemist, still dubious about his motives for helping us.

"So where were you going when we caught you this morning?" I asked, scuttling to keep up.

"Kenver's ship is just around the headland in the next cove. A few of his men are waiting there to sail me down to the island near Land's End."

Ren grimaced at him. “For what purpose?”

“That’s where he sent all our womenfolk and children. They were told to set up the signal fires to lure the foreign ships in for trade.”

It was just as I’d suspected. Kenver had been selling our tin and setting up his own trade partners all along. Before we could express our disgust at this latest betrayal, Nectan veered off the beach and began yomping up and over the dunes.

“This way. It’s not as steep as climbing the cliff face.” He yelled back over his shoulder. Our warriors ran after him, worried that it was a trick to escape. I wasn’t so sure. After all that he’d told us, I was starting to trust the man. Ren lingered behind, helping me over the slippery sections of loose sand until we could scramble onto a well-worn track up to the cliff path.

After a short but steep walk, Nectan pointed out the spot where the trickle of water ran over the rocks. The exertion of climbing made us all sweat, but the faint breeze and clean air restored us in no time. Ren filled our bladders while I splashed myself with the chilled water. It was good to wash the filth of burnt huts and sick men from my skin. More than anything I wanted to strip off and roll about in the cool stream, but there was no time to waste. I had to stew the mullein to give to those in pain.

Ren pushed the stoppers into the necks of the bladders and cupped his hands in the spring. As he brought the sparkly water to his mouth, he stopped and looked up at Nectan. “You say that there are three water sources in the tunnels?”

“Yeah, but one has practically dried up. I’ve never seen such a dry summer as this season in my life. Old shafts that were abandoned from previous flooding are now bone dry." Nectan said. "Makes it much easier to travel between the valley and the gorge, I can tell you."

The jolly fellow had no idea why we were smiling and Ren and I were not about to tell him.

# CHAPTER TWENTY-FOUR

There was much to prepare and all had to be done with the utmost care and timing. Our men, and indeed our headstrong Chief, needed a lesson in stealth and there was only one person among us who excelled in that department. The problem we faced was that she was both female and a youngster herself. The men may have treated Senara as one of their own on the Long Hut benches, drinking ale and singing bawdy songs, it was quite another matter taking advice about strategy from her.

Ren and I discussed as much as we could on our way back from the cliff side spring, quizzing Nectan over the position of the tunnels with the steepest inclines and those which housed the greatest numbers of Alchemists. By the time we were back with Tallack on the beach, Ren was able to explain his idea to the warriors in some detail by adding to the map in the sand.

I hovered at the side of my nephew, wondering how well he would receive the plan, it having come from Ren instead of being a product of his own mind. He certainly looked pensive and fraught. Ever since his lover was skinned and left hanging in the woods to taunt him, Tallack had become broody and unapproachable. I guess that was to be expected, but I did miss the light-hearted boy he used to be. Responsibility and grief make martyrs of us all.

The Chief listened and watched as Ren scored the sand with the stick, naming who among the men he thought suitable for each of the tasks ahead. When it came to Senara's part in the scheme, the men blew out air over their teeth. No doubt they all thought themselves to be her equal or better, but Ren and I knew that only she had the requisite skills and without her, the entire enterprise would fail. There was a long moment of tense, nervous silence as we all eyed one another in the circle. Senara kept her sight on the Chief, despite the seething stares all around her.

At length, Tallack looked down at the map, rubbing his forehead absently as he thought. "This will take a number of days to arrange." He said without averting his gaze. No one spoke while we awaited his decision. Eventually, he turned to face Senara. "You really think you can do what Ren is suggesting?"

There was not a moment of hesitation. She nodded her head with vigour. "I can, Chief."

"It'll take courage and accuracy…"

"I understand and I'm ready. I won't let you down." She adjusted the strap of her quiver across her chest and held her head high. There was something about this young warrior girl that defied explanation. Was it her dogged determination or her unfailing loyalty that inspired confidence? I wasn't sure, but whatever it was, Tallack saw it too.

The Chief smiled. "I believe you. Everyone, get to work."

It was like a pall of gloom had lifted from the beach. Occupation lightened the moods of all the men, even the discontented and envious ones. They glared and scowled whenever they caught sight of Senara, but the hope of victory spurred them on to work late into the night. Ren insisted that the majority of the tasks were carried out at the farthest reaches of the valley, so as not to alert any of the Alchemists hiding in the gorge about our plan.

The horses took the brunt of the heavy lifting, dragging lumber into position. Without Kewri and our fallen men, everything took twice as long to accomplish. Senara chose to make her own preparations away from camp alone. I can't say that I blame her given the importance of her part and the animosity that it stirred up with the men. I suspected that she also needed time to practice her skills. So much relied on her success.

My duty lay with the injured. The mullein brew was not as powerful as willow bark in relieving pain and the sea weed wrapping on Kewri's back failed to reduce the blisters on his shoulders. Once or twice, I caught him shivering despite the warmth of the day and the gentle breeze. He was hot and clammy and a faint foetid smell of rot hung about him.

I had to avoid rupturing those blisters. The fewer open wounds about his person, the better. Either way, he really needed a hefty dose of something strong, like poppy resin. How I wished that my kit bag was filled with several pots of the stuff. There was no other option but to walk to the marshland, hike up my tunic and wade into the reeking mud in search of mace reed. It didn't take long to find a patch but it had already been heavily harvested. When animals and birds are scarce, they are a rich staple among our people and many other tribes.

All I required was enough fresh leaves to split and scrape the clear jelly into a wooden bowl. It was slow work, especially since I needed every drop of the gooey substance I could lay my hands on, but still quicker than grubbing about in the foul water to collect roots to cook and smash. My shins and calves were chilled through to the bone, while my hands toiled instinctively, skimming the ooze into the bowl with a firm scoop of my thumb. I found myself humming softly, barely noticing whenever one of our men thundered past on horseback as they sped up the valley. They were so careless. At the rate they were going, Kenver would discover our plot long before we could finish the preparations.

When I had collected a bowl full, I slipped and skidded out of the muck and on to drier ground carrying my precious cargo wrapped in damp leaves back to the beach. Where the jelly had coated my forefinger and thumb, I was bereft of all feeling. It was enough to reassure me that it could be of some use to my giant friend.

After a quick rinse in the sea, I was ready to begin the job I'd been dreading. Only the wounded men and Nectan were left to keep the fires burning and our belongings guarded. Nectan pulled a face when I told him that I needed his help. For someone who'd endured day after day toiling in the mines, so close to the demons of the Underworld, he showed surprising cowardice. He shuddered and recoiled when I asked him to gather more seaweed and change the wrappings of some of our men. Maybe I was being too harsh. Not everyone can cope with the sick and injured. For me, blood, guts and pus were a daily occurrence.

Avoiding the inevitable, I chose to apply the reed slime to Kewri's blistered areas first, hoping that it would lessen some of his discomfort. As I smeared the taut skin of his shoulders, I examined the damage to his lower back. The stitches made in haste had not held fast.

Many had torn through the brittle edges leaving sagging gaps between those that remained. Each section wept with sticky humours.

"Bite down on this leather strap, my boy. This will hurt." It doesn't matter how softly you say those words, they cannot ease the pain that follows. I felt Kewri tense under my touch. His entire torso clenched as he endured the agony. Placing all five fingertips on the charred flap of flesh, I gently tested how far it could be shifted. It was the only way to determine if the tissues beneath were starting to reattach, or whether the entire area was likely to rot and would therefore need to be removed.

His mournful grunts and murmurs almost broke my heart, but he bore the pain with the same dignity as before. There was strength in the giant yet. Satisfied that the flesh had begun to knit, I concentrated on the open sections of the join. If I could get the festering patches under control, Kewri stood a good chance of recovery.

The first step was to clean away the bad humours and filth. With cupped handfuls of sea water from a pail, I delivered a steady trickle over the broken stitches until much of the charring and fragments from the wrapping had washed away. If the Belgae Tribe had not confiscated my best shears, I could have trimmed off the dead sections. As it was, I didn't trust my hand with Nectan's blade to do a good enough job. There was a possibility that I could make things much worse. When his back was clean, but raw as fresh meat, I smeared what was left of my mace reed paste over the edge of the skin flap. The numbing effect should have taken the edge off the pain while I made a balm for the rot.

Had we been back at the island compound on the Exe, I would have instructed Kewri to lay still on his front with his back open to the fresh air. On the beach, however, every gust of wind delivered fine sand to coat his troubled flesh. All I could do for him was to lay a clean section of damp hemp cloth across his back for protection and wait for Ren to return from the valley with the other herbs I needed.

When the men did finally walk down to the beach for the night, Kewri's fever had taken hold. I could barely get him to drink water to counter the sweats. His shivers were so violent, he was shifting in the sand like a babe. Several times, he tried to cover himself with some of the rescued furs, but I couldn't let him wipe off the jelly I'd applied.

Ren led his horse right up to us at the main fire. It was laden with dripping bundles. "We've had a stroke of luck." He grinned, handing me the reins before starting to unload his steed. "Anyone would think we'd sacrificed a couple of goats to the gods to be blessed with such a haul."

I grew impatient with him, fearing for Kewri's worsening health. "Did you get my willow bark?"

"Huh? Oh, yes, and the burdock. Couldn't remember whether you said the leaves or the root, so I brought the whole plant." He seemed more interested in the sopping wet bundles suspended from either side of his pony. A second horse and then a third arrived just as Ren unhitched the lengths of soaked linden bark, each laden with a similar quantity of the goods. "Kenver must have hoped that we'd not find them. They were trailing in the river upstream." He looked at me as though I could perform miracles. Did he really think I had the time or the strength to split and twist that lot into rope?

I raised my brows and pursed my lips, holding out my hand. It took a moment for him to comprehend my frustration. His expression crumpled into sadness when he glanced down at Kewri laying by the fire. His jubilance crushed, Ren untied a sack hanging from the horse and handed it to me.

"Thank you. This should make all the difference to his recovery." I hated to think that I'd trampled on what little hope he'd found. I gave Ren's forearm a little squeeze and smiled. "You may just have saved Kewri's life." I waited long enough to see his weather-beaten face light up, before returning to treat my patient.

The medicine didn't take too long to prepare. Smashing a little peeled burdock root and the willow bark between two large pebbles was easy, waiting for them to stew in the hot water over the fire was the hard part. While it cooled a little, I took what duck fat I'd saved and began working in the chopped burdock leaves to make a salve against the rot.

When the brew was ready to drink, I couldn't get Kewri to cooperate with me. "Please sit up, lad. It'll taste something awful, but it'll help with the pain and bring your fever down. The burdock should clean your blood before it starts to fester." I waited for some sign of understanding, but he just groaned and ignored me. "Kewri, please sit up."

Ren saw my struggle and called the men over to assist. It was not an easy manoeuvre, tipping him onto his side to avoid further harm to his back, and lifting his shoulders enough to pour the liquid down his gullet. I thought he might react to the bitter taste but he just swallowed it without a murmur.

There was nothing more I could do for him. The men rested Kewri in the sand on his belly and set to work on preparing the linden bark strips for twisting. While I scaled and gutted a few trout and a couple of flat fish they'd caught, Ren told me about their progress in the valley. He explained how they overcame some obstacles early on in the day by felling a few storm damaged trees that were partially uprooted, thus saving them time and effort using axes. His main concern was in being spotted by the Alchemist watchmen.

Thanks to Nectan, we now knew where the lookouts were posted and could avoid them. I worried that the speedy preparations put too much strain on our surviving horses. The men were exhausted too and at greater risk of injury. With so few of us left, we had to preserve our fighters at all costs.

Senara didn't return to camp that night, nor for the three nights that followed. Nectan and I took it in turns to keep watch over the wounded and forage for food and wood for the fires. Kewri had his ups and downs. He almost scared me to death on the third night, with his raving sweats and thrashing about, but by dawn of the following morn, his fever broke. He ate a little for the first time in days and was well enough to sit up and wash himself - much to my relief.

The men worked long days and some of the nights to set up the foundations of our plan, and by good fortune or the will of the gods, come late afternoon of the fifth day, we were ready. Senara crept out of the dunes to join us around the fires. She carried with her a number of plucked waterfowl and a quiver packed with new arrows. I believe she meant the food to be an offering of peace to the men, but it failed to charm them. They grew surly and quiet when she lingered at their fire making her as uncomfortable as they could. In the end, she left the birds at their feet and sat with my nephew, Ren and me.

The sun was far from setting, it being so close to the solstice, but we all needed to rest before dark. Kewri offered to see to the horses while Nectan and I prepared the wildfowl for roasting. As much as I wanted to appear calm and confident in our scheme, my hands were trembling as I slashed open the birds to yank out the entrails.

Nectan noticed my jitters and gave me a warm smile. "It'll be fine, Fur Benyn. There's nothing to worry about." He whispered, which only served to make me more anxious. The entire scheme rested on the information he'd given us. He certainly seemed to be confident, which was suspicious in itself. Whose side was he really on? Had he set us all up for a catastrophic failure? From captive to ally in a few short days, I was starting to doubt my trust in him. It would certainly be a clever ploy if Kenver deliberately placed Nectan among us, someone capable of influencing our actions.

I spent much of the evening mulling over my thoughts on the matter. Kenver couldn't have known that we would spare Nectan's life. Neither was it likely that anyone would volunteer to walk into enemy hands, risking the same torture our crewman, Treeve had endured. Since his capture, Nectan had plenty of opportunities to escape, yet he stayed close by and made himself useful. He never spoke about the Alchemists, nor his family while we worked together on the shore. The man was either the greatest tactician that ever lived or was genuinely indifferent to the fate of his clan leader. Either way, I found myself hanging on his every word, looking for signs of duplicity.

As the sun dipped below the cliffs at our backs, Tallack and the warriors bedded down to rest. Kewri and a couple of the least wounded kept watch, padding along the dunes and scavenging what useful wood they could for the fires. Neither I nor Senara slept. For one, the evening was still and humid, my clothes stuck to my back and my lank grey locks matted at the nape of my neck, but seeing the men drift into sleep gave me a measure of confidence. I was sure their anxiety would show if they believed our plan would fail.

When the moon reached its peak in the sky, I knew that Kewri would return to wake Tallack and the warriors. Away from the fires, it was undeniable that the strength of the moonlight would not help our endeavours. We'd hoped for the cover of darkness, but were left wanting.

Senara caught me gazing skyward and shrugged. She gathered up and secured her weapons about her person. "Can't be helped, Fur Benyn. I made a sacrifice to the Morrighan for protection. Let's hope she heard me."

Tallack stood up and faced the young woman, holding out his arm to her. "Go with blessings, Senara."

She tucked her dagger in her belt and clasped his forearm. "You'll have control over the mines by sun up, Chief. Just you see." It was only then that I caught the tiniest whisper of doubt in her voice. A tremble that propagated along her bottom lip as she smiled.

Tallack held on to her arm for a moment longer, the firmness of his grip intended to convey his trust in her. When he let go, she turned and ran along the beach to the cliff path. Every one of us watched her shapely silhouette shrink into the gloom.

# CHAPTER TWENTY-FIVE

The warriors left shortly after Senara. Each had a specific place and role to play in the plan. Kewri and Nectan walked alongside my horse as we scrambled up to the ridge top between the two valleys. Despite the disadvantages of the powerful moonlight, it did afford me a decent view of proceedings as they unfolded.

My pony whickered and snorted from the exertion of climbing the steep valley side. Dismounting, I hitched its rein to the branches of a woody shrub out of sight and joined my friends at our high vantage point. The trees above the fast-flowing river cast long shadows on the dry ground. There was not a puff of wind, nor a foraging animal in sight.

"Are you sure that we're in the right place?" I whispered, leaning from one side to another and scanning the rise for signs of life. Kewri said nothing. He just held out his arm and pointed to a thicket beneath a clump of alders. It took me a while to see what his young eyes had already spotted. Beneath the rustling boughs of a tall tree hid an Alchemist watchman, his pale cheeks a stark contrast to the shadowy bushes in which he lurked.

Just as my sight had picked him out among the undergrowth, he vanished. There was not a sound, nor any hint of foul play, but we all knew his fate. Senara had just taken her first victim. I imagined her dangling by the legs from the overhanging branches and slashing through the man's throat before he could sound an alarm. Kewri was grinning at me as though he could read my thoughts. I'd almost forgotten their former relationship. He knew her better than any of us and truth be told, still admired her greatly.

By the time I turned my head back to the sight of her first kill, she was already positioning herself for the second. I could see her balancing on a higher branch of the same alder tree, straddling the bough and taking aim with a deadly arrow nocked.

Moving along the ridge top, I was able to see her quarry. He was young, no more than twelve summers, and gazing up at the moon. How could he have known that he'd made it easy for the bolt to whistle through the air and pierce his neck with a perfect shot? The poor lad had just enough life left in him to grasp at the shaft, slick with his pumping blood as he crashed to the ground. I should have been sickened by the death of one so youthful, but all I could think about was how telling it was that Kenver would force the least experienced of his clan to complete their duties on the night watch.

Nectan and Kewri relaxed, fascinated by the spectacle. They made themselves comfortable on a couple of dry rocks while I paced about less certain of our shield maiden's success. Two of the gorge watchmen had met their fate. Three remained, and they would present a much harder challenge. Two stood behind the sturdy barricades of the entrance to the largest tunnel. I knew it well from my time treating injured miners following a cave in during the winter. The stretch of land outside the barricade was bare of vegetation, allowing their ponies to pull carts of rock and stone. I saw no carts, nor ponies, just a wide-open space most likely laid with more traps. It certainly had what looked to be a fresh layer of sand strewn rushes laid across the bare earth. What better way to conceal another of Kenver's wicked pits of death?

Senara was still some distance from those guards, further down the gorge. Another, much broader watchman lay in her path. From his swagger, I'd say that this miner was older and at least twice her size. As stealthy and swift as Senara was, he still spotted her long before she could get close enough to surprise him.

She froze, her strategy had failed. My hand leapt to my mouth to stifle my cries. I was sure that he'd shout to his clansmen; summon all those on guard to assist him, but he did not. Perhaps he thought her too small to be a threat, we will never know, but he grabbed a thick staff as long as he was tall and thundered towards her. Still Senara did not move, her feet rooted to the hillside, her hands level with her hips.

"No!" I cried, too scared to watch and too dazed to look away. He was less than a boat length from her and gaining speed along the river bank. He raised one end of the staff high, preparing himself for a crushing blow down on her fair head.

My nails dug into my palms but I felt no pain. A rush of emotion flooded my head at the thought of burning another of our friends on the pyre. Kewri swayed, clasping the sleeves of his tunic in sudden panic. Only Nectan seemed to be enjoying the events as they played out before him.

Why wasn't Senara running? There had been more than enough time to slip away and disappear from such a hulking great brute, yet her feet were stock still. Other than the snapping of twigs underfoot, his grunts and puffs were muffled by the rushing waters of the river. Before his staff could land on her skull and crack it open like a nut, Senara reached to her belt, whipped out her dagger and threw it with alarming precision into the man's face.

His head snapped backwards; his mouth gaped open as her dagger embedded itself to the hilt in his left eye. It took another moment for his body to slump; first to its knees, dropping the staff as he fell, before tumbling forward onto a soft bracken death bed. Senara wasted no time in mourning. She kicked his shoulder until his corpse rolled over, allowing her to retrieve her blade. I could tell from her swift escape that she was not troubled by her encounter in the slightest.

How I wish that the men could have seen her courage and fortitude. I'm sure many would have turned on their heels and fled in the face of such an enemy, but not she.

There were just two guards left to dispatch. Both had the protection of stone and wooden blockades, a paling wall and probably three or more hidden pits filled with spikes, if experience had taught us anything. I couldn't see a way for her to approach. The Alchemists had spent a lifetime guarding their hoard. They knew every rock and crevice in the gorge. Every weakness would have some kind of trap set in addition to the guards.

It was the one area where Nectan's information was vague. He claimed that he had no involvement in the defences and scant knowledge of any planned traps. At the time of his telling, I'd found that hard to believe. How could someone as senior as he, not know about the preparation of siege walls, yet be so accurate with the watchmen and their look out posts? Something about Nectan did not add up. He seemed to be enjoying the whole situation far too much for my liking.

Senara disappeared into the undergrowth and out of our sight, leaving the dead man on the slope shrouded by ferns. Kewri let out a huge lungful of air, I suspect he'd been holding it for some time.

Our relief was short lived. From where we stood, we could see the heads of the last two guards above the defences. They were peering through the hurdle fences between the rocks and posts. From the head bobbing and speed of their movements, I guessed that they sensed something was wrong. Perhaps the dead guard had let out a particular warning sound, a bird call or something that I'd missed during Senara's calm encounter. Whatever had spooked them looked set to ruin our whole plan.

If Senara waited much longer to kill them, they would summon the entire Alchemist Clan from deep within the tunnels. Our numbers were too few to confront them head on, and we were scattered right across the two adjacent valleys.

It was my turn to hold my breath. Nectan sat chewing on a strip of dried meat, Kewri fidgeted on his rock and I paced along the ridge top in a growing fog of panic.

"Maybe I should ride down and distract them." I muttered, knowing that it was a foolish suggestion the moment it left my lips, but I felt so helpless. Kewri said nothing, sensing that I was just speaking my thoughts.

Nectan took my offer seriously. "You can't do that, Fur Benyn. Who would tend to the sick? Do you think Kenver would spare you after all that's happened?" I couldn't tell if his concern for my wellbeing was genuine or whether he felt it was simply the right thing to say under the circumstances. Either way, it didn't assuage my suspicions. Despite my misgivings, his argument was valid.

I shook my head, muttering my agreement to his common sense. What use is a stupid old woman in such matters? Kenver had let me live once but he'd made it plain that his leniency would not stretch further.

Every moment we waited seemed an eternity. My mouth dried, I chewed the sides of my fingernails until they bled and still there was no sign of our brave young warrior. The moon began its descent and as the night wore on, my hope faded.

"She can't afford to leave it any longer." I wailed. "The guards are restless." I turned to Nectan. "Can't you tell? They can sense trouble."

Nectan nodded. All hope swept out of me, leaving me empty inside. She'd failed us. All our preparations were for nought. I closed my eyes and imagined all the horrors that Kenver and his men could inflict on a young woman until the tears began to flow.

Before I could express my grief, Nectan pointed ahead. "Don't give up just yet, Fur Benyn. There she is." His smile reappeared. "Can you see her on the rock face above the defences?"

In the shadows, shielded from the moonlight, I could just make out a slender figure clinging to an outcrop of rocks. "How in the name of the gods did she get there?"

My amazement triggered a little chuckle from my giant friend. It came as no surprise to him. She must have climbed right up over the side of the gorge, edged along the top and clambered down sheer cliffs and scree slopes to position herself above the mine. Was there anything this girl couldn't do?

My breath came in short gasps as I watched her lunge between two overhangs separated by a sizable gap, until she was holding on with just her fingertips above the entrance to the tunnels. The guards were straining to see over the fences and paling walls a short distance from the mouth of the mine. They hadn't heard her approach from behind.

"But how can she get to both of the men before she's discovered?" I hadn't realised that I was speaking aloud. Nectan shrugged, Kewri stood up and paced along the ridge for a better view.

It didn't stop my loud musings. "Even if she could throw two blades at once, they would surely cry out. That would spell disaster."

Nectan joined Kewri and me further along the peak of the gorge. The humidity was cloying, rattling my wits further still. Senara edged along the overhang by her fingertips, her entire body swinging freely in mid-air. When she was level with the massive rocks bolstering their defences, she kicked one leg up and hooked an ankle over the ledge.

"What's she doing?" I couldn't keep silent. Every anxious thought I had just tumbled from my lips.

"She'll have planned all this out, Fur Benyn. You can be sure of that." It was the first thing Kewri had uttered for half a day. I had to be content that he was right. Clamping my hand over my mouth, I sucked in air and held it while we watched the young woman hoist herself up onto the ledge and crawl to the top of the massive boulder.

From there, she slid down silently to the space behind the watchmen, slipping the blade between her teeth and unwinding the long leather straps of her sling shot.

"She'll never fire that off without them noticing," I stammered, leaning against Kewri for support. "It'll make too much noise…" I barely finished my thought before Senara had loaded the ball of stone into the sling, whirled it about her head and let go with a snap of the wrist. One of the straps skittered free, launching the stone with such momentum, it caved in the skull of the guard.

He fell against the hurdles and posts, startling his companion. The young lad was too slow to react or yell for help. Senara was already poised with dagger in hand. The man opened his mouth to scream, but she was quick. Her blade slashed across his windpipe in an instant, spilling foaming blood down his chest as he fell.

The defences shielded her victims from view, but I knew that she would not have let them linger in their dying throes. She took a moment to check that they could no longer raise the alarm, before clambering up the walls and returning the way she had come.

In no time at all, she reached a high trail above the mines. Stopping low in the moonlight, she ignited a bundle of kindling attached to the head of an arrow with her flint.

The glow brightened to a full flame as she nocked it in her bow, and with her stance wide and proud, she pulled back the string and sent it high into the night sky. It seemed to hang suspended for a while, slowing its course before falling to the ground. If there were any stray Alchemists abroad, they too would have seen the signal, but none would respond to their cries. The five guards in the gorge were making their way to the Underworld.

Even if they could find a way to warn Kenver, we were too far into the plan to abandon it now. I clasped my hands together as Tallack, Massen and our remaining warriors crept along the river bank carrying the boards and planking to lay over the sand and rushes. There was no way we would fall for Kenver's tricks twice. Picking their way through the dense undergrowth, they heaved the ladder-like contraptions over the gullies and thickets, ever higher into the narrow gorge, until they were just shy of the clearing. Hunkering down in the bushes, they waited.

I started to worry that Ren had missed the signal way up stream. Although I'd not seen the preparations myself, he'd described the huge pile of tree trunks, rocks and gravel that the men had amassed above the tightest bend in the river. The massive load was held back by two large stakes driven into the sandy soil.

All was silent and still once more barring the gush of the white water below. Kewri and I exchanged glances, baffled at the delay. Nectan returned to his rock and scraped out the bowl of his pipe.

"Should one of us ride along the ridge to see if Ren's in trouble?" I said, directing my gaze to the idle Nectan. He pretended not to hear me, blowing out the charred weed until it whistled clean. My liking for that man plummeted in that moment. I grabbed my bag and slung the strap over my head. "Neither use nor ornament, the pair of you." I muttered, but loud enough for them both to hear me.

As I tensed my muscles to slow my descent down towards my pony, a distant rumbling noise stopped me in my tracks. It was followed by a hollow banging of wood against wood and the cracking and splintering of rock and branch. I cocked my head in the direction of the sound, but I heard no more. Scrambling back to the ridge top, I hurried over to Kewri. “Was that it? Do you think he’s done it?”

The giant lifted his shoulders to his ears, pulling a face. “We’ll soon find out.” He said, looking down at the fast river below. The green rocks jutting out from the channel frothed with the swirling power of the tumbling water, every pool spun with hypnotic grace. All three of us trained our attention on the frantic pace of the crystal-clear stream crashing down the steep creek towards the sea.

“Nothing’s happening.” I said, revealing my impatience. “It hasn’t worked.”

Nectan lifted his face to the sky and shook his head. He didn’t need to voice his scornful thoughts.

It was gradual at first, a lessening of the rush and hiss, until the flow was reduced to that of a trickle. We stood close together and waited for the plan to unfurl.

“I can’t bear this,” I said, hurrying to the head of the trail leading into the gorge. “They aren’t all evil like Kenver. I have to save as many as I can…” and with that, I slid and tumbled down the steep bank to the valley floor.

# CHAPTER TWENTY-SIX

Kewri and Nectan dashed after me, leaving the poor pony to fend for itself. I had to be close enough to lend support to any of our men, yet not get in their way. It didn't take long for me to trip and stumble down the track to the drying riverbed and cross the slippery rocks to the opposite bank.

I couldn't hear the water at first. It was snaking its way from the hidden tunnels at the head of the river to the lower, much larger mine shafts near to the valley floor. Then a rumbling began, different in pitch and tone to the first time. The low hum became a dull roar mingled with echoing screams of frightened men.

Tallack roused his warriors, ordering them to push the lengths of timber and ladders across the clearing in front of them. Where the rushes and sand gave way, the Head Hunters were able to steer the boardwalks over the spiked pits until the ends were resting on firm ground. Four men crossed as quickly as they dared, before lifting the sharpened paling structures that blocked them from the hurdle gates ahead.

In the stillness of the summer night, the roaring flow found several exits, gushing out of the rocky cliffs with enough force to sweep away the barricades and tunnel reinforcements. Those shafts further up the valley filled with unsuspecting miners were swept up by the current and carried to the surface, coughing and spluttering. Most were too fatigued or injured to fight, surrendering themselves to Massen and the Sea Warriors who waited for them on the trail path with spears aimed at their heads.

Back at the main entrance, two more of our strong men slashed the ropes securing the hurdles between the posts allowing our warriors safe passage over the pits and into the space beyond the defences. Tallack and the Head Hunters stood with sword and spears at the ready. If he hadn't already drowned, or had his head caved in by falling rocks and timbers, Kenver would have no choice but to surrender.

Muffled hollering and shouting preceded a tiny rivulet of water sloshing out of the tunnel. The diverted stream had insufficient volume to fill all the connected tunnels. Most of the water flowed from a steep gully carved into the hill side. Some ran from the abandoned shafts at the lowest level of the gorge.

Those men that were left inside the main tunnel entrance could not go deeper for fear of drowning and yet would not venture out and face Tallack and his men. A few of our warriors lit torches and wedged them in the post bindings of the defence wall. Others helped Massen drag the captives from the side shafts and bound them at their wrists and ankles.

"Shall we go in after them?" One of the Head Hunters growled. "The more time they have to get their wits about them, the more dangerous they'll be."

"No, let them wear themselves out treading water or struggling up the lethal tunnels. It might be warm out here, but the icy river will chill their bones in there.

With any luck, Cernonnus will drag them into the Underworld, saving us the bother of dispatching them by blade." Tallack sneered over his shoulder at his grinning men.

That was when the first of the Alchemists launched themselves out of the tunnel, roaring and wailing and thrusting their spears at our men. Two stayed in the mouth of the entrance, firing off arrows at anything that moved.

"Take cover!" Tallack yelled, before a blade hurtled past his cheek and found its way into the neck of the archer. Stunned, Tallack turned around to see Senara hopping between the tall boulders, spinning her slingshot over her head. I might have known whose hand launched that knife. It was rapidly becoming her favourite move.

Massen charged into the entrance, deflecting the stream of arrows with his shield until he was close enough to barge the second archer. He smashed him into the rock face until his skull was a bloodied mess of hair and bone. The mighty Sea Warrior used the momentum of his spinning bulk to shove more miners from the safety of the tunnel and into the sharp spears of our men. Another quick lunge and Massen retreated, swiping his sword in a vast arc at shoulder height, almost beheading a miner as he ran.

There was no sign of Kenver, yet more of his miners spilled out of hiding to strike sparks with the blades of our men. Many were cut down by Senara and our archers before they could complete their battle cries and lift their spears. Others managed a couple of jabs and lunges, before our warriors opened their bellies. In a matter of moments, it rained entrails and blood.

Splattered in the gore of our enemies, Tallack's patience wore thin. "Come out you coward and face me like a man!" There was no doubt as to whom my nephew was referring. More and more Alchemists ventured out of the entrance, some in a rage, others meek and timid as though Kenver had pushed them from the safety of the tunnel as a sacrifice to the gods. Few had the skill or experience to stand up against our warriors.

The bodies were piling up in the small space between the cliff and the defences, their blood ran underfoot and drained into the spike filled pits. I crept closer, edging my way up the slope and avoiding the run off and slick mud from the flood.

Kewri straggled behind me, his face pinched with pain. As I drew level with the clearing, I looked over my shoulder at him. For every step he made forwards, he slid further back on the sludge. Despite every effort to hurry, Kewri made no further progress.

Nectan was nowhere to be seen. Whether he was hiding through cowardice or had switched sides again to help his fellow clansmen, I could not say. Neither could I really hate him for such a crime. It was obvious that only a few of Kenver's loyal clan agreed with the siege. These people were Nectan's friends and relations. It would take a hard heart indeed to turn wholly against them.

Under the pale moonlight, it was easy to see where the pits lay ahead. Their sand covered rushes and thin supports were swept aside. I was able to squeeze myself tight against the defences, where the paling walls had stood, until I was able to see through a gap in the remaining hurdles.

Something stirred from within the tunnel entrance. Tallack, Massen, and the closest warriors made ready for an attack. With a swiftness that startled me, Kenver came out running, flanked either side by his trusted men. Tallack readied his mystical sword, swiping it through the air in a display of dominance. It did not deter the Alchemists.

Most of the miners brandished spears and shields, managing to deflect Senara's and the other archer's bolts. One knocked the feet out from under the shield maiden. She toppled off her perch, high on the huge boulder, and fell into the rocks and bracken on the outside of the defences with a winded groan.

Another miner twirled about on his heels, striking out at anything that lay in his path. At least one of our men was slashed across the thigh with his spear, another took a jab in the gut but miraculously stayed upright long enough to yank the spear from the Alchemist's hand. The stricken Head Hunter crashed to the ground, holding in his guts. Without his weapon, the miner lifted his shield high above the Hunter's head, ready to crush his skull.

Within moments, Senara was back up on her rock and showering the Alchemists with a quick-fire round of shots from her leather sling. Down they went, one after another as the shield maiden took out her spite on anyone who dared to cross her path. One shot laid low the whirling miner. He fell down in the churning mud right next to our gutted warrior. I had to get to him, try to save his life, but the closer I got to the gap in the defences, the more our men pushed me back.

Kenver squared up to Tallack with a blade of equal magnificence to that of our chief. From the smug grin on Tallack's face, he had not noticed the Alchemist's sword glimmering with the same silvery sheen as his own. My nephew lurched forwards, eager to take the head from Kenver's shoulders. With both hands clasped about the hilt, he drew it back to shoulder height and swept it at our enemy.

Kenver was swift to react. He raised his sword to meet that of our leader. The blades clanged together with a deafening ring, neither man prepared to give way. They locked their strength against one another, baring teeth and snarling. Despite the raucous scrapping and thrashing fists and blades all around, I could not tear my gaze away from them.

Matched in height and weight, I'd hoped that my nephew's youth would give him an advantage over the older man, but I hadn't accounted for the Alchemist's experience. Kenver squared his shoulders and pushed from the hip, forcing Tallack to slide backwards in the mud. Before he could regain his footing, Kenver twisted his wrists, circling his sword in an arc until he could thrust it up towards my nephew's chin.

The whites of Tallack's eyes shone in the torchlight. He hadn't anticipated the move. Arching his back, he jerked his face out of the way, but the tip of Kenver's blade caught his chin. It sliced clean through the flesh like he was made of pork dripping. Kenver followed this with another cross cut, his full strength directed into the downward force. Shaken and bleeding, Tallack was just able to meet the sword with his own, but his body was twisted and unable to deflect the blow. The mystical blade, sent through me from Cernonnus himself, was flicked from Tallack's grasp.

"Watch out, boy!" I yelled, but it was too late. His heels teetered on the edge of the spike filled pit at the mouth of the defences. He had nowhere to run and a poised sword, moments away from cutting him down. Kenver grinned, lifting his blade high for the killing blow. He did not see Massen's great hulking body staggering backwards from a lunging spear. They collided with a series of grunts, shoving Kenver a few steps closer to where I clung to the hurdles.

Tallack tried to regain his balance, tilting his shoulders forwards and scampering on the shifting soil. The trickle of water turned into a flow of mud, washing out the fine clay and sand until it crumbled into the pit below. The ground could no longer support his weight. He fell down the inside wall of the gaping hole, grabbing out at anything that could slow his descent.

My poor old heart almost stopped. I shut my eyes and bit down on my knuckle. I didn't want to see him impaled on the sharpened poles lining the pit. There were too many painful memories of impaled loved ones swimming around in my head as it was, losing Tallack would be my end. With Kenver so close, though, I couldn't afford to dally. He was just as likely to run me through as turn and finish off my poor nephew.

As it was, the collision with Massen had altered Kenver's priorities. He seemed keen to avoid such a huge warrior. Stepping behind an unsuspecting miner to his left, he shoulder barged the young man into Massen's path, allowing him to scurry back to the edge of the pit.

I hurried along the hurdles and posts, until I was close to the fighting but shielded from the main thrust of the skirmish. Kewri yelled from the riverbank, begging me to return to safety. I knew he was right, of course. This was no place for a meddlesome old woman, but the need to help Tallack overwhelmed me. My family was shrinking in size every moon. As frightened as I was to discover his fate, seeing his body was preferable to the agonising uncertainty.

Kenver smirked and positioned himself at the edge of the pit. From his expression, I thought the worst had passed; that I'd lost my nephew for good. It was when he crouched down and jabbed into the hole with his sword that I knew Tallack was still alive. I drew closer to Kenver's right hand side where I could just make out my nephew's shape in the darkness. He was clinging to a tree root embedded in the pit wall, just an eagle's wingspan from the top.

More miners found their courage and streamed from the opening, outnumbering our few men. Those with decent blades fought two Alchemists at a time, relying on the crack shot of Senara with her leather sling to even out the sides. As they spilled out between the defences, I clawed along the broken hurdles with faltering steps. That wretch, Kenver was determined to send our Chieftain to the Summerlands long before his time. I couldn't let that happen.

After the countless winters we'd sent grain to his settlement, the slaves Tallack took to bolster the tin production, the privileges afforded to his kin, this rogue leader chose to rebel against a family who'd ruled fairly and wisely for generations. This was the thanks we got for all the healing treatments and tinctures I'd made for him, the comfort I gave to his children and the injuries tended following several accidents.

My thoughts simmered in a mire of stinking hatred as I watched him poke and jab at my helpless nephew clinging on for his life. This was not a time for reflection and regrets. This was a time for vengeance. I took a long slow breath and unsheathed Nectan's dagger from my belt. It felt at home in my palm as I tightened my grip, clenched my teeth and lunged.

The bronze tip fractured on its way into the muscle and sinew of his back, but that didn't stop me. He squealed like a stuck pig when I rammed it in an upward thrust towards the most vital of all his organs. I knew where the heart would be, I'd cut out enough dead ones in my time. I only stopped pushing when my fist was flush with his back and covered in his squelching blood. Shock muted his voice. Kenver lived just long enough to twist his head to see who'd robbed him of life, before he fell.

The fresh corpse of the treacherous kyjyan, Kenver toppled over the edge and landed on the sharpened poles below. I heard his spine snap as it buckled and slumped to the base of the pit. Only one of the spikes managed to bore a hole through his body, but it was enough for me to be sure that he could no longer be a threat. A fitting end for someone who'd inflicted such torture rather than face up to his daughter's lies and deceit.

I never expected to survive what I'd done. I turned around to face the enemy, my tunic and face dripping with blood. It took a few moments for the miners to realise that they no longer had a brutal leader commanding them. No one giving them orders to fight and kill their own tribe's folk.

One of our men lowered his spear into the pit, allowing Tallack to crawl out. He stood by my side. "Red suits you, Aunt. You should wear it more often."

Despite the seriousness of our situation, I couldn't help but titter. He retrieved his sword from a short distance hence and returned to my side. With a peck on my cheek, he whispered, "Nothing you do or say will ever vex me again."

Only then did the enormity of my actions dawn on me. I'd taken a life with my own bare hands, used a blade to kill and not cure. My gut twisted, sending bile into my throat until it burned me inside. Were it not for the confusion and noise all about me, the stink of spilled innards, the pools of muddied blood, the screams of the maimed and injured, I'd have lost control of myself. Shock froze me to the spot, unable to move.

By the time Tallack had skirted around the edge of the defences and mounted the boulders alongside Senara, most of the miners had dropped their weapons and were prepared to surrender to the mighty Massen. Those stubbornly refusing to admit defeat were encouraged to look up at our young Metern of the Dumnonii.

The moon bathed him in a victorious glow, as though the god, Lugh had picked him out in a beam of his own. My chest swelled with pride when he lifted the Sword of Cernonnus and shouted at the warriors to lay down their spears.

"Take a good long look at your opponents, men. They are not enemies, nor foreigners. We are all brothers on the battlefield, are we not?"

Senara coughed loudly, making my nephew grin.

"Brothers… and sisters. The point is, we are one tribe, one family, and none deserved to die this night, or any night. Kenver forced you all to carry his grievances, made you hide like cowards in the tunnels. His fight is not ours. Let us begin again with one aim together. We'll make the Dumnonii the most feared, most envied and most respected tribe in the whole land." He waited while his Head Hunters and Sea Warriors roared and whooped their approval, but few of the miners joined in with their revelry. Tallack did not seem to notice. I suspect the relief of ending the siege in our favour was all that mattered.

It was only then that I grabbed a torch and went in search of my giant friend on the slopes above the dry riverbed. Kewri was close to tears when I found him sitting on a rock grunting in pain. A dead man lay at his feet, caked in silt and mud from the flood.

"That's not Nectan is it?" I said, barely concealing the anxiety in my voice.

The giant shook his head. "Just a young fool who thought he could take me on and win." He tipped backwards and winced. "He very nearly did."

I wondered if he'd ripped out his stitches again, but chose not to ask. Instead, I said, "So, where's Nectan? I've not seen him since the fighting began?"

# CHAPTER TWENTY-SEVEN

Enquiries amongst the men yielded no information regarding Nectan's whereabouts. Tallack sent one of his men to retrieve my pony from the ridge top but he came back a short time later empty handed. When I mentioned my concerns about Nectan, Tallack dismissed them immediately. I'd caught him at the wrong time to get any sense from him. He was too giddy about his victory and the continued rule of our family over the tribe.

Between him and our warriors, the relief was profound. They joked and teased one another, cleaned off their weapons and instructed the miners to take care of those dead Alchemists lost in the skirmish. Our clans had suffered fewer fatalities and the siege was finally at an end. There was cause for celebration, but I could not forget the pyres of the last quarter moon.

At dawn, Ren rode from further up the valley to join Kewri and me, before we began the slow walk down the gorge to the beach. Some of Tallack's reliable men stayed behind to make sure that the remaining miners didn't try to take Kenver's place and cause us more distress. It didn't seem likely, given that we knew the location of their womenfolk and children and could threaten all kinds of unpleasantness to assure their cooperation.

Our men also needed to remove the makeshift dam of tree trunks and rocks from the river. The tunnels had to drain fully before mining could begin again. All in all, there was much to be done, not least the binding of our Chief to two new brides who awaited him on the fire ravaged moors to the east.

Ren gave me his horse to ride. He walked alongside with Tallack, Kewri and Massen. Their jovial mood grated on me, but I couldn't quite figure out why. There was something not right about the way Nectan had vanished from the fight. He'd made a seriously advantageous deal with Tallack for leadership of the Alchemy Clan, and yet he'd disappeared before claiming his prize. Why would he have done that, unless he was sure that we would fail?

We stopped briefly to fill our water bladders and let the pony drink from the spring before rounding the headland onto the beach. The ocean was unusually calm and blue; there was not a cloud in the sky. Heat from the sand played tricks with my eyes, as though Tallack's grand ship was shimmering out in the bay.

As my pony waded through the tidal river emptying into the sea, we spotted Nectan next to our burned-out fires further along the beach. He saw us approaching and started walking to meet us halfway. His grin seemed forced; his greeting too effusive. He stuck out his arm for Tallack to grasp. "I am so pleased to see you all. What an incredible victory… I knew you would prevail. I take it that Kenver is no more?" He acknowledged our nods and blew out his cheeks in relief. It made me wonder how soon into the battle he had fled.

I glanced beyond him to the horse near the cold embers. It was loaded with the bedding furs we'd rescued from the hut fires, and bags of our meagre food stores and belongings. He saw my curious look descend into seething anger.

"I've packed your horse for you, Fur Benyn. I…um… didn't think you'd want to linger, especially if the plan didn't tilt your way. I was just devising an escape route for you, in case… well, you know."

Tallack failed to notice the squirming weasel clutching at lame excuses. "That was smart thinking, Nectan, and good of you to want to protect my aunt. As it happens, we'll need to journey up to the northern mines. Kenver's brother has taken control there too."

Sometimes, I despair at how blind my nephew can be. I sincerely hoped it was just his youth that made him so trusting of people.

Nectan leaned his head to one side and frowned. "There's no need. I can get a message to my boys at the mine. Clemo is as hated as Kenver was here. They can rally the men to overthrow him, with your blessing, Chief. When that kyjyan's out of the way, my lads can keep everything running for you in the meantime." He seemed to have everything trussed up neatly and all arranged in his favour.

While Ren and a few others prepared to paddle out to Tallack's boat, I followed my nephew around trying to make him understand the folly in trusting someone such as Nectan so soon after we'd dispatched Kenver, but he would not listen. Tallack had spent little time with the man, and Nectan had a way of seeming useful and compliant whenever he was close to the Chief. As far as I could tell, we were simply swapping one rogue with grand ambitions for another. I said as much to Ren, when we were alone, but he quickly dismissed the issue.

"What do you want me to do, Mel? I don't have as much influence over Tallack as you seem to think." That was all he would say on the matter.

We rested for a while on the beach, exhausted but too agitated to sleep. I covered my eyes with my cloak to blot out the sunlight, but the trapped heat made it even more uncomfortable. Later in the day, Tallack gave Massen specific orders, before we rowed out to the Phoenician ship in the small boat.

My words of caution must have sunk into my nephew, since he insisted that Nectan sailed with us to the bay where land ends. Ren and I stayed close to the Alchemist, asking him more and more questions about the island where the miners' women and children were hiding.

He explained that Kenver had discovered more tin deposits some time ago, but had managed to keep it a secret from all but a few close friends and relatives. Kenver's youngest and only living son spent most of his time there, signalling foreign ships with lit beacons on the seaward side of the island. Those that dropped anchor carried exotic goods in exchange for our tin. That must have been how Kenver got hold of such fine weapons, many that were different in shape and metal to our usual ones.

During our voyage, tacking against the wind and currents, I tried hard to get Nectan to explain the process of turning rocks into pure tin, but he refused. I thought he might crumble and tell all when Ren stood over him with his hand on the hilt of his dagger, but he would not talk.

"It's more than my life's worth to tell you, Fur Benyn, much as I would like to. The magical ability is passed from father to son on the fourth moon after spring equinox. I was initiated when I'd seen twelve summers. Only the chosen families ever get to learn the ways of the rocks. If they speak of it to anyone outside that sacred bond, the gods would cut out our tongues and strike us dead with a lightning bolt so vicious, it would wipe out our entire family, women and children too."

I glared at him, assessing the truth in his eyes. That sounded like a tall tale spread about to scare the young, but for someone as cowardly as Nectan to risk death rather than reveal the secret, it had to be true. Mind you, he can find his courage when he has no other choice. He managed to talk his way out of slaughter when Ren and I caught him leaving the tunnels. He's a slippery one and someone I vowed never to trust.

By the time we were closing in on the bay where the land ends, I remembered the missing purple pennant from the ship. It had been present for every journey I'd taken with my nephew in seasons past, and it had barely faded from the sun at all. It was a colour that I'd only ever seen once before, worn by the Phoenician Prince who had caused me so much heartache and pain. I wondered how many foreign sea snails had to die in order to achieve such a rich hue.

We sailed all through the night and arrived at the bay as the sun was falling again in the sky. I knew that Kenver's son would have spotted us. There was no way to sneak about with such a conspicuous vessel as ours. We should have ridden around the headland from the mining settlement with Massen and his crew, travelling in Kenver's ship. That would have enabled us to use stealth in our approach. All we could do was hope that none of the woman were armed. They couldn't defeat us, but no one wanted to use force against them.

Tallack, Senara, Nectan, Ren and I took the row boat ashore first. It was high tide and the gravel causeway linking the mainland to the island was deep under water. It gave us time to think of our options.

"I'll row around to the rocky cliffs at the back and scout out the island, Chief." Senara offered, keen to prove herself again.

"Nice offer, Senara, but that won't work. Kenver's lad will have the youngsters hidden and keeping watch. You can't creep about on the ocean like you can on land." Tallack tried to mask his amusement, turning away from her. The girl was from homesteader stock. She had no experience of the sea at all.

"We'll wait until the tide changes at dusk and walk across. They can't get off the island without us noticing." Tallack said, settling down to rest.

"They'll hide." Nectan said, jabbing his thumb over his shoulder towards the tall craggy rocks jutting out from the sea. "They'll be hoping that you're just passing. There's a slim chance that they've never seen your fine ship before, Chief. They could mistake you for a foreign trader. Better to wait until dark to see if they light the beacons."

I couldn't see that being the case at all. Tallack's fine Phoenician ship was the pride of our tribe. Having spent the winter season in and out of the mining settlement at Bentewyn, there wasn't an Alchemist this side of the River Sid who didn't know the craft well. Was Nectan deliberately delaying us so that he could get a message out to the island? If that was his aim, what purpose did it serve? Kenver's youngest and sole surviving child would likely prevent our passage across the causeway given the chance. How he planned to achieve that, would decide our own actions.

Ren caught a fat goose from further inland, a couple of the warriors set about making fish traps and I collected firewood with Nectan. None of us were idle, barring Tallack, who sat brooding on the beach. When the fire was lit, I sat opposite, waiting for him to reveal his thoughts. Before the light failed entirely, we saw Massen's crew sailing Kenver's ship into the bay.

"That should be enough proof to the whelp that his father no longer holds sway over these lands." Tallack said, leaning on his sword as he hoisted himself onto his feet. The causeway should be dry enough by now. Let's hack off his head and be done with it."

Senara peered up at me to intervene. It was as though we both had the same notion, but she was reluctant to speak out.

"Chief, if I may suggest an alternative course?" I was trading on the good will I'd accrued from killing Kenver, not sure how long his favour would last. Tallack flicked his head around and stabbed the end of his sword back into the sand. I took this to mean that he was prepared to listen, but his expression was grim and unforgiving.

"I know the boy well from my time with his family. Would it not be prudent to at least speak with him first? I can walk the causeway alone and tell him the news of his kin. If he will not yield, you can always run him through later." All those around the fire kept their heads low, their mouths closed. Kenver's son had seen too few summers to be tested as a warrior. He was no more than a child. From the looks on the warriors' faces; none relished the task of slaughtering him or his mother.

"Fine, do it your way, if it pleases you, Aunt, but take Senara with you. If he cuts up rough, take him down as swiftly as you can." Tallack gestured for one of his men to hand Senara his shield, while another was sent to prepare a torch for us to light our way.

Ren grabbed my arm before we set off. "Let me come too."

I smiled and tapped his hand until he let go. "If he sees it's just two women, he won't feel threatened. Frightened boys lash out. Calm ones talk."

Senara walked a step ahead of me, close enough to slip the shield across my body if we were met by raining arrows. In her right hand, she held the straps of her leather sling. My arm ached from holding the torch aloft over the pitted gravel path towards the island.

The Alchemists had erected defences at the far end of the causeway too; a tall wooden palisade blocked our way with a gate as high as ours back at the compound on the Exe. Every so often, Senara glanced backwards, as though she could sense movement behind us. It was probably the motion of the sea lapping the edges of the shingle.

There were no fires visible, nor torches to reveal their preparations. We had no idea whether their walls were lined with archers, or their children with slings. Nevertheless, we stepped closer until a squeaky voice called out.

"That's close enough, state your business." His voice cracked.

"Ho there!" I bellowed up to him. "Do you remember me?" I searched my memories for his name, but drew a blank. "I am Meliora, healer to the tribe. I stayed in your father's hut over winter."

"I remember you. Your kin poisoned our water, made everyone ill. Some of my friends died."

It was not a good start. Tallack's half-brother, Paega, was involved in that incident. No apology or explanation was likely to make any difference to this boy's opinion of me. Taking care of foreign trades and the safety of the women and children was a huge responsibility for someone so young. I could hardly fault him for taking such a stance.

"That was unfortunate and out of our control." I scuffed my feet in the shingle, ashamed at my family and all they had done. "Why don't you open the gates so we can talk properly?"

"You must think me a fool, Fur Benyn. I'm fully aware of the warriors creeping about the rocks by the shore. You'd have me welcome and host those who murdered my brother and sister?"

I spun about, confused for a moment. Senara nodded to a rocky outcrop a short distance away. Ren and two of the Sea Warriors bobbed into view. They'd sneaked along the edges of the causeway behind us, keeping low and out of sight. Senara was aware of them the whole time. What keen eyes the boy had. I wasn't about to tell him that I was the one who'd driven a blade into his father's back.

"The conflict between our clans is over. We are united as one tribe once again. Open the gates and no one will be harmed. You have my word." I glared at the men peering over the rocks. Tallack was among them.

"Tell those men that we have a great many archers trained on them right now and my father is on his way with more warriors." Again, his voice broke half way through his threats.

Tallack came out from his hiding place, followed by a number of his men. "That's about as much as I can take, Aunt Mel." He clamped his hand on my shoulder, using his grip to move me backwards. "Your father is dead, boy. His rebellion failed. If you don't open the gates, you, your mother, and all your friends will die too."

I heard a little gasp from behind the palisade wall, and then soft cries of despair. My heart went out to Kenver's wife. She'd lost everyone except this young boy at the gate tower. I hoped that her panic and grief would be enough to talk the boy out of his stubborn revolt. It was not.

The lad screeched so that we could all hear. "Then you will pay for his death." His cry was desperate and filled with pain. He ordered his little band of untested warriors to fire their slings and arrows onto us. Senara lifted her shield above my head. Tallack stepped aside as a rounded rock landed at his feet. A small volley of flint-headed arrows stuck in the gravel or were easily deflected by our men. None found their mark.

# CHAPTER TWENTY-EIGHT

Before the women and children could reload, Tallack nodded to a single archer on his left. I watched the warrior take no more than a moment to aim the nocked bolt before launching it at Kenver's son. I heard it hit the lad with a familiar squelch of spurting humours, followed by a dull thud as his body slumped against the watchtower floor. I closed my eyes to the sadness welling up inside me. Loyalty to his father had claimed another life. Would he spend eternity in the Summerlands? I wasn't sure. One so young would not have had the chance to earn his place at the side of those fallen in honourable battle.

Our men did not wait for Tallack to give further commands. They charged at the gates and forced them open before the pitiful attempts with sling shots could do any damage. When the miner's wives and children realised that the insurrection was over, they put up no more resistance. They gained nothing by risking their lives. Kenver's widow no longer held power over them. As soon as they were able, they handed her over to Tallack in return for leniency.

By daylight, Ren and the men had uncovered a massive trove of jewels, weapons, tin, copper, gold, and more importantly, a huge store of traded Frynkish grain. The bounty was so unexpected that Tallack ordered Ren to find a suitable sacrifice to honour the gods watching over us. We'd been fortunate indeed to have secured their favour in recovering the mines.

While Massen oversaw the transfer of grain and metal into Kenver's ship to take back to the Exe, Tallack spoke to some of the Head Hunters. He tasked them with the job of helping Nectan while he began his new role as clan leader.

The Chief allowed me to select a few choice items from the hoard before the Sea Warriors carted them away. With the binding ceremonies looming close, I took two delicate brooches inlaid with amber beads and a jewelled dagger as offerings. I was also able to replace a couple of the knives lost to the Belgae from my medicine kit.

I suspect that my nagging doubts about Nectan had played on my nephew's mind, since I overheard him tell one of the men to send word if Nectan did anything suspicious or untoward.

Before we set sail in Tallack's vessel the following day, Kenver's widow was brought before us. One of the other women had caught her with a rope suspended from a supporting beam in her hut. The noose was about her neck when they stumbled in and stopped her from taking her own life.

"What do you expect me to do about it?" Tallack huffed, sheathing his sword and gathering his bedding furs in a roll. "If she wants to die, let her."

The women pleaded with him to take her back to the compound on the River Exe, to give her useful employment, but he would not budge.

"I've no use for the wife and mother of traitors. Tried that before. Won't make that mistake again." He lifted his things into the row boat and gestured towards me to follow. I knew to whom he was referring. The Skotek Novantae Chief and his sons had turned against us. It had been my idea to save the life of the troublesome daughter. I kept my mouth shut this time around. Tallack used to be so kind, so forgiving. This is what happens when you see your lover skinned and strung up for the crows. I wondered if he'd have shown more mercy if she had chosen another method to kill herself.

Nectan stepped up. "I'll take her on, Chief, make sure she has food and shelter, but she'll have to work like everyone else."

Of course, he would take her under his wing. He would make her a slave after her family had treated his so badly. That poor woman had suffered so much in her time, she hardly deserved that fate. As we pushed off and rowed out to the bay, I watched her drop to her knees, sobbing. I doubted that she would live much past the solstice. Her grief was absolute. If she failed to take her own life once, her determination would be all the more pressing.

Kewri and Senara were given the choice of vessel in which to travel. I urged my giant friend to sail with Massen straight back to the compound at the Exe. His injured back needed time to heal, not more trudging across moorlands under the relentless sun. Senara was keen to be present at the binding ceremony to support her friend, and I suspect, her lover, Endelyn. Somehow, I couldn't imagine Senara wearing a colourful robe with flowers woven into her hair. I could be wrong.

Our trip back along the coastline was swifter in this direction. Both the current and the wind was with us and the mood of the menfolk buoyant and cheerful. We rattled along at such a pace, we overtook Massen in Kenver's boat and pulled into shore where the River Yealm empties into the sea.

It was late in the day when we arrived, but it being so close to the solstice, there was still plenty of sunlight left. There was another half day's walk to Gutter Tor on the moors ahead of us. The black smoke of heath fires billowed into the sky. I was convinced that we were all thinking the same thing; to get back on the ship and sail to the Exe and safety, but no one spoke.

When my nephew's mind is made, there is no convincing him to alter course. He promised his mother, Endelyn and the father of the new Duro bride, that he would be bound by midsummer's day, and he was determined to keep his word.

The problem lay before us; how could we cross the moors to the sacred circles by the tor without being burned alive? None of us knew whether the womenfolk and elders would even be at the stones, given the dangers involved. Even though we'd had word from a messenger that they intended to set off from the settlement on the Exe, they could easily have turned back.

Tallack's jaw clenched. He scanned the horizon and pointed to a trail leading north. "We'll skirt the edge of the moors until we can pick up a safer route heading east. The onshore coastal breezes should keep the fires at bay until then."

I knew that he'd planned to trade with local homesteaders for horses to speed our journey, but the moorland settlers had long since abandoned their fields. Those in the surrounding regions had fled to our camp on the River Exe. The place was deserted. We had no other option but to walk the charred landscape over ridge and valley, kicking up the ash and snagging our ankles on the brittle stalks and branches left behind.

The going was tough, and I'm ashamed to say that I slowed them down, particularly where the shallow valleys gave way to steeper ones. How I longed to be on horseback, keeping up with the men and earning my place with my skills at healing. They did their best to hide their frustrations, but I could tell they resented my presence.

Ren and Tallack took us on a longer route not just to avoid fires, but to accommodate my aching joints. I implored them to go on ahead, happy to catch them up at my leisure, but Tallack would not hear of it; I'd saved his life and he felt he owed me.

At dusk, we rested for a while next to an abandoned chalk pit. I knew this countryside well. Under different circumstances, I would have collected some of the white dust to thicken my balms and scour my cooking pots. The eerie orange glow on the horizon kept us moving. It lay in the opposite direction to that of the setting sun, and reduced us all to an anxious silence as we walked. Shortly after dark, we picked up the course of the River Plym, making our navigation to Gutter Tor easy.

"Which of the sacred circles did Endelyn choose in the end?" I asked.

Tallack's head tipped forward. He stared at his toes treading cautiously along the winding riverbank. "Um… I can't recall."

"But there are four sets of stones surrounding the tor."

He flapped his hands in my direction. "Don't fuss. We'll just look for their fires."

He couldn't see me roll my eyes in the darkness behind him. How in the name of Cernonnus were we supposed to distinguish between the orange glow of a few small fires from the moorland blazing in the west? I felt the warmth of Ren's hand brush against my arm. It wasn't comfort so much as food and rest that I needed, but I didn't rebuke his kindness.

The River Plym snaked to the west, steering us ever closer to the angry skies and stinking air. Two of the stone circles were close by. The area where I knew the first to be was dark and lifeless. The second circle was above us at the peak of the hill beyond. We had no way of knowing if our elders waited for us there. Senara volunteered to run up the hillside and scout the circle for us, leaving Tallack, Ren and I to rinse ourselves down in the cool water of the Plym.

I soaked a cloth and wrung out the excess, passing it to my nephew. "Is there a wood henge at Yellowmeade?" I asked him, my memory hazy from the trek.

"No, but there is at Drizzlecombe, down in the gorge to the south of the stones."

"Then my best guess is that Endelyn will have chosen that for her binding ceremony." I slipped off my shoes and dangled my feet in the river. The sensation was blissful.

"Why do you say that?"

I looked at Tallack and frowned in disbelief. "Do you know how much preparation she's put into this ritual? Becoming the Ruvane of our tribe is all she can think about. She's occupied all the Long Hut slaves for the best part of a full moon's cycle, stripping the alder trees and dying expensive fabric for her gown and those of her maids. She sent out messengers to look for her old priest friends from the Nine Maiden's circle, and probably many others besides."

The Chief scratched the tiny flies crawling at his hairline. "So?"

There were times when he was beyond my patience. "The stones at Drizzlecombe are blessed by her clan. The henge in the valley nearby is beautiful. There are so many flowers and shrubs, it's almost as though it's under the protection of the goddess."

"Not if the heath fires get there first."

He had a point. Most of our journey was across a blackened wasteland where heathers and shrubs once grew in abundance. Only when we reached the Plym River, did the grass and mosses return to cushion our steps.

I waited for Senara to return with a growing sense of dread in my chest. As I predicted, she did not find the women and elders at the top of the rise. We marched on late into the night, ever westward and closer to the red blaze in the summer sky. The breeze had picked up, cooling our faces. When the moon was high above our heads, we could see the flames licking the ridge top in the distance.

Hurrying along the opposite bank of the Plym, my jitters increased with every step. Ahead of us, we could see the elders scattered among frightened ponies, trying to gather their belongings ready to flee. Endelyn was in the midst of them, her arms high, her head tipped back in one of her customary poses where she claimed to be communing with the gods. I could see her bulging belly silhouetted against the fire light. The child inside her was growing fast.

As we drew near, The Chief's mother shrieked at the elders and their wives to pack up and leave. They were all so fraught, few noticed our arrival. Senara dashed over to the priestess and together they pressed their foreheads together, sharing a moment of joy. It was a touching scene. Even their puppy bounded towards the young warrior in greeting. Behind them, the wooden henge of life was lit up with torches and decorated with flowers and ivy tendrils, carted all the way from the Exe.

When the priestess turned to welcome Tallack and me, I saw her gown in all its glory. The robe was almost as vibrant as the curls in her hair. The sunset colours from the alder bark dye framed an arrowhead shaped section of deep purple cloth, stitched from her chest to her swollen belly. I couldn't suppress my smile. Endelyn had taken the pennant from Tallack's ship to incorporate into her bridal gown.

Her attending maids were similarly clad, with paler gowns of their own. Theirs differed only in the absence of the purple strip of fabric. She had created a magnificent setting for her ascension to the position of Ruvane, spoiled only by the threat of the wild fires.

"Thank the goddess that you've arrived." Endelyn exclaimed, cupping Senara's face in both hands before approaching the Chief. "I was beginning to think you'd never come." She stroked Tallack's chest and wound her arms about his neck in an enforced embrace. "We should begin the binding ritual immediately." Endelyn nuzzled her face into my nephew's neck and looked set to stay there.

Tallack peeled the priestess's limbs from his body and stepped aside. "Mother!" He called out to Cryda. "Did you bring the Duro bride along as I asked?"

Endelyn slumped, her freckled face puckered in dismay while all eyes turned to the fair-haired girl on Cryda's arm.

"I did, son. Her name is Gytha." Cryda held out the girl's hand, encouraging Tallack to clasp it in his own. I don't suppose I was alone in seeing the alteration to the sullen Duro from when we first saw her at the crossing on the River Sid. Her yellow hair was pinned in curls around her radiant face, her blue gown cinched at her narrow waist, her pale limbs dressed with a single golden armlet. Even I could detect the impact it had on my nephew. The poor dazed dolt took her hand in his and blinked so slowly I believed him to be drugged.

Cryda shot me with a wicked grin. "Isn't she a beauty?"

All Tallack could manage in reply was a satisfied hum, similar to that emitted whenever he ate roasted boar.

His mother was not finished with her introductions. She lifted a graceful arm towards a warrior who bore the neck tattoo of the Durotriges. "This is her brother, Hedley, come to assure the safety of his kin. He brings with him some charming young men too."

Tallack bristled at the notion of a Duro warrior having enchanted his mother in such a short space of time. The Chief released his new bride and took the forearm of the brother he would gain from the ceremony. The two men regarded each other with suspicion. Hedley, being shorter, had to stare up at my nephew. I could see that the Duro had greater strength in his grip. Tallack flinched from the pain as Hedley dug his fingers into our Chief's muscles and squeezed.

"Glad to have you take such good care of my… our kin, Hedley. You are most welcome."

The Duro nodded in return, careful to retain his stern expression. "A long-overdue union between our tribes, Chief, but under the circumstances, I think it prudent to retreat from the moors and conduct the ritual elsewhere." There was something irksome about his manner, as though he expected our entire tribe to jump at his suggestion. He dropped the Chief's arm and turned his back to us, in readiness to leave.

It may have been common sense, but his manner of delivery only served to rile Tallack even more. "Scared of a little heath fire, Hedley? We have ample time for the ceremony." The fearful mumbles and muttering among the elders grew loud enough to warrant a venomous glare from the Chief. "Make ready, Priestess," Tallack called out. "We'll have this matter sorted in no time at all. We can celebrate with a feast when we return to the compound."

People scurried about the place, gathering posies and offerings, moving agitated horses from the henge of life and preening for their part in the joint binding of Tallack to Endelyn, followed by Tallack to Gytha.

Recovered from the Chief's slight, Endelyn rallied at the thought of finally becoming the most powerful woman of the tribe. "Tallack, I have asked my friend from the Nine Maiden's circle to conduct the ritual. I should very much like you to be friends with him too." She beckoned the willowy creature over for a formal introduction.

"Not now, Priestess. Let's just get on with it." He waved them away and trotted through the tall uprights of the henge to his position at the farthest end. Scowling, Endelyn picked up the fabric of her trailing gown and summoned her maids to assist her. They fussed about, carrying her flowers and tending to the fallen tresses curling over her shoulders.

Hedley and I exchanged an exasperated look, before taking up the eastern and western sides of the inner circle reserved for close family members. Cryda and

Ren took a northern and southerly point, while the elders claimed random places in the outer fringes of the henge.

The priest picked up a long staff and untangled the braid of beads, bones and feathers attached to the end, before strolling at a casual pace to the centre of the circle.

I heard one of our most revered elders bellow to him. "Move faster, won't you, before we are all burned alive!"

He only said what we were all thinking. The wind had altered direction, fanning the flames onto the slopes of the valley in which we stood. It brought thick black clouds to cover the sky and a chill that we'd not felt in more than four moons. Tiny hot embers travelled on the breeze, igniting the parched shrubs all around us. Some of the elders stamped on the burgeoning fires but there were too many sparks to stop them all.

Before Tallack could call an end to proceedings, Endelyn handed her posy to one of her maids and glided into the centre of the inner circle. "Do not fear, my people. All will be well. I shall ask the goddess to protect us." Throwing her head back, Endelyn began her tiresome chanting in a mystical language known only to the highest of priests from her clan.

Babbling and muttering for a few moments, she then tipped her head forward to speak in our tongue. "Cerridwen, Mother of All Life, hear me now. Grant us your wisdom, your protection and your blessing, so that we may forge a new generation of peace and prosperity among our people and those of our new friends, the Durotriges. May the fruit of this union continue the line of Dumnonii from this day until the end of all days." Her voice rose until she was yelling the last part above the noise of the crackling blaze that sprang up a short distance behind her.

Most of the elders sank to their knees, making their own promises to the gods. Gytha scampered across the henge and into Tallack's arms for protection. At the time, I wondered what had induced such folly, when her brother was but a few footsteps away. It was when I saw the expression on my nephew's face that I understood her actions. He wrapped his arms about her slender young body and whispered words of comfort into her ear.

The flames ate vast swathes of the dry sedges along the valley floor, creeping closer every moment. Ren pocketed his offering and walked over to me. "We must dowse ourselves from the river and walk along its course to safety." He wasn't prepared to wait for our Chief's instruction. Grabbing my hand, he tugged until I followed. We led the charge for others to leave with us.

"Wait!" Endelyn yelled, turning her face skyward. When no one listened to her command, she repeated herself. "Wait! Can't you hear it?"

We stood still and tried to ignore the roaring of the flames. A bright flash illuminated the sky, blinding us all for a single moment. The deep, continuous rumble, echoing throughout the valley, made us all gasp.

Heavy raindrops fell shortly after, flattening our hair and leaving us all with our mouths agape in wonder. By the time the clouds burst, the elders and their wives were all in awe of Endelyn's powers.

"She is favoured," said one woman.

Her husband agreed. "She has the ear of the gods."

Another shouted, "We are saved!" More of them began chants of, "Bless you, Endelyn. The Mother has chosen you."

The priestess spun slowly in the centre of the henge of life, taking in the collective adoration. My attention stayed on Tallack and the Duro girl. She was sobbing with relief, her lack of tears masked by the rain streaks down her face. Tallack saw only the bedraggled bride in his arms. Our Chief was utterly smitten.

When the clamour finally reduced, the priestess urged everyone back to their positions in readiness for the ceremony. Ren and I waited for a signal from our Chief, a nod or smile permitting the continuation of the binding.

"Chief?" I shouted above the cracking thunder and forked lightning overhead.

Tallack inhaled sharply, jogged from his witless state. Taking the Duro girl by the shoulders, he held her at arm's length and gazed into her deep blue eyes. "I've changed my mind." He announced. "Gytha will be the new Ruvane of the Dumnonii."

Ren shut his eyes and sighed. "Here we go again."

***

If you enjoyed this novel, and have a moment spare to express your opinion, **a review would be greatly appreciated**.

**Historical note from the author.**

Recent studies into the genetic makeup of Bronze Age Europeans suggest that they did not possess the genes to enable full digestion of milk as adults. While the data set was extremely small, it would indicate that an intolerance to animal milk was present in the general population for many thousands of years. This being the case, it is reasonable to assume that despite an intolerance, such a readily available food source would not necessarily have been dismissed, nor would it have affected all within a community. With this reasoning, I have chosen to include the use of milk and milk products in the series, mainly due to archaeological evidence supporting the production of cheese for millennia. According to Dr S Charlton, from the department of archaeology at the University of York in 2019, processing the milk into other products reduces lactose and makes it more palatable and easier to digest.

For more information on the rest of the series, please go to: www.carantocpublishing.com

**JOIN MY READERS' GROUP AND RECEIVE THE EXCLUSIVE EBOOK NOVELLA**

**PAGAN FURY**

**Three unsuitable lovers.**
**Two valuable metals.**
**One critical mission.**

The Dumnonii have no copper for their forges. Without a new supply, there will be no more bronze weapons for the inevitable battle ahead.

Joint Chieftain, Tallack, must cross the western ocean to negotiate an alliance with the obstinate Dathi of the Ivernii and complete an impossible task to gain his trust.

Can he succeed where once his father failed?

Join the young warrior and his crew in a lust fuelled, intense quest on the shores of Iwerdon and find out for yourself.

**This story takes place between book one, Pagan Death, and book two, Pagan Curse. Please be aware that there will be spoilers that might ruin the enjoyment if they are read out of order.**
**Join here:**

www.carantocpublishing.com

**About the Author**

Sam Taw is the pen name for fiction author Sam Nash. Sam is committed to delivering novels in two distinct genres, historical thrillers and a unique blend of science fiction and international espionage stories.

She lives in a small village in the south of Northamptonshire, in the UK but dreams of one day owning a woodland on the Cornish coast.

For information regarding the work of Sam Taw, please visit:

www.carantocpublishing.com

For information regarding the work of Sam Nash, please visit:

https://www.samnash.org

Printed in Great Britain
by Amazon

70896086R00174